IN DEFENSE OF DELIA

In Defense of Delia

A SANGAMON NOVEL

Pat Stoltey

THORNDIKE PRESS
A part of Gale, a Cengage Company

LIBRARY OF CONGRESS CIP DATA ON FILE.
CATALOGUING IN PUBLICATION FOR THIS BOOK
IS AVAILABLE FROM THE LIBRARY OF CONGRESS.

ISBN-13: 978-1-4328-9472-6 (softcover alk. paper)

Published in 2024 by arrangement with Patricia A. Stoltey.

Printed in the USA
1 2 3 4 5   28 27 26 25 24

ACKNOWLEDGMENTS

Many thanks to all those who've read and critiqued earlier versions of this novel, including my beta reader, Diane Cheatwood, and present and past members of Raintree Writers: Brian Kaufman, Kenneth Harmon, Brigitte Dempsey, Jim Davidson, Beverly Winter, April Moore, Katherine Valdez, Laura Mahal, and Gordon MacKinney.

To my editor, Deni Dietz, I am always grateful as she is a great teacher as well as editor. To Five Star/Cengage and all those who are involved with making a manuscript into a book, thank you.

CHAPTER ONE:
COMING HOME

Village of Sangamon
State of Illinois
September 1838

Delia Pritchard rode into town on the Palouse stallion she called McAllister, leading a sorrel mare with a young boy astride. She knew they would attract the whole town's attention. The seven-year-old black child would cause talk. Even worse, Delia was fighting pain from a bullet in her shoulder.

She hadn't figured on being recognized at first sight, especially considering her sorry state. It had been thirteen years since she'd left, just after her sixteenth birthday.

But Jeremiah Frost stepped onto the front porch of his general store and called her out the moment he saw her, raising his voice to make sure she heard every word. "Tarnation, we got trouble back in Sangamon. As if we haven't already had enough to last a lifetime."

A pregnant woman with blonde hair tucked into a snood walked out the door to stand by Jeremiah's side. In seconds, a girl in yellow gingham danced across the porch, twirling a parasol that matched her dress. She stopped next to Jeremiah and reached for his hand.

Delia sat up straight, not an easy move with her arm in its belt sling. She looked the grocer in the eye, then glanced at the woman and girl at his side. *If that's Jeremiah's daughter, she must have been born after I hightailed it out of this place.* The pretty woman standing next to Jeremiah didn't look old enough to be the girl's mother. Perhaps he had worn out the old wife and got him a new one. The child looked to be about nine or ten. And wearing real gingham. *The general store must be doing well. Too bad the poor child looks like her pa.*

Before Delia moved out of earshot, Jeremiah added one more comment. "Elizabeth, you stay away from that gal on the big spotty horse. Her middle name is Trouble and that's exactly what she'll bring to our town."

"Who's that boy?" said Elizabeth, talking as loud as her daddy. "Looks like he's near burnt to a crisp."

Jeremiah snorted and turned his back on the riders. He yanked the girl inside by her wrist. The woman glanced over her shoulder for one more look as Delia rode past. Then she followed Jeremiah into the store.

Delia ran her fingers around her collar to make sure her rat-tangled hair remained hidden under the flat-brimmed hat she'd taken from the man who'd once owned McAllister. She also had the man's saddle-bags, rifle in its scabbard, Colt revolver, and the belt now draped over her shoulder to serve as a sling for her left arm. Even thinking about him — the wandering artist who'd shown up one day and died the next — made Delia sad. The artist wasn't prepared to fend off thieves and killers. Good people had no business roaming around this country alone.

The Palouse plodded past the store, kicking up dust balls and crumbling the smaller dirt clods. Wagons had left deep tracks during the rains that usually marked springtime in the Sangamon Valley. Everything dried up when summer came, so the ruts were now hard as rock.

Delia rode on, guiding the horses around the furrows, still thinking on Jeremiah's cantankerous wife and what might have happened to her. Still wondering what folks thought as they passed Delia on the road or watched from their front doors. A man's shirt and pants worn almost through at elbows and knees and filthy from days of wear without a washing. Big patch of dried blood on the back of her left shoulder. Boots with scuffed-up toes and horse shit caked on the heels and soles. *Lordy, do I ever need a hot bath.*

Just beyond Jeremiah's place, three men sat on wooden chairs in front of the feed store, their boots resting on the top rung of the porch railing. Delia didn't recognize the first two. The third, Colin Pritchard, put his feet down, unfolded his lanky frame from the chair, and stood for a moment to watch Delia and her companion approach. Then he walked to the porch steps, widened his stance, and folded his arms across his chest. "What the hell are you doing here, Delia?"

"I've come home, little brother." Delia studied Colin's appearance. Thirteen years had not been kind to him. Hands roughened by years as a smithy, face weathered from exposure to the sun and his fire pit.

That's if he had taken over their father's business, as she'd expected.

"This ain't your home no more," he said.

"I'm not staying long. Got a bullet in my

shoulder. It hurts bad enough I can't use my arm. I need to get patched up. Can we stay in the room behind the stable? It's only for a few days."

"Is the law after you?"

"No, I don't think so. I had a disagreement with a man who didn't take to my young friend here. He called the young'un awful names and offered to buy him because he needed a whipping boy. When I started to ride off without a word, that son of a gun shot me. I guess he was aiming to kill me and take the boy and my horses."

"How'd you get away?"

Delia glanced at the other men on the porch, then winced as she leaned forward. "Is the doctor in town?" she asked. "I don't feel much like talking right now."

"You killed that man, didn't you? And you say the law ain't after you?"

"Nobody knows what happened, Colin, except this boy here. And he's not going to say anything."

Delia's brother turned his attention to the child who sat straight in the saddle and clutched the saddle horn with both hands. The boy's hat shaded his face as he leaned forward and patted his horse on the neck. He wore no shirt under mud-stained overalls. His boots looked about two sizes too big for his feet. The sole on one flopped loose at the toe.

"He's a Negra," Colin said. "There's abolitionists hereabouts. They find him in Sangamon and think we're keeping a slave here, there'll be hell to pay. You a slave, boy?"

"He's not a slave, Colin," Delia said. "His pa, a freeman, got hanged near Shawnee-town by a gang hunting for runaways. His ma, well, she got worse, according to the boy. I found him hiding in the big woods, all hunkered down and shaking like a scared rabbit."

"And you came here for help, Delia? Don't you reckon that's a mite stupid after what you done? Bringing that boy here to boot. I think you must be out of your mind."

Delia looked at the other two men on the feed store porch who were listening to the conversation with interest. "What about you two?" she said. "You think my brother should turn me away when I might fall off my horse and die any minute now?"

One of the men shrugged. The other leaned forward and brushed the dust from his boot. The first man pointed along the road in the same direction Delia headed. "You know where the smithy shop and stable are. Go on past them. At the saloon, take the road to the right. We got us a full-time doctor now, name's Ernest Hemmer. Doc Hemmer. He'll take care of you."

"Thanks. I'm mighty grateful a few folks around here have a kinder heart than my own kin."

The man scowled. "Don't put a lot of stock in my kind heart, Delia. Most of this town remember what you done. Folks will not take you to their hearts. Could be they'd run you out of town on a rail. You take the boy with you and keep him out of sight. We don't have none of his kind in Sangamon."

Delia looked at the boy and smiled. "Don't pay them any mind, young'un. This world is full of ignorant men." Colin's harsh words hurt worse than Jeremiah's or this other man she couldn't place. Maybe she'd made a big mistake. Maybe, as Colin said, she was plain stupid.

She tapped McAllister's flank with her heel and led the way. As she passed the stable, she noticed the addition to its east side, more stalls visible from the road. At the saloon, now a bigger and fancier building than the one built of logs and mud she remembered, she guided the horse to the right and urged him to walk a little faster. By the time she found the cabin with the doctor's shingle hanging out front, she was hunched over the saddle horn, trying to fight her nausea. She wondered if the pain made her sick . . . or the fear of dying.

"You doing okay, Miss Delia?" the boy said. "There's the sign. Office of Ernest Hemmer, M.D."

"Yes, I reckon it is." She guided the Palouse to the rail and sat still, trying to get her feelings under control. Delia had figured she'd get patched up by her brother with a prod fired in the blacksmith's shop and a bottle of horse liniment if the old doctor wasn't in town. Hard to believe a real full-time doctor had moved to a little place like Sangamon.

There used to be a visiting preacher, too, but she saw no signs of a church. The new saloon occupied the biggest lot on Main Street. It sat at a junction, so anyone passing through town would see its huge sign. Apparently drinking and carousing ranked higher in importance than praying, but nothing new about that.

Delia wondered if Colin had a wife and kids now. Kids. She looked over her shoulder to check on the young'un. Her whole arm shrieked with pain. Sweat broke out on her forehead and she moaned.

"You okay, Miss Delia?"

A smothered chuckle escaped her lips "I will be soon as we get this doctor to fix my shoulder."

Would she come out of this mess alive? She sure didn't want to be buried here without benefit of a preacher or a blessing. Her ma had delivered Delia and Colin in this same town without a doctor and no baptizing, either. Full circle brought her home, but she didn't want to die in this hateful place. Full circle be hanged.

The doctor's office sat near the road, while a second cabin had been built to the side and rear. Small rocks lined the dirt path to the front door in an effort to hold back the sparse, dried prairie grass. Delia sat for a moment, still in the grip of gut-stirring pain, hoping someone would come out to help.

"Hello," she called. In the silence that followed, she glanced at the boy. "I reckon I need to get inside on my own." She dropped the Palouse's reins across his neck, trusting him to stand still until she signaled him to move. Kicking her feet free of the stirrups, she swung her right leg over the saddle and slid off the horse in one smooth move. The landing wasn't as easy as she planned. Her hand jerked free of the belt sling. A jolt of pain shot from her shoulder to her fingers.

She staggered and dropped to one knee.

The boy jumped off his horse and ran to her side, grabbing her uninjured arm at the elbow. It was enough support to keep Delia from landing face-first on the hard-packed dirt road. She gasped and bowed her head. "Oh, damnation, that hurts. If I had that son of a whore in my sights, I'd shoot him all over again."

"You hurting bad, Miss Delia?"

"Yeah, young'un, but I'll be okay." She smiled at the boy and took a few deep breaths, letting them out slow and easy. The pain eased a little. Then she turned her stern look on the child. "How many times do I have to tell you. You don't have to call me Miss Delia. Delia will do fine. Now run inside and get that doctor for me, will you? I don't think I can stand by myself."

The boy sprinted up the path to the door and opened the latch. "Doctor, doctor," he cried. "Help!" When they heard no answer, the boy disappeared inside. A minute later, he returned, trailed by a middle-aged man carrying a black bag.

"What happened?" the man asked as he rushed to Delia's side.

"Got a bullet in my shoulder."

"Can you walk if I help you?"

"I think so. But take it slow, Doc."

16

He set his bag on the ground and gently helped Delia to her feet. "Would you get that bag for me, son?"

Delia's heart jumped. She hadn't run into too many people over the last few days who treated the boy with kindness. Calling the boy "son" was a nice thing for the doctor to do.

After her impulsive decision to take the boy with her to Sangamon, she'd wondered if any good would come of it. If she couldn't defend the child, bounty hunters looking for runaways would get him. Her hope that her brother would provide shelter for her and the boy had proved to be a foolish notion.

Inside the doctor's spacious office, a high bed with a thin mattress and pillow took up considerable space. Two cabinets with glass doors flanked a table against the wall. An assortment of doctoring tools lay on a white cloth. A stack of folded rags sat at the rear corner of the table. The air smelled sharp, like homegrown corn whiskey with a kick. Delia's eyes watered. The doctor was going to save her life, had to save her life. She let her thoughts go soft at the edges and melt away, relaxing her muscles to help ease the pain.

Doc Hemmer guided Delia to the cot,

holding her upright when her legs went wobbly. As she tried to scoot her rear end onto the side of the bed, she bumped her hand again, waking her out of her stupor. "Shitfire!" she cried. "That hurts like hell." She grabbed her hat and flung it onto the floor, no longer giving a hoot about her appearance.

The doctor waited while Delia got herself settled, her legs dangling over the side of the bed, then he gently lifted the belt and removed it over her head. He eased her left hand onto her thigh.

"Do you think we can get your shirt off without you passing out?"

She shook her head. "Cut it off. I can't stand any more pain right now. It's a damn ugly shirt anyhow."

"Could you use a drink?"

"Hell, yes, I could use a drink. Maybe a whole jug. You got something powerful?"

"I do, in the cookhouse. I'll be right back." The doctor went out a door at the rear of the cabin and returned with a full tin cup. Delia sniffed the contents, winced at the whiskey fumes, and emptied the cup in a few swallows. "Give it a minute," she said.

Doc busied himself at the table.

Delia glanced up to check on the boy's whereabouts. He stood at the end of the bed, watching the doctor gather supplies — a big pair of scissors, a lethal-looking knife with a bone handle, and a brown bottle with a glass stopper. Delia focused on the tool's sharp edge, then finally looked away and tried to concentrate on the back wall where three documents in wooden frames hung in a row. Delia squinted to see better, but they were too far away to make out the words. She hoped they all said Doc Hemmer was well educated and fully trained to dig around in her shoulder and dispense whatever medicine she needed to get well.

Another door at the back of the doctor's office was open. A narrow, low bed sat against the side wall. A fat pillow lay at the head, and a blue-and-green appliquéd quilt covered the thick mattress, the edges tucked in tight.

Turning her attention to the doctor, Delia noted his shined leather boots with only a tiny bit of dust on one toe. He wore a blue-denim oversized shirt over brown pants. He appeared to be older than her, perhaps thirty-five or forty. His brown hair showed no gray. He wore it long to his shoulders, tied at the nape with a strip of rawhide. His eyes were brown and kind. Calluses stretched across the base of his fingers.

"You live in that little room?" she asked.

"No, that's for patients. I live in the other cabin by the cookhouse."

The mellow warmth of the drink had spread from Delia's gut to the rest of her body, except for the shoulder that felt on fire. Still, waiting would make it worse. "You can cut my shirt now," she said. "Where's the young'un? He doesn't need to watch this."

"I'm doing fine right here, Miss Delia." He'd moved to stand behind her, next to the bed. "I can catch you if you fall."

"I won't need catching. You go on outside and tie the horses to the railing. And bring the saddlebags and my long gun inside. That new Colt, too. We might be here awhile. Doc, you can start now. Let's get this done with."

The boy ran out the door and returned in less than a minute, dragging the saddlebags along the floor and clutching the rifle and revolver to his chest.

"Careful, young'un, those guns are loaded."

The boy dropped the bags. He handed Delia the rifle and lay the revolver on the bed.

The doctor picked up the weapons without asking, briefly examined the handgun and placed it on his worktable next to the pile of rags. He propped the rifle against the wall by the front door. Delia didn't care what he did with the guns. Asking for another cup of whiskey was the thing highest on her mind.

"Young'un, you go on over and sit in that rocking chair. You don't need to stand so close."

The boy did as she told him, dragging the saddlebags alongside. He picked up Delia's hat on the way and laid it next to the chair. He didn't sit but stood where he could watch the doctor's every move.

When Doc Hemmer put the scissors down, he gently peeled away the fabric stuck to Delia's arm and shoulder with dried blood.

"Looks bad, don't it?" she said, her teeth clenched against the new pain from the reopened wound.

"Probably not as bad as it feels. There's no redness on your arm or back. The entry wound is small, so there's likely just one piece of shot to deal with."

"Can you get it out of there?"

The doctor put his hand on Delia's forehead. "I'll do the best I can."

"I have a fever, don't I?" she said. "I guess that's why I feel so ornery. That and the pain."

The doctor walked around the bed to stand in front of Delia. He looked her in the eye and put on what she would call a serious doctor face. "You do have a slight fever, but it hasn't killed you yet. I need to clean out that shoulder. Don't worry. I've done this before. Served in Alabama during the Creek Uprising. It won't take long and then the rest will be up to you and how fast your body recovers. You'll be ready to move on in a week or two."

"A week or two? I can't be here that long. The town won't put up with it. My own brother won't put up with it."

"Who's your brother?"

"Colin Pritchard."

The doctor stepped back, glanced over at the boy, then at her. The corner of his mouth turned up as if he wanted to smile but didn't quite dare. "So, you're the gal they call Trouble. I always thought you were one of those tall tales used to scare children and entertain the old folks."

Delia grimaced. "It isn't funny. It might be mostly tall tales you've heard, but the folks in Sangamon won't look kindly on my troubles, that's for sure. You need to get me moving faster than two weeks. It would save all of us from a mess of squabbles with those that don't want us here."

"We'll see what happens. Did you plan to stay at Colin's place?"

"The room behind the stable is what I asked for. I doubt he'll let me. And I know he won't let the young'un in his house."

"Then you'll stay here."

"And the young'un?"

"He can stay as well. What's his name?"

Delia turned toward the boy, and said, "Tell the doctor your name."

"It's Andrew Jackson, sir! I was named after a president of the United States."

The doctor raised his eyebrows and looked properly impressed. "If it's okay with you, young man, I'm going to call you Jackson."

"Yes, sir. Sir, is that your name on the sign out front?" Jackson asked.

"Yes, it is. You can call me Doc Hemmer or just Doc."

"Where'd you live before you moved here?" Delia asked.

"I grew up in Ohio, then went to school in New York. Joined the army for a spell. I've only been here a year."

"What made you pick this village from hell?" Delia asked.

"Jeremiah Frost advertised for a full-time doctor in about every newspaper east of the Ohio River. I had left the army and hated the idea of returning to my old life, especially now that my parents have both passed. With the country's finances going bad, it seemed more exciting to follow the pioneers, help out a town that had a need."

Delia shifted her position and winced, then tried to ignore her pain by focusing on Doc. "When I lived here, an old doctor spent part of his time in Sangamon but mostly loaded up his horse and buggy and visited farms and settlements for miles around. If you got sick, you might survive if he was close by, or you might die if he wasn't."

Doc frowned. "There's a terrible shortage of doctors in these parts. Lots of folks dying before their time."

"That's what happened to Schoolmaster Billings, too. He taught us our lessons when the schoolhouse first got built, but he got a god-awful disease called scarlet fever that turned him red all over. Killed him and two or three of the children. The young'uns dying near broke our hearts, but none of us minded the schoolmaster meeting his maker. That man was so mean he snapped a bullwhip at any child who didn't pay attention. He left marks on my arm for talking out of turn and beating up boys."

"That's why they call you Trouble? Jeremiah said you were a wild child but beating on boys doesn't seem all that bad."

"There's more," Delia said. "If you heard that much, I'm surprised you don't know the rest of my story. Jeremiah thinks the worst, I know that. He told his little girl to stay away from the likes of me. My brother wouldn't even give me directions to your cabin. Took a stranger to take pity on me and send me your way." Realizing the whiskey had taken hold of her tongue and set it wagging, Delia chewed on her bottom lip and looked at the floor.

"I'm sorry that's the way things are for you," Doc said. "Let's get that shoulder fixed and we'll see how fast we can get you headed out of town."

Well, that's what I asked for. But Delia felt a twinge of hurt anyway. She'd hoped, at least for a moment, the doctor would become her champion, that he would help her find a place to hide out for a while. Now it sounded as if he, like everyone else, wanted to get rid of her.

Delia heard the door of the cabin open and close. A woman walked around the bed and stopped. She looked at Delia's face and bared shoulder, glanced at Doc Hemmer, then removed her feathered green hat.

An odd hat for summertime, Delia thought, desperate to find things to distract

25

herself from her misery. The woman hung the hat from a nail on the wall and stood beside Doc with her hands at her sides. Her dark-blue muslin dress was spotless, her white collar lacy and prim.

Delia felt a flush mark her cheeks as the lady raised her eyebrows.

"Mary, you're just in time," Doc said. "I'm about to remove a piece of lead from this young woman's shoulder and clean the wound. We'll need to treat her here for a few days to prevent blood poisoning."

"I heard. I let the children go home early so I could help."

"Miss Pritchard, this is Mary Proud. She's the schoolmarm now. I'm also teaching her to be my assistant."

Delia looked at Mary curiously, her name vaguely familiar. "You've lived in Sangamon a long time, haven't you?"

"Yes."

"But you weren't the next schoolteacher after Billings died."

"No, that was Sarah. She's now married to Jeremiah and expecting her first child."

"So, you live in the room behind the schoolhouse?"

"Yes," Mary said. She abruptly turned her back on Delia, then stopped when she spotted Jackson in the rocking chair. "Who's this?" she asked.

Doc explained as he gathered more supplies from the worktable and placed them on the bed next to Delia.

Mary wrinkled her nose. "Perhaps a bath for the boy when we're finished here?"

"That would be kind of you," Delia said. "We haven't been near a washtub or even a cold-water creek since I got shot. I reckon I could use a bath, too."

Mary went to Doc Hemmer's side. "What should I do first?" she asked.

Doc handed her a small stack of clean white rags. "Be ready to wipe away the blood."

CHAPTER TWO:
NEW DOCTOR IN TOWN

When Doc Hemmer arrived in Sangamon in the summer of 1837, he found the state and the town very different from the eastern part of the country where he'd grown up. His most frequent visitors in Sangamon — the lady farmer, Miss Annie Gray, and the self-appointed town leader, Jeremiah Frost — were also the town gossips. Not that folks back in Ohio hadn't passed on tales about their neighbors, but these two Sangamon residents were champions at the art of chatter with little regard for the truth in their tales or the consequences of telling all they knew, or thought they knew.

From Jeremiah, Doc learned about the gory death of Mary Proud's son, the demented Caswell, and the disappearance of Caswell's much younger half sister, Jo Mae. The old Indian called Fish and the young preacher, John Claymore, had left town the same day, Jeremiah confided.

"Suspicious, don't you think?" he asked.

Doc had nodded and then tried to forget all gossip about Mary and her family.

Annie Gray was eager to describe the sudden illness and death of Jeremiah's wife. "Sad, so sad," she told Doc, shaking her head. But her expression turned sour as she went on to tell of Jeremiah's rapid recovery from his loss and his courtship of the town's lovely schoolteacher, Sarah.

"Quite unsuitable," Miss Gray said, shaking her head. She leaned closer to Doc and whispered, "Sarah has a fondness for whiskey. She should not be watching over Jeremiah's daughter, nor should she be having children of her own. Good thing Jeremiah's oldest are away at school. They'd have a few things to say, I'm sure."

Annie and Jeremiah competed to see who could tell Doc Hemmer the most lurid stories about Mary Proud — beginning with how she'd come to Sangamon as a widow with a young son — then shared her bed with the itinerant French trapper who fathered her daughter, Jo Mae. Doc tried to let these stories go in one ear and out the other.

Jeremiah claimed he couldn't believe the change Mary had undergone as she gradually reformed her dependent and lazy ways, volunteered to tutor children and assist the schoolteacher, and eventually became the replacement instructor when Sarah married Jeremiah and became pregnant.

Annie seemed determined that Doc should know the terrible life Mary had lived and that Annie had kept the family from starving. "I also made certain that little girl, Jo Mae, stayed safe from Mary and Caswell, especially while Jo Mae was with child and living with the old Indian."

Doc stared at Annie, not knowing whether he could believe such an appalling tale about a child.

Annie sighed. "I suppose losing both her children in one day made Mary realize she had to change or die."

Although the rumors about Mary Proud and her past varied from one gossipmonger to another, most painted her as a sad victim of circumstance and a shining example of how one can recover from a sordid past and become a pillar of the community. Once Doc Hemmer met Mary for himself and had occasion to treat her for minor afflictions while conversing on various topics, he found her well spoken and well educated. Over time, he learned she came from Philadelphia, but she seemed unwilling to say more. Older than he, she treated him like a youngster, as though she was his sister or friend.

When he eventually asked if she would like to work for him when she was not teaching, she surprised him by showing reluctance. He won her over with his promise to train her in everything he'd learned about medicine and surgery. He could afford to pay Mary for her time. With his large inheritance at risk as the country's economy deteriorated, Doc had abandoned Ohio, taking his funds in gold and silver specie from the Cleveland Bank. On the trip west and when he finally settled in Sangamon, he had hidden his hoard well. She finally agreed, telling Doc she could not bear to be idle, especially during weekends and summers. She said she feared that inactivity might leave her too much time to dredge up bad memories and dwell on past indiscretions.

Doc Hemmer forgave anything in Mary's past without knowing exactly what needed forgiving. Except for Miss Gray, the townsfolk had already given Mary a pass on whatever bad things she'd done, so he had no interest in asking questions. He understood her need to use her mind for good purpose, to live for the present day. He often pushed memories of dead or brutally injured soldiers from his own nightmares. He and

Mary each claimed a traumatic past but chose not to bring up more than necessary.

"You plan to hire Mary Proud?" Annie Gray had exclaimed in surprise.

"I certainly do," the doctor said. "She has a quick mind and will make an excellent doctor's assistant."

"But —"

"Never you mind, Miss Gray. This is not your life to live. Now tell me, what ails you today?"

Miss Gray had sucked in her breath, lowered her chin, and glared at Doc Hemmer. She then pursed her lips as though ready to give him a piece of her mind.

"Tut," he had said. "Is it your lumbago?"

She relaxed her shoulders. "It is. I strained my back again when I tried to pull the mule away from my garden. He balked, then jerked to the side. The rope I wrapped around my waist tightened, and he pulled me off my feet."

"The treatment will be bed rest, Miss Gray. No bending or lifting for a month. I always tell you the same thing."

"And I always tell you that I can't take care of my farm without bending or lifting."

"You're getting —"

"Don't you dast tell me I'm getting older, Doctor Hemmer. I'm no older than you."

He knew that wasn't true. Annie Gray had at least ten years on him, which would put her in her late forties. He was too much of a gentleman to correct her on such a delicate matter.

"Then you must resolve to be more careful in the future, Miss Gray. For now, perhaps you can ask for help from your neighbors. There are older boys who do little more than run about town tormenting each other. Hard work would go far toward applying that excess energy to good cause."

"I will not have a passel of young ruffians tearing through my garden and chasing my mule."

"Let me ask around Sangamon to see if any of the boys might be willing to help. If we arranged for one assistant at a time, perhaps there will be little disturbance to worry about. Watching one young man at work would not tax your energies unfairly, would it?"

Miss Gray had ducked her head to agree. "I'll trust your judgment," she'd said. "About the boys helping on the farm." Giving Doctor Hemmer a sharp glance and raising her eyebrow, she'd added, "But I do not trust your judgment about Mary Proud. You'll be sorry if you take her on as your assistant."

Hemmer had turned away, strode to the front door of his office, and held it open as a pointed dismissal. She'd left in a huff with her chin held high and her shoulders rigid.

Sadly, he thought, that exchange didn't stop Miss Gray from coming to his office at least twice a month, usually with the same complaints about her lumbago, but occasionally with another injury to her body, accidentally self-inflicted with one of her farm tools.

The partnership he developed with Mary involved nightly study sessions with his medical books and her active participation in treating each of his patients. Mary's gentle touch and her kindness helped temper Miss Gray's stubbornness as well as curb the woman's sharp tongue.

"Miss Gray kept my children and me alive when I fell on hard times," Mary said. "I needed food most of all, something Miss Gray could supply in abundance. Despite her criticisms and her tendency to pass on every bit of gossip she hears, she does good works in the name of our Lord. Perhaps she fancies herself one of God's helpers."

Hemmer glanced at Mary's face to see if she was joking, but she appeared quite serious. She read her book for a moment, then turned the page. When she realized he was watching her, she laughed. "A silly notion, yes? Annie Gray as the right hand of God? Can you imagine her preaching a sermon or setting the punishment for those of us who have sinned?"

The camaraderie Hemmer and Mary shared, the time spent in teaching and learning, and their ability to work side by side, whether in the doctor's office or the doctor's garden and chicken coop, helped forge a bond no one in the Village of Sangamon could break.

Doc Hemmer had thought about Annie Gray many times over the last year, wondering if her mind was aging even faster than her body. The woman was not ancient by any means, but it was clear her physical strength had declined. Mary also told him Miss Gray's life had been hard, but was best not discussed, especially with Annie herself. The ramblings of the lady farmer could stir up trouble. Sangamon did not need any more trouble.

Chapter Three:
Annie's Life Changes

Annie had indeed noticed her memory problems, her declining strength, and her tendency to fall asleep in her rocking chair long before her usual bedtime. Getting old scared her. The thought she might die alone terrified her. More and more she pushed herself to stroll around the town, chattering about this and that with anyone who would listen.

After failing to convince Jeremiah he should not marry Sarah, Annie had stomped out of the general store and all the way to her farm before she realized she'd meant to buy a sack of cornmeal. It would have to wait. She did not want to see Jeremiah or Sarah again until she could do so without showing her rage. *Best to forget. Forget everything.* Annie and Sarah must put their secret intimacy to rest the same way Annie and Mary Proud had buried the secret about Caswell's murder. Best to never talk about it. Best to never think about it.

Annie had needed a distraction when Jeremiah instructed her to stay away from Sarah. For a time, she concentrated on the newest arrivals in town. The two hat-shop ladies appeared one day, sharing very little information about who they were and where they came from. Annie shopped for a new hat and asked a lot of questions.

She also wanted to learn more about the man who built the fancy new saloon and promised to turn it into a place for travelers to rent a room and buy a meal. He certainly bore watching to make sure he didn't include a brothel in his plans. The residents of Sangamon could never tolerate the presence of whores in their town.

Mary Proud no longer seemed like the same person. Annie had criticized and judged her behavior for years while still offering gifts of food and midwifing when Mary's second child came into the world. They could never be more than nodding acquaintances. Such a pity.

Annie tried to learn more about Mary's transformation. From a slovenly creature a mere four years ago, Mary had blossomed into a productive and gracious citizen of Sangamon. She cleaned herself up and tutored children that Sarah seemed unable to help. Mary built a quilting frame, with Colin Pritchard's help, where she sat for hours, creating new patterns and then teaching the craft to others. She started a quilting circle that included Colin Pritchard's wife and the two hat-shop ladies. She did not invite Annie to join. Annie knew why, and knew it was for the best. Nodding acquaintances they would remain. But it still annoyed her to be excluded. Perhaps that small humiliation explained why Annie persisted in her belief that Mary was not fit to be a schoolmarm or tend to the doctor's patients.

Annie also wanted to learn more about Mary Proud's father. He had visited Sangamon briefly and, according to Jeremiah, promised Mary he would return soon with a load of building lumber and nails. He wanted to build Mary a new house. The falling-down log cabin she'd lived in for years had been taken over and remodeled by the hat-shop ladies. For now, Mary lived in the small living space attached to the schoolhouse.

The new doctor presented another mystery for Annie to unravel. Distinguished and handsome, his arrival in town led to an eruption of injuries and complaints that prompted Annie to stop by Doc's office at least once a week. Annie continued to seek his care for her ailments, even after he hired Mary. With Annie's view of the doctor's office and cabin from her barn door, she always knew when Mary went to the school and left the doctor alone. Only then would she hustle to his office and explain again why Mary might not be suited to nursing.

Annie looked forward to the new traveling preacher's return more than any other event in Sangamon. He'd only visited once so far, well over six months before, and for the life of her, she couldn't remember his name. This new circuit-riding man of God had captured the town's attention with his youthful vigor and his comforting way of talking to the people instead of preaching at them as though they were all sinners and he the only righteous person in the world. Before his arrival, the town had been deprived of the Lord's Word for more than three years, ever since Preacher Claymore had vanished along with Jo Mae Proud and the old Indian. Just as well. Preacher Claymore knew what happened the day Caswell Proud died. If he had stayed on in Sangamon, he might have said too much during one of his sermons. The whole town did not need to know what happened that day in the woods.

After Sarah married Jeremiah, and Doc Hemmer would no longer listen to Annie's gossip about Mary, Annie felt abandoned. The townsfolk were tired of her scatter-brained and annoying ways. Talking to herself became her comfort, her own voice one of reassurance and strength. She tried not to let anyone hear, knowing they would tell each other she'd gone crazy as a loon.

The new preacher had said he would visit twice a year. Now the only one who would suffer through an afternoon at Annie's table without complaint, he took up a major part of Annie's thinking.

CHAPTER FOUR:
SARAH'S LIFE IN SANGAMON

When Sarah Wallace first arrived in Sangamon in 1828, her schoolteacher life was made miserable by more than just rowdy and undisciplined children. At first, Sarah had been relieved to have a friend like Annie Gray in this wild place, someone to help her adjust to the primitive Illinois frontier. But their friendship changed as time went on. The elegant and refined Sarah, as she saw herself, grew increasingly lonely because of her shyness and inability to control the ruffians in her classroom. That isolation left her vulnerable when Annie intruded on Sarah's privacy and became uncomfortably familiar. As their relationship became more intimate, Sarah craved Annie's touch, even when overcome by shame.

Sarah withdrew to her small room behind the school and rarely ventured from the building unless she needed supplies from the store. Terrified the townsfolk would discover the women's secret, Sarah suffered from night terrors when left alone. What if Jeremiah fired her, or a bunch of folks ran her out of town? Or ridiculed her in public, shunned her? Annie would surely turn on Sarah to save her own reputation. Alone and destitute in this backwoods state, Sarah would die.

The peddler brought the antidote to her fears on his regular trips through the region. One bottle of whiskey lasted Sarah through several weekends, her excesses often overflowing onto Monday.

The passing years brought more upheaval. Mary Proud's son died a violent death, but no one discovered who did the killing. Caswell's young sister disappeared, as did the old Kickapoo Indian who lived by the river. The preacher, John Claymore, who always said something to make Sarah weep, left and never returned.

But Annie Gray continued to visit Sarah's room whenever she pleased, accepting no protest or excuse. Sarah's drinking was a problem for Annie, who claimed the whiskey would lead a body into the flames of hell. She emptied Sarah's bottles when she found them. Sarah divided her supply and found excellent hiding places. That one act of rebellion against Annie's hypocrisy kept her sane. If Sarah killed herself with whiskey, she'd be free of that horrid school, free of Annie, free of Sangamon, and free of her tawdry life.

With nowhere to go, no family to help, Sarah believed nothing would ever change. Then Jeremiah's wife, weary from pregnancies and stillborns and years of hard work, struggled to deliver the late-in-life child she'd never wanted. The baby died. Jeremiah lost the boy he had hoped for after all those years. His wife died a day later. Jeremiah was left with one child still at home, his daughter, Elizabeth.

The funeral turned into a village affair. Annie dragged Sarah to view the body and sit through a long sermon delivered by Annie herself. Sarah wept when Jeremiah sobbed and moaned, his anguish so real that she leaned forward and placed her hand on his shoulder. He seemed not to notice. Sarah removed her hand when Annie glared in disapproval.

On Sarah's occasional trips to the general store over the next couple of months, she observed Jeremiah's apparent grief. That's how long his mourning lasted. Two months. Then Jeremiah began to woo the unmarried women in Sangamon. Sarah understood right away that he sought a wife.

When Jeremiah called on the outwardly pious and hardworking Annie Gray, she rejected him with disdain.

"The man thinks he can take over my farm and then work me to death," she told Sarah. "The old fool!"

Mary Proud had turned her own life around after her son died and her daughter ran away. But when Jeremiah tried calling on Mary, she promptly pushed him out her front door, where Annie happened to be passing by.

Sarah listened thoughtfully as Annie reported Mary's words: "Get on with you. I like my life the way it is. When my father returns, I'll have a new house. I would not care to have a husband take over the deed just because I'd become a married woman."

The two newest residents of Sangamon, the hat-shop ladies, were single but too old for Jeremiah's courting. That left Sarah the only other single lady in town old enough to marry a man of Jeremiah's age.

The first time Jeremiah called on Sarah, she giggled as though delighted with his attention. Until Jeremiah's wife died, it had never occurred to Sarah she'd find a suitor. The more she considered Jeremiah's interest, the more she realized he offered an escape from Annie's clutches. Sarah didn't know him well, but assumed he knew nothing of her friendship with Annie. He certainly was not aware of her weekends alone, hiding in her room, drunk as a farmer at the saloon on Saturday night. If he'd learned about that, she would have been fired long ago.

When Jeremiah finally proposed, she quickly accepted.

Then she tried to explain her decision to Annie.

"He offers me a better home than this room behind the school. I might have children. I've always wanted children, but supposed I'd grow old a spinster teacher, supported by the townsfolk with never a life of my own." Sarah felt no guilt about lying to Annie. Truthfully, she hated the idea of being pregnant, but hated the idea of continuing her present existence even more. Annie's protests barely registered.

"Sarah, he'll work you day and night in that store, then make you do the cooking and cleaning besides. You'll be with child most of your days and still be a slave to his demands. You'll be mother to that incorrigible Elizabeth who gets everything she wants."

"But this is what I choose, Annie. I'm going to marry Jeremiah."

Annie had approached Jeremiah in his store after hearing the news. "I understand you want to marry Sarah," she said. "That would be a terrible mistake."

Jeremiah gave Annie his full attention. "Why would you say that?"

"You need a woman who knows hard work, one who is strong and healthy, one who is good in spirit and action. Sarah is none of those things."

"I know more about Sarah than you believe I do," Jeremiah said. "You may keep your thoughts to yourself."

"She drinks whiskey!" Annie blurted out.

"I thought you were her friend. Why would you tell such terrible lies about her? When Sarah and I are married, she'll have no more need of your company. You'll stay away." Jeremiah had pulled a bag of flour from the shelf behind the counter. "Now, do you have an order to fill? If not, I'm a busy man and have no time for gossip."

CHAPTER FIVE:
THE RECOVERY BEGINS

Delia's shoulder pain was slightly dulled by the cup of whiskey, but the ache didn't stop her from observing how well the doctor and Mary worked together. Both assured Delia that all would be fine as they helped her relax onto her stomach on the bed with her bad arm hanging off the side. Mary suggested Delia turn her head away from the doctor and administer her own anesthetic as needed.

"An anesthetic? What is that?" Delia asked.

Doc held up a bottle and swirled the liquid before removing the cap. He tipped the bottle toward Delia's face, so she raised her head and took a whiff.

"This is called ether," he said.

Delia lay her head on the pillow and relaxed. "It doesn't smell too bad, but I never heard of it before. Why not give me another cup of that whiskey instead?"

"Ether is an uncommon way to send a patient to sleep, I admit," the doctor said. "When I studied medicine during my days at university, we played with ether for fun."

"Putting yourselves to sleep? Doesn't sound like fun to me."

The doctor laughed. "Young men do very strange things in the name of fun."

"Well, I have no experience with young men at a university," Delia said.

"Like most new ideas, acceptance of ether as a method of anesthesia will take time."

"Why is that? Too dangerous? Are you using me as some kind of test patient?"

"No, not at all. Blame it on the doddering old fools who spend years ridiculing new ideas before they're forced to accept change. Only on the battlefield could we experiment without supervision, keeping the practice secret in fear of being charged with using poison against our own soldiers. When we were about to inflict additional pain and suffering on the gravely injured, we scorned the rules."

Doc Hemmer stopped and cleared his throat. "Sorry, I'm pontificating. I shouldn't be going on like that. The ether will work better than whiskey, and most assuredly better than biting on a stick. You'll feel relief from the pain, and you'll be asleep while I clean out your shoulder."

Delia moved the ether-soaked rag Mary had placed in her hand close to her face but pulled it back as she looked the doctor in the eye and asked, "Will you swear an oath this won't kill me?"

The doctor placed his hand over his heart. "Yes, I swear."

As soon as Doc Hemmer touched the wound, Mary guided Delia's hand to her nose. Delia pushed the rag away. "The pain has been bad for days. I've had nothing but whiskey to settle it down. I can take it a little longer."

At that instant, the doctor probed the bullet hole with something sharp. Delia screeched, pressed the rag to her face, and sucked in a deep breath. She sighed as her hand relaxed and the cloth dropped to the side. "Sorry," she whispered. "I didn't think it would hurt that bad."

"I'll scrape aside the crusted blood so I can see what I'm doing. It's going to hurt worse when I poke deeper. If I were you, I'd put that rag over your nose and keep it there."

Delia tried to raise her head but failed. "Hey, young'un, you still in here?"

"Yes, Miss Delia."

"Delia."

"Yes, ma'am."

"Don't you want to go outside so you don't have to watch this?"

"That's not a good idea," Mary said.

Delia looked at the woman who stood at the bedside with her hand close to the ether rag. Mary's forehead creased as though worried the boy would do something bad, or something bad would happen to him. "He's not safe outside?" Delia asked.

"There's some who don't want his kind in town."

"You mean they don't want Negroes here?"

"They don't want the abolitionists to come around and accuse us of keeping slaves. I'm sure you've heard of the Reverend Lovejoy who was murdered near St. Louis last year?"

"Of course."

"There's plenty of folk around this part of Illinois who own a slave or two, but no one here in Sangamon. We don't want that kind of attention. We've had enough violence in this town. No sense inviting trouble."

Mary put her hand to her mouth as though she couldn't believe her own words. "I'm sorry," she said. "I didn't mean you."

"It's okay," said Delia. "I see how the wind is blowing. It's going to blow me and the young'un out of town as fast as we can go."

"Let the boy stay inside while you're here. He can sit in the other room and look at a book. Can he read?"

"I reckon," Delia said. "He read the sign out front of Doc's office. I haven't had him around long enough to ask that kind of question."

"I can read mighty fine," Jackson said.

Delia closed her eyes as Mary bustled about, her skirts sweeping the floor as she pulled books from wherever she had them stored and chatted to the boy as they moved farther away. When Mary returned, she placed her hand on Delia's forehead. "She's burning up."

"I know," Doc said. "Let's get this done."

Mary retrieved the white cloth and wet it again from the glass bottle. She placed it in Delia's hand and pushed the hand closer to Delia's face.

At the next touch of the doctor's scalpel into her wound, Delia pressed the cloth to her nose and breathed as deeply as she could.

When Delia woke, her stomach heaved, and her left arm and shoulder throbbed with the kind of pain she hadn't come close to experiencing with the lead shot. She tried to move her head to the side so she could puke on the floor instead of the bed. Any movement made the headache and nausea worse. She lay as still as possible with her eyes closed.

Mary's voice cut through Delia's pain. "You're feeling sick. Chew this sprig of peppermint. It might help."

Delia felt the herb touch her lips and then press into her mouth. She moved the mint around with her tongue, then bit into the peppery wad. She tucked the mint into her cheek like a plug of tobacco and let the smell and taste flavor her saliva until she could swallow. The nausea eased, but Delia feared to move her head.

As she took stock of her body and its position, she realized she still rested on the doctor's high bed in the front room of the office. She lay on her stomach, her head turned to the right. Her left arm no longer dangled from the cot but stretched along her side. She carefully turned her head to view the damage. Her shoulder and upper arm were heavily bandaged, her arm secured to her waist with a soft cloth binding. Wiggling her fingers took concentration, but they moved like they were supposed to move. The effort, however, hurt like the devil.

"How long was I out?"

"For the surgery? No more than an hour. When you let the ether rag drop away, I held it over your nose awhile longer. I don't think you felt much. You've been asleep ever since, near on three hours. How's your pain?"

"It's bad."

"When Ernest returns, and he's sure the anesthetic has worn off, he'll give you laudanum. I'm not allowed —"

"It's locked away?" Delia tried to raise her head to look around, but she couldn't see much on the doctor's worktable or whether the glass cabinets had locks. If she had to get out of town in a hurry, she'd need to take some of the drug with her. Steal it if need be.

"Yes, he keeps it locked away."

"I guess it's dangerous if you use too much."

Mary's voice dropped to a near whisper. "Especially dangerous if found by a child. That's what happened here before Ernest moved to Sangamon. The old doctor left town soon after. Just as well. I think a horrible fate awaited him at the hands of the girl's mother."

"A little girl died?"

"It was an accident, but no one in town would forgive the old man for his carelessness. He should never have left the drug on an open shelf."

Did she read my mind about stealing? Delia thought of the boy she'd taken under her protection, thought how she'd feel if she carelessly caused his death. Dang! The notion made her heartsick. That emotional reaction was one more problem. She had no business getting that close to any human being, especially a child. Not the way her life had unfolded. *I can't afford to get soft.* She needed to find a home for the boy as soon as she could.

"Are there any of those abolitionists around here?" Delia's words came out of her lips as incoherent mumbling. She repeated her question in an effort to speak more clearly.

"I don't know," Mary said. "A man and woman traveled through town not so long ago, and they had two dark-colored women in their wagon bed, sitting on heaps of loose straw. They stopped here for Doc to tend to a bad cut on the man's hand. I figured the colored women might be runaways."

"Anything bad happen while they were here?"

"No. They took a chance staying out in the open, but they came straight here and moved on that same day. The man and his wife could be abolitionists, but that's guessing. Haven't seen them since."

Mary paused, then touched Delia on the hand and whispered, "You'd give Jackson to the abolitionists?"

Delia sighed. "Can the young'un hear us?"

"I don't think so."

"I don't know what to do. I can't be much help to the child if I'm always on the move. He won't get a good home; he won't go to school. What was I thinking?"

"You thought you couldn't leave him alone after his parents were murdered."

"The doctor told you?"

"Yes. But you must know, he can't stay here. I don't think Jeremiah would let the boy go to school."

"Jeremiah still runs the town, then. Does everyone in these parts feel that way?"

"I'd say yes about most in town. Doc is one exception. He looks on all folks as just folks. They could be naked except for Indian feathers in their hair, and he'd do his doctoring same as for anyone else."

"What about you?"

"Doc is a good teacher," Mary said.

Delia turned her head to the other side while she pondered Mary's answer. It was a hard thing for some people, this learning how to look on all folks as just folks. Hard feelings started early in some, later in others. For Delia, her own hard feelings could be blamed on her father and the cruel men she'd known along the way. It wasn't color that got her dander up. It was men.

Turning her head caused no dizziness, no nausea. "Do you think I could sit up now?"

"It will pain your shoulder, but we could try," Mary said. "Why don't you roll a little to your right first? Slow and easy. Then I'll support your good shoulder while you move your legs off the bed. We'll let you sit there for a time."

It was a struggle, but one Delia accomplished without crying out. Hiding her pain, both mental and physical, had become a habit. With her legs dangling from the side of the bed and her right hand gripping the edge of the thin mattress, Delia fought a wave of vertigo. Mary jumped to stand in front of her and push her hand against Delia's chest. Even that small contact caused the muscles in her left side to throb from her shoulder and arm to her fingertips. She moaned, then bit her lip.

"Do you want to lie down?" Mary asked.

"No, this is good." Delia managed a weak smile as she met Mary's concerned gaze. "But I won't try to stand yet." She looked around the room, noted her saddlebags and hat on the floor next to the rocking chair at the rear of the cabin, her rifle leaning against the front wall, and her handgun still sitting on the doctor's worktable. "Where's the young'un?"

"In the bedroom. I gave him a stack of books that I must mend before I take them back to school. I think he's in another world."

"He really can read?"

"It appears so. I watched him for a time while you slept. It didn't seem to matter whether the book was for beginners or older children. I am certain he reads the words."

"And yet, if we stayed here in Sangamon, he could not attend school."

"Oh, surely you're not thinking of staying here. Not after all that's being said —"

"What's being said? Who's doing the talking?"

"I'm sorry, Delia. I haven't heard the talk myself. I've been here the whole time. The doctor walked your horses to the stable and asked Colin to rub them down and give them stalls and feed. A small group of men, some of them with their wives, demanded your brother send you and the boy out of town. Doc told them he'd performed surgery on your shoulder and that you'd be staying until your wound healed. There was much fuss about that, and the worst of the protests came from Miss Annie Gray. Do you remember her?"

"She has a farm on the edge of town, if I recollect right. Why would she care about us?"

Mary studied the ceiling a moment as if she might find the answer written in the oak beams. "I doubt it's personal. She's had rough years with her farm and other problems I don't care to gossip about. Her religious notions have become confused, her judgments no longer based on the Christian beliefs she held to in the past. We wonder if she's gone off in the head, but no one wants to bring on one of her anger fits, so the men let her rant and rave when something like this happens."

"Something like this? You mean me showing up with a young'un the wrong color."

"Yes, I guess. But Miss Gray is also carrying on about you, saying that you're an outlaw, that you've killed men and should be run out of town or —"

"Or there should be a hanging?"

Mary looked at the floor. She removed her hand from Delia's chest and stepped to one side. "How do you feel now?"

Delia took a deep breath. "The dizziness is gone. Could I have water?"

"A few sips until the doctor returns." Mary brought a half-full tin cup from the pail by the door. She watched Delia's face while relaying more of Annie's gossip.

"Miss Gray said you've robbed banks. And something about consorting with a gang of men making fake money. She's getting so strange in the head these days that it's hard to know what to believe." Mary reached for the empty cup in Delia's hand but remained standing nearby.

She's waiting for me to tell her what's true and what's not. "Don't worry, Mary. I'm not a danger to you or the doctor. And I'll leave as soon as I can so as not to put you in harm's way."

Mary set the cup on a low wood shelf next to the water pail. She dragged the rocking chair near the bed, sat, and folded her hands in her lap.

Delia didn't want to tell more. She looked around the cabin and pretended a great interest in everything from the framed documents on the wall to the medical books that sat on shelves. When she ran out of things to look at, she studied the bandage that held her arm to her side, wiggled her fingers again to make sure they worked, and dried the palms of her hands on her pants leg. That small movement of her left hand sent sparks of pain through her shoulder.

"Might I lie down on the bed now? Perhaps on my back this time?"

"Could you hold on a few more minutes? The doctor will return soon. He can give you something for the pain, check the wound and add more medicine for the poisoning. Then I'm sure he'll want you to eat. That will prevent the laudanum from upsetting your stomach. Once all that is done, you'll sleep. Most likely through the whole night and another day."

"These clothes," Delia said. "They're not clean."

"When you lie down again, I'll remove the pants and give them a wash. Your shirt is ruined but the doctor has one that will fit. May I take off your boots now?"

"I can only hold on to the bed with one hand."

"Oh, of course. Perhaps the boy can help."

Mary got up, went to the bedroom, and returned with Jackson. While she supported Delia's position on the bed, Jackson gripped Delia's left boot and tugged. When it suddenly came free, he landed on his rear end on the floor. He laughed, jumped to his feet, and went to the other foot. This time he stayed upright. "How are you feeling, Miss Delia?"

"I'm feeling better, young'un."

"Jackson. Doctor said y'all should call me Jackson."

"Okay, then. Jackson. You know we'll be staying here for a short time, a few days for sure. Some of that time, I might be sleeping because of the medicine the doctor will give me. You'll be minding the doctor and Miss Mary with please and thank you and not bothering them with any troubles. Is that understood?"

"Yes, ma'am. And I can help with chores. I know how to sweep the floor, slop the hogs, empty the chamber pots and curry the horses, if you got a wood block I can stand on. Does the doctor have hogs and horses, Miss Mary?"

"I'm afraid not, Jackson. But I'm sure he'll find chores right here in his office to keep you busy. For now, you can go on back to the books. Are you hungry?"

"I'm always hungry."

"In that room where you've been reading, there's a tin of sugar biscuits on the table. You help yourself to two biscuits, and we'll eat a whole meal soon."

Mary watched the boy run into the bedroom, then seemed deep in thought for a moment.

Delia had a flash of remembering. "You're

Mary Proud that lived in that old run-down cabin at the end of the road, aren't you? You had two children."

Mary did not move, did not turn to face Delia. "That life happened a long time ago. I no longer have any children. I'm going to the cookhouse to light the fire. I'll be a few minutes." She bustled out the back door.

Delia grabbed onto the edge of the high bed for balance, hoping the doctor or Mary would return soon. It was clear Mary hadn't taken kindly to getting the table turned on her, to be questioned instead of doing the questioning. Perhaps now there would be no more inquiries from Mary about Delia's reputation and the stories that Annie Gray told about the day of the fire or the years after.

CHAPTER SIX:
MARY'S PAST

After she escaped Delia's questions, Mary hid in the cookhouse for a few minutes, waiting to calm her mind and shove her bad memories away. But some things she could never forget, no matter how much she tried.

Delia's questions triggered one picture after another, dropping through Mary's mind as though viewed through the new Wheatstone stereoscope the doctor had ordered from England. She hoped the pictures she'd see with the new contraption would be more beautiful and more calming than the ones she now fought to ignore.

The worst was her memory of the day Caswell died. One of five witnesses to the bloody murder, Mary watched her son's throat open under the hunting knife, paled at the sight of blood flowing down his chest and onto the new spring grass at the riverside. Except for the killer herself, Mary remained the only person left in town who knew the killer's identity. She would never tell anyone what happened that day, not even Doc Hemmer. She would never reveal the murderer's name. In one way, her son's death tore her heart out of her chest. In another, his death gave her back her own life with new heart and fresh hope.

The many times a month she ran into the killer in the Village of Sangamon raised fresh waves of pain. They never spoke to each other about Caswell's death, never acknowledged anything in their acquaintance except the cordial greetings of neighbors who would never be friends. But each chance passing, each brief exchange, blew the memory at Mary with a force that left her breathless. An enraged and hate-filled Caswell running toward his half sister Jo Mae, the killer stepping forward to intervene, the hunting knife slashing across Caswell's throat, the gushing blood and horrible sounds he made as he fell to the ground. Again and again, she remembered. Again and again, she shoved the memory away.

The days that followed Caswell's death were less vivid in her mind. A federal marshal had come to town. Mary told him she didn't know what happened, didn't know where her daughter went, and that she had a vicious headache.

What happened to Jo Mae remained a mystery to this day. Mary did not lie to the marshal about that. As soon as Caswell fell, Mary fled the woods and ran to her decrepit little cabin where she huddled on her bed for hours, crying and shaking in fear.

She had a terrible headache the day the marshal asked all his questions. She had not lied about that fact, either. After he left, she went back to bed. She couldn't remember how many days passed before she got up again.

At first Mary wanted to die. She sat on the edge of her rickety bed, her hair hanging in matted knots around her dirty face, her dress stained with grease and sweat. In her hands, she held the bottle of laudanum the doctor had prescribed for Caswell's injuries from a lightning strike that had burned part of a nearby tree. She'd only given him a small amount from the bottle. Mary could end her miserable existence with less than half of the remaining liquid.

But Caswell's death also freed Mary to live, released her from the burden of a demented, unmanageable son. Her future had once seemed to hold nothing but misery and an early death. Now possibilities grew with each passing day.

She had poured the drug into the pit

under the outhouse and threw the bottle in, as well. That day four years ago she'd begun her recovery and reentry into the town's daily life.

Now, established as the schoolteacher and the doctor's assistant, Mary tried to avoid thinking about her former life. The curiosity she'd shown toward Delia's history backfired when Delia began asking questions of her own. Questions. Too many questions led to too many memories. Thinking of the past made Mary feel trembly inside. Her hands felt cold and clammy.

Think about something else.

Mary walked to the fireplace in the cookhouse and used a metal prod to stir the coals and revive the fire. Adding a few clumps of dry grass, then two logs, she built the fire hotter to boil well water for drinking and for coffee. After that, she planned to hang a soup pot from the hook and put a freshly killed chicken to simmer for several hours with a few carrots and turnips from Doc's garden. Mary swung the pot of water on its hook to sit directly over the fire.

The distraction did not work. The nervous shakiness inside Mary's chest grew worse. Turning to the food cupboard, she pondered the remedy Doc sometimes used for his patients when they had the vapors — the bottle of whiskey. Primarily used to soak hunks of venison to soften the meat and temper the flavor, it had medicinal benefits as well. She tipped the bottle to her lips, swallowed once, and choked as the fierce burn hit the back of her throat. Once the bottle sat on its customary shelf in the cupboard and Mary's eyes stopped watering, she dried her palms by smoothing her hands over her skirt.

After taking a deep breath, and then another, Mary pulled a slice of peppered venison jerky from the jar by the stove and bit off enough to flavor her mouth. She chewed and swallowed. Vowing to leave Doc's whiskey on the shelf in the future, Mary gathered the tools she'd need to kill one of Doc's chickens.

It had become a habit for her to prepare food in Doc's cookhouse and carry meals for herself to her room at the schoolhouse. The practice served them both well.

Chapter Seven: Visitors for Delia

Delia almost dozed off while sitting, something that could have been disastrous if she fell from the bed. Her back to the door, she stiffened when she heard the rattle of the door handle and footsteps cross the wood floor.

"It's me." The doctor's voice sounded anxious, even agitated. "How do you feel?"

Delia tried to turn her head to see Doc but discovered her neck had stiffened and become painful. She listed her aches and pains and general complaints.

Doc stepped in front of her and put his hand on her forehead. "Did Mary give you any water?"

"Yes. But I'd like more. She feared I'd get sick, so I didn't get as much as I wanted."

"How long have you been sitting?"

"Long enough. Mary didn't want to move me again without your help. She's bringing me something to eat. She said I should have food in my stomach when I take pain medicine." Delia bowed her head to hide the tears leaking from her eyes. Now that the doctor had returned, she could stop fighting the pain and ask for help.

Mary whisked into the room with a steaming cup that smelled like meat. Delia's mouth watered. She hoped that was a good sign. At the same time, the doctor approached with a small, corked bottle. He poured a few drops of liquid onto a ladle and held it to Delia's mouth. She took the full amount at once, grimaced, and swallowed. Then she took the hot cup in her hands and sipped the weak meat-flavored broth until it cooled enough to drink the rest.

"It's tinned broth from the general store," Mary said. As soon as Delia finished, Mary retrieved the cup and set it on the table.

Mary stood on one side of the bed and the doctor on the other to gently lower Delia onto her back. Doc lifted her legs as she reclined.

"Dear God, that hurts so bad," Delia said.

"The medicine will help you soon," Doc said. "You'll sleep for a long time, perhaps through the night and into tomorrow. When you wake, I'll check the wound and change the dressing. After that, we'll move you to a chair and you can have real food . . . if your stomach will tolerate it."

"What about the boy. You'll watch out for Jackson?" Delia's words sounded slurred to her own ears. The throbbing in her shoulder and arm had already eased, the edges of pain softened to the point of bearable. She did not hear anyone answer her question about Jackson.

Delia awoke to the smell of strong coffee and side meat crisping over a hot fire. She tested a small adjustment to her shoulder's position, gasped at the pain, then lay very still. When she opened her eyes, she discovered Mary and the doctor watching.

"The pain won't go away quite yet," Doc said. They helped Delia sit, tended to her shoulder, then eased her off the tall bed and guided her to the rocking chair. Her left arm was no longer bound to her side, making it easier to walk, but no less painful if she bumped her hand or arm. Once Delia settled into the chair, Mary covered her shoulders with a shawl and tucked a quilt around her bare legs. The doctor pulled a three-legged stool close to the rocking chair. "Mary will bring the chamber pot in a moment," he said. "I'm afraid it will take two of us to help you."

"Let me rest here first. I don't think I could —"

"When you're ready."

Mary returned moments later with coffee, a cup of broth, and a plate of side meat and biscuits. "This is breakfast," she said. "You slept all night."

"Sip the broth before you try solid food," the doctor said. "If you feel no nausea, you can nibble a few bites. That will help you tolerate more laudanum without getting ill. You need more sleep."

"Where's the young'un?" Delia asked. She sipped the strong coffee first and felt a rumbling in her stomach and a rush of saliva in her mouth.

Mary offered the broth next, holding the coffee cup as she watched Delia like a hawk. Slightly uncomfortable at Mary's intense supervision, Delia drank slowly. She eyed the plate of hot food. *It smells so good.* No longer worried about Mary, or Jackson for that matter, Delia reached for a slice of meat and a biscuit.

"He's in the cookhouse, on his second helping," Mary said. "He has a mighty big appetite for such a small boy. Before that, he was up early to watch the chickens. They're chasing grasshoppers, running every which way. We got that bath in as well.

I filled the tub inside the cookhouse and handed him a big rag and a bar of soap and let him take his time. Jackson has a wonderful laugh. Have you noticed?"

"I'm afraid we didn't have much to laugh about between the time I grabbed him and when we rode into Sangamon."

Mary didn't say any more. She left the room with the empty plate and cup. When she returned from the cookhouse, she had fresh coffee for Delia and for herself. Jackson followed her into the room, peering around her long skirts.

"Howdy, Jackson," Delia said.

He stepped around Mary so Delia could see him from head to toe. He carried a chamber pot as though presenting Delia with a gift. "Howdy, Delia."

"My goodness. You look different. What happened?"

He giggled. "You know. I took a bath. And Miss Mary washed my britches, and she gave me this shirt."

"It's a mighty big shirt." The shirttail hung almost to Jackson's knees, and the sleeves were rolled up so much they created puffy bulges just below his elbows. "What else have you been doing while I slept off the hurting from this old shot-up shoulder?"

"Not too much. I wanted to go see the

horses, but Miss Mary said I had to stay here. Doc Hemmer told me he'd take me there later, but I know I could go by myself. I remember right where the stable is."

"Best to do what Mary and the doctor say," Delia told him.

All three adults and Jackson looked toward the front of the cabin when a horse whinnied outside. The doctor strode to the door and flung it open. Just as quickly, he stepped through and pulled the door shut.

Mary hurried to the front window and opened the slats they'd kept partially closed against the morning sun. "It's your brother."

"No doubt come to see how I'm faring and how soon I might leave Sangamon behind. The stories told about me are so bad, I'm sure he's worried."

"Worried you'll shoot up the town? I hardly think —"

"No. More likely worried I'll draw a bad sort to Sangamon. The people I lived with in Cave-in-Rock are a bad lot."

"Is that the place way south by the river?" Mary asked, apparently encouraged by Delia's open mention of the outlaws at Cave-in-Rock. "I've heard stories, too. Did you live there when you got shot?"

"It's a very long story. One I'd best not tell in front of this young'un." She looked at

Jackson and realized he still held the chamber pot. "Set that down by my chair. I'll use it in a bit."

"Should we be concerned they'll come here?" Mary asked.

"I don't think they know where I am, Mary. They sure don't know why I left Sangamon in the first place . . . except for . . . well, like I said, it's a long story best left for another time."

Mary came away from the window and carried Delia's cup out of the room. When she returned, she took up her vigil. "Colin is leaving. I thought he'd come inside to see you."

Delia's laugh sounded hard, even to her own ears. She glanced at Mary, then put her hand to her forehead and rubbed as though she could erase her thoughts. "Is the doctor coming back inside now? I need more of that medicine."

Mary retrieved the pillow from the bed and brought it to Delia. "Will you be able to rest in the chair?"

Doc Hemmer returned before Delia could respond and sat on the stool in front of her. "Your brother wanted to know how soon you'd be able to travel. When I said you couldn't ride a horse for at least two weeks, he offered to take you and the boy away in his wagon. 'Where would you take them?' I asked. He said, 'Straight to hell, for all I care. Just get her away from Sangamon. There's a reason they call her trouble. That's something we don't need here.' "

Mary gasped and put her hand over her mouth.

Delia laughed again, meaning to ease Mary's mind, but the sound came out harsh and angry. "There are things you don't know about me, Doc. Things even Colin doesn't know. It's best you don't ask questions."

Jackson walked to Delia's side and patted her hand. "Why doesn't your brother like you?"

"I might have beaten him up too many times when he was a young'un like you," Delia said.

Jackson laughed, a genuine merry sound that made Delia smile in return. "You didn't."

"Okay, I didn't. It's too hard to explain right now. I got bad pain in my shoulder. I need to take my medicine and rest for a time."

The doctor took the hint and fetched the bottle and ladle. This time, she received a mere taste. "More than that and you'll likely fall out of the chair," he said.

Mary brought another biscuit, this one slathered with honey, to take the bitterness away.

Delia thanked them, then tapped Jackson's hand. "I'll be using that pot now, and then getting more sleep. You stay out of the doctor's way and be polite to Miss Mary. Read more of those stories. When I wake, you can read one to me."

Jackson didn't argue. He returned to the bedroom with the books. With Doc and Mary's help, Delia wrestled with the pot then sat back, exhausted. She stuffed the pillow behind the right side of her neck and leaned into it to relieve the pressure on her injured shoulder.

Before Delia drifted off, a soft whisper caught her attention.

"Doc," Mary said. "I can tell you some of what happened. The part before she ran away from home."

Someone knocked on the doctor's office door. Delia heard nothing more.

Doc found the hat-shop ladies on his doorstep with a basket covered by an embroidered cloth. "Just a social call," said one.

"To bring these johnnycakes for the little boy," said the other as she tried to see inside the doctor's office.

"We thought your patient and the little one could use some company," said the first. "May we come in?"

"Perhaps tomorrow," Doc Hemmer said. "My patient is sleeping, and the child is going to take a nap as well." He reached for the basket, said "Thank you," and eased the door closed.

CHAPTER EIGHT:
ABOUT THE HAT-SHOP LADIES

Ella Lee and Sally Fay Cramer were sisters. Twins, if the truth be known. Born forty-two years ago in Kentucky, thieves and counterfeiters by trade, they had traveled west to escape the law and the wrath of their victims. Passing fake money was not the worst of their crimes, either. Ella Lee and Sally Fay had robbed two stagecoaches at gunpoint and had then crossed the Ohio River to Ford's Ferry, where they learned all about being river pirates. Always one step ahead of the law as they added to their savings, the sisters finally decided they were getting a bit long in the tooth to continue their unlawful endeavors. They hitched their two horses to a wagon, loaded it with supplies they might not find so easily on the frontier, and journeyed west into Illinois.

Their arrival in Sangamon, the year before Delia's return, was accidental, a side trip taken to avoid an outbreak of smallpox in a small town on their route between the Indiana state line and the city of Springfield.

"Such a quiet, peaceful countryside," Ella said as they passed straight through Sangamon and out the other side, turning south on the river road.

"The river, the trees, it's lovely," added Sally. "Should we turn back?"

"Whoa, whoa." Ella tugged on the reins to reinforce her command. The horses stamped their feet and snorted. "Have we gone far enough to escape those who want us jailed?"

"I believe we have," said Sally. "Let's go talk to folks."

They stopped first at the general store where proprietor Jeremiah Frost greeted the sisters, spinsters who looked so much alike folks often called them by the wrong names. They told Jeremiah they had migrated from Pennsylvania with their wagonload of fabric, needles, and thread and had a contact in Philadelphia who could ship new goods as soon as he received an order. In addition to their stylish hats, the ladies created matching bags.

Jeremiah seemed enthusiastic about their plans. "We need genteel folks like you to help the town grow," he said. "A new business to attract the wives of farmers on

Saturday, the fine presence of proper ladies to set a civilized example, an incentive for the men to behave as gentlemen. We've long suffered a shortage of new business in Sangamon. Once this river has been made navigable, more and more will seek opportunities in Sangamon. You and your shop will be most welcome, I assure you. And you will have an advantage over those who follow."

"How might we arrange for a place to live and establish our shop?" Ella asked.

Jeremiah directed the ladies to the owner of the cabin once occupied by Mary Proud and her children. "It needs repair," he said. "And the addition of a space to display your finery. But you'll find the location satisfactory, not too close to the saloon, so ladies won't be offended by the noise or bad behavior of those who imbibe."

Ella and Sally exchanged a look, agreeing without speaking aloud. "We'd like to see this cabin right now, if that's possible," Ella said.

They paid the rent and moved in immediately. "We'll supervise the repairs ourselves," Sally told the owner, "to make certain the changes meet our requirements." Both were confident they could nag and push to get the work done in a timely manner.

Ella and Sally unloaded their supplies, piece by piece, and carried them inside without assistance. The very heavy, long chest that sat on the bottom of the wagon under the smaller boxes gave them more trouble than anything else. They jockeyed the chest back and forth, lowered it to the ground, then dragged it inch by inch until they pulled it inside and shoved it against a wall.

Ella unlocked and opened the lid of the chest. The carefully packed contents seemed undamaged. The newest model of Hall-North carbines, a few new Colt Ring Lever rifles, and ammunition for both, all stolen from an army warehouse, would hopefully prove a lucrative source of income in the future. On top of the chest, Sally placed a brown-and-green quilt made of assorted felt squares, two small pillows covered in blue silk, a stack of felt remnants and gewgaws, and a wooden head used for shaping hats. "That should discourage prying eyes," she said.

Ella and Sally regarded their handiwork with folded arms, exchanged another of their glances, and sat at the lopsided wood table to have a cup of tea.

"Genteel," said Ella with a nod.

"Indeed," responded Sally with a sly smile.

They hoped to make the acquaintance of more Sangamon residents in the coming days. Many had passed the cabin but directed only curious glances their way. No one had called on them. No one had offered to help.

The sisters noted the cool reception but didn't take offense. They preferred each other's company over that of strangers. Focused on increasing their inventory of hats to show, they agreed to take their time trying to win over the townsfolk. They would set aside their solitary pursuits and act friendly when necessary. They could do anything when it came to their business. Rehashing their history for the townsfolk, however, never became part of the plan. Rarely discussing their past even when alone, the two sought to establish new identities and respectability with their elaborate hats and bonnets and their idle conversation.

"Let's start with the teacher. She goes directly to the doctor's office when school lets out," Ella said a few weeks after moving in. "We can introduce ourselves to both at the same time. I'll wear the blue cotton bonnet and you can show off your green felt with the feathers."

Mary had welcomed the ladies graciously and escorted them to the cookhouse for tea. Doc quickly escaped their presence to, as he said, clean his office after the last patient. When Mary admired Sally's green felt hat, Sally removed it and placed it on the table. "A gift," Ella said. "You'll be the first in Sangamon to wear one of our creations."

Ella remarked several times after that meeting that Mary wore that one hat on occasion but seemed to have no others. "She doesn't even wear a bonnet in the heat of the day."

"Shocking," Sally answered.

Not long after they called on Mary, the ladies met Annie Gray. As all three waited in line at Jeremiah's general store, Ella tapped Annie on the shoulder and said, "We haven't met." She introduced herself and Sally, then politely waited for Annie to return the gesture.

Instead, Annie pursed her lips, stared at the hats the sisters wore, then raised her eyebrows. "I'm a farmer. Feathers and bobblety-jobs are too hoity-toity. I won't be buying your flibbertigibbet monstrosities." She moved closer to the counter, sighing as though the waiting was too much to bear.

Sally had leaned toward Ella. "Shocking," she whispered. Ella's eyes narrowed as she glared at Annie's back.

A year later, the two ladies were even more shocked when a white woman in men's clothes and a young black boy rode their horses into town.

"Haven't we seen her before?" asked Ella.

"Perhaps near Ford's Ferry?" Sally mused.

Ella frowned. "Hmmm. This might be a problem."

The next day, when another stranger rode into town on a spotty paint mare, the ladies exchanged one of their knowing glances.

"Sangamon is becoming quite busy, but not, it appears, with folks likely to stay and buy our hats," Ella said.

"I agree," answered Sally. "I wonder who that handsome young fellow might be. Perhaps Jeremiah will know."

CHAPTER NINE:
PREACHER JOHN CLAYMORE

It had been more than three years since the preacher made the long circuit through Illinois and western Indiana to see the folks who had long relied on his Presbyterian teachings. In most places, townsfolk greeted him as an old friend dropping in for a long overdue visit. He wasn't sure he'd receive the same welcome when he reached Sangamon for this last time. When he left that little town over four years ago, he'd escorted young Jo Mae Proud and her baby, along with the elderly Kickapoo Indian known as Fish, and the three-legged, partially blind Old Dog, from Sangamon to New Salem.

They had all witnessed the murder of Jo Mae's brother, Caswell, then fled to avoid being accused of the crime. None of the witnesses wanted to see Fish or Jo Mae, or the preacher for that matter, questioned and maybe accused by a federal marshal. No one from Sangamon tried to stop them. As far as the preacher knew, no one had tried to track them down later.

Now more than a day's ride from Sangamon, John sat astride his aging paint mare and stroked her neck with his fingers. She was skittish that morning, for no apparent reason. No rattlesnakes, no wind, no threatening rumbles of thunder, no sign of wolves. A low cloud of dust hung over the road in the far distance, closer to the town of Danville, not far from the Indiana state line.

Staying put for the moment, John looked over the Illinois countryside, the prairie tallgrass turning dry and yellow in the September preview of fall, the wildflowers long past their spring and summer bloom and shriveling into the soil. A few trees had begun to change color, but most were still green and fully leafed. He looked to the east again. The dust cloud seemed a little closer.

Could be a gang of stagecoach robbers. Or folks moving into Illinois from Indiana with wagons and horses or oxen. Who can tell from such a distance? John guided his horse off the road and into the woods so he could watch those on the road without being seen.

The paint didn't like standing still. The longer they stayed in the same place, the more agitated she became. To ease her distress, John dismounted and pulled her feed from his saddlebags. With the grain and a drink of water from a creek, he distracted the horse enough that she stopped her nervous dance. He hoped she wouldn't whinny or rear and try to run, but a calm hand on her muzzle seemed all she needed. They stood together in the woods, the horse and the preacher, and waited.

Almost an hour later, the first sounds of creaking leather and shuffling feet reached the preacher. By then, he'd sat on the ground and leaned against a tree, the horse's reins in his hand to prevent her from wandering too far or bolting at the first sign of trouble. John scrambled to his feet, brushed a few ants off his clothes, and mounted the horse. He guided her closer to the road and peered past the trees.

What he saw caused him to rub his eyes and look again. There were more people than he'd ever seen in one place outside of St. Louis in the state of Missouri. Militia, dragoons, and Indians on horseback, Indians and loads of their possessions in wagons, and more Indians on foot, shuffling at a slow pace, stirring up enough road dust to give the mass of humanity an eerie, ghost-like blurriness. Old men and women, younger adults, children and babies. Sometimes one fell, slowing the others until the

Indian on the ground revived or others carried the sick or exhausted to a travois. Or to the bed of a wagon that eased into the crowd on its mission to secure the dead or those about to die.

John had heard of the militia assignments to escort tribes west in the government's continuous attempts to rid the land of Indians. The tribes still claimed ownership and refused to sell their land. Renegades chose not to live in harmony but instead steal livestock and sometimes murder settlers and burn their homes to the ground. The relocation process had accelerated after President Jackson signed the Indian Removal Act in 1830, but John Claymore had not seen the policy in action before. The forced mass exodus of the People to make way for a new invasion of whites seemed heartless on paper. When viewed firsthand, however, the sight proved near unbearable.

As the Indians, soldiers, and volunteers reached the woods, John moved onto the road and approached the two men in the lead.

They stopped, one with a hand on his holstered pistol, another with his long gun half out of the scabbard secured to the front of his saddle.

John raised his right hand. "I mean no

harm. I'm a circuit minister for the Presbyterian Church. May I be of service here?"

One of the soldiers laughed. "For these heathens? What help could you be that's not already provided by the esteemed Reverend Father Petit?"

John shifted uncomfortably in his saddle. "Who are these people and where are you taking them?"

"Potawatomi tribe from Indiana. We're moving them across the Mississippi. Government is giving them new lands."

"Are they going willingly?" John asked.

The soldier who'd answered the first time responded again. "Heathens don't do nothing willingly."

Another leaned toward John as he shoved his pistol back into the holster. "Not really heathens, you know. They seem to hold Father Petit in high esteem and pray with him during mass."

John looked at the men, women, and children, many now sitting on the road with their heads in their hands, the children crying. A few of the elders had climbed from their carriages or wagons and sprawled on their backs as if catching a little much-needed sleep. He spotted the black-robed priest far to the rear, moving from one child to another, patting shoulders and offering ladles of water. "They seem resigned to their fate."

"I suppose," the first soldier said. "It's hard to argue with armed men on horseback."

"How long have you been walking today?"

"Since just after the father conducted mass at dawn. We'll stop soon and set up a camp, get everyone fed and rested, then set out again tomorrow at first light. We might get to the river in ten days or so if we don't lose too many more stragglers. We waste a lot of time burying the ones who don't survive."

"Have there been a lot of deaths?"

"The ancient ones and the babies. Maybe twenty so far."

"Will you have burials this evening?"

"Five or six, I reckon."

"I could come along and say prayers at the graves."

"Grave, not graves. You can suit yourself, Preacher, but it don't make no difference to these here heathens what you do. They're as godless a bunch as ever lived on this earth."

The second soldier frowned and exchanged a glance with John.

The preacher thought about Fish, the one Indian he'd grown to know well, and how much that Indian had shared about the spirit world, the Kickapoo chief and prophet Kenekuk, and God's plan for taking back the lands from the whites and restoring them to the tribes who'd been displaced. John hoped this ignorant militia volunteer would live long enough to see that happen.

"I see," John said. "May I walk among the Indians now and meet Father Petit?"

"Not a good time, Preacher. We have to keep moving." The soldier turned his horse and shouted to his company alongside the road. "Let's go. Pass the word."

Those Indians who could stand struggled to their feet and returned to their carriages or horses. Others plodded forward on foot. A few kept their heads down as though watching their feet and willing them to move. Those who rode in front in carriages held their heads high, their eyes on the clouds or the distant horizon. None made eye contact with John.

Those few who could not get up were dragged to the side of the road and left for the wagon. Walking among the Indians with a bucket and a tin ladle, Father Petit talked, offered water, and shook his head as though unable to believe he participated in this horror. He glanced at John once, then looked away. As the group moved forward, Petit mounted an old swayback horse that looked as though it might collapse at any moment and rode alongside the Potawatomi.

Before the wagon could reach the nearest stragglers, John slid off his horse and approached one of the old men. With one hand on the Indian's shoulder, John bowed his head and sought the words that might offer comfort. The Indian shrugged off John's hand and pointed toward Father Petit. His loyalty lay with the Catholic priest.

The other Indians seated or sprawled on the side of the road wore their bruised dignity and exhausted bodies as a mantle of defeat. They had no use for a Presbyterian preacher who had found them by accident and would continue on his own way, providing nothing more helpful than talk. He climbed on his horse and let the weight of the moment settle on his body and stifle his breath.

He stayed at the edge of the woods and watched until the whole group had passed. Their forms began to waver in the dust like a heat mirage. For a while, he couldn't bring himself to get on the road and follow. He would be on the same path for the next couple of hours, but he didn't think he could bear seeing more, knowing he could do nothing about it.

John wore this sense of failure like a cloak, using it to explain why he planned to leave his ministry behind. No matter where he'd gone and how often he'd preached, he never felt he'd made a difference. Folks had a way of showing up for Bible meetings or Sunday preachings, acting like they sought salvation, but he knew as soon as he left a town, old ways crept back within hours. Saloons thrived. Brothels sprang up out of nowhere. Gambling. Killings.

Talking a blue streak with a sermon here and a prayer meeting there wasted everyone's time, most of all his.

The biggest blow to his heart and soul had happened in New Salem four years ago when he'd showed up at his parents' house with Jo Mae, her baby, and Fish. John's mother, the woman he'd thought closer to God than any other human he knew, turned out to be as hateful and judgmental as any devil he'd encountered in his worst nightmares. When he visited New Salem in more recent years, he stayed with his friends and called on his father but did not see his mother. That was another fault he claimed. He had been unable to forgive the woman who'd bullied him into the religious life and only then revealed her very un-Christian side.

Religion tried to eat his soul as it had devoured his mother, turning her into a model of heavenly devotion rather than wife and caregiver. John now realized his whole adult life may have been based on lies. God might exist. But if He lived, why did He allow his People to be so mistreated?

As the dust gradually settled in the distance and the Potawatomi disappeared, John thought of what his future might be like without his ministry. He sometimes thought he could believe more in the Kickapoo spirit world than the Christian Heaven.

The Potawatomi, called heathens by the militiaman, most likely had religious beliefs similar to those of the Kickapoo, but the legends would vary, the prophets bear different names. Who deemed the Christian God any better, any more powerful, than a god worshipped by the Indians?

John nudged his horse to a faster walk. The sudden need to move away from the tragic migration overpowered his concern for the suffering. John couldn't take it anymore. He took the next road that would lead him closer to Sangamon.

Put the Potawatomi out of my mind. Think of why I'm here and what I need to do now.

A few months ago, John had traveled to St. Louis to follow up on rumors about a potential migration west, great wagon trains with guides and armed guards to travel across the plains, some intending to go all the way to the ocean. Although he'd considered traveling with one of the wagon trains as a preacher, his Presbyterian masters had not agreed to his request. Still, he would go when the time came, no matter what the masters said. Abandoning the ministry was his other option, and that's what he would do. It was time to change his life.

This one last visit to the towns on his old circuit might never have happened if he hadn't met two very different individuals in St. Louis, both with past attachments to the people in the Village of Sangamon. The population of St. Louis had quickly grown to nearly nine thousand people, and with its location on the Mississippi River, it was destined to become a great hub of trade and commerce. Men of means who desired adventure gathered there in great numbers to discuss the promise of fertile soil and other riches that might be available once the Mexicans abandoned their claims on the western lands. John had toyed with the idea of heading west himself, so he located the meeting place and mingled with those doing most of the talking. John had immediately recognized the French trapper

Henri de Montagne — the man who fathered Mary Proud's daughter, Jo Mae — when the Frenchman described in his heavy accent the terrain and the dangers west of the river.

The mountain man had recently traveled to the Kickapoo reservation where Fish, Jo Mae, and her child now lived. When he left the reservation, he carried a letter Jo Mae had written to her mother. Henri told John he didn't want to return to Sangamon, but Jo Mae had been so hopeful that Henri had promised to see the letter delivered. At first John, not that eager to return to Sangamon himself, declined to take the note. He finally relented after Henri explained why it would be better for the preacher to deliver the letter. Henri de Montagne had not left Jo Mae's mother under friendly circumstances, so an unexpected return would likely cause Mary pain and embarrassment, and might result in bodily injury to the trapper.

As John had continued to attend the St. Louis gatherings and listened to the big dreams of the most adventurous, he learned the names and histories of the men present. One of those men turned out to be Mary Proud's father. After they met formally, John accepted his letter for Mary. Her father explained that his lumber and construction business had failed, and his promise to bring the supplies and build Mary a house in Sangamon would go unfulfilled. Instead, his letter outlined a plan to go west when the wagon trains officially organized. He included an invitation to Mary to join him in St. Louis in the interim and travel to the Pacific coast when the migration began in earnest.

Two messages now rested in the preacher's saddlebag, both intended for Mary Proud, a woman he didn't care to see again and who might even be dead by now. But the messages were important. He had agreed to make the effort.

This mission to deliver the letters kept John moving toward Sangamon. When he trotted along the river the afternoon after leaving the Potawatomi, he turned onto the main road to enter the town. The sameness made him stop and look around. Only a few new cabins filled the considerable space. Two new businesses added to the growing main street. The general store looked the same as before, except for the pregnant lady standing in the doorway and the child hopping around on the porch.

The lady, familiar, saw him and smiled. Sarah. John tipped his hat and rode on past. He would check out the rest of the town before asking about Mary Proud.

Noting the stable had been expanded and even sported a sign advertising a buckboard and a buggy for let, John stopped to see if the room at the rear of the building remained available for him to stay overnight. Perhaps two nights. He needed to rest his body and his soul.

CHAPTER TEN:
THE LETTERS

Preacher John Claymore settled into the room behind Colin Pritchard's stable with a sigh. His saddlebags sat on the floor by the door, and his rifle lay across the small table. John pulled off his boots and stretched out on the sturdy bunk, the rough horse blanket spread over the straw mattress scratchy against his neck. The bed was even less comfortable than the last time he'd visited Sangamon. No doubt many travelers had used this small room over the years, packing the straw into a rock-hard mass. Pritchard probably left the bunk unchanged to discourage long stays.

It doesn't matter. I won't be here long.

But a couple of days of solitude before meeting with Mary Proud would be a welcome interlude. He had asked Pritchard if Mary still lived in the same ramshackle cabin as before and blinked in surprise to hear she now taught school and resided in its attached room when not assisting the new doctor in his office.

Meeting the doctor might be a pleasant addition to his plans. He didn't view all potential reunions with the same optimism.

The Good Lord knows how much I dread meeting Annie Gray again.

After his embarrassing attempt to court the lady farmer four years ago and her firm rejection, John wondered if he'd ever feel comfortable around Annie again. Unlikely. But he doubted a meeting could be avoided. She had always known everything that happened in Sangamon. Without a doubt, she'd hear of his return before he had time to rest.

A sharp knock on the door followed those thoughts as though fulfilling a prophecy. John sat up and pulled on his boots, then walked to the door and threw it open.

"Preacher Claymore, I've so looked forward to seeing you again!" Annie Gray stood outside the door holding a basket close to her waist with both hands. "I brought you a loaf of fresh bread, a jar of my raspberry preserves, and a spoon that must be returned to me when you finish. With the basket."

John accepted the gift and stepped aside as though to invite Annie into the room.

"Oh, no, sir, that would not do. But I ask

that you let me know your plans for a prayer meeting so I can spread the word and prepare. We've had no well-attended gatherings since you left, not even when the new preacher passed through. Seems only you can bring us together."

"That's kind of you to say, Miss Gray, but I'll not be having a meeting. I'm here simply to deliver letters and let everyone know my replacement will be in this part of the state again before Christmas."

"No meeting? Why not? You're here, you're a preacher, and we're all sinners. It's your duty."

John shook his head. Without looking at Annie, he walked to the table and placed the basket next to his rifle. "Thank you for bringing this food, Miss Gray. I'll return the basket and the spoon as soon as I can."

"But your duty to this town," she said in an indignant tone.

"No. I no longer have a duty to this town. I have resigned from my Presbyterian ministry and will move on west to see how I can better serve this country and myself."

"Yourself?" Annie could not have sounded more incensed.

John faced Annie again and noted her raised eyebrows and pursed lips. She had a pinched look about her face, reminding him

101

that luck had been on his side when she rejected his awkward proposal. For that he thanked any old god that might have intervened.

"Yes, Miss Gray, my duty to myself."

"Well!" Annie hesitated a moment as though she would say more, then flounced away from the door and along the path to the road.

John suspected Annie headed straight toward Jeremiah's store where she could spread the word. She would make John the talk of the town for a few hours, no doubt leading to more visitors. Even if he had to give up the straw mattress and the roof over his head, he knew the solitude he craved waited just outside of town on the trail.

So be it. I'll take a nap, deliver the letters, go meet the new doctor to be sociable, then move on.

A gentle knocking woke John from a sound sleep that he thought could not have lasted more than fifteen minutes. He yawned and pulled on his boots before answering the door. Running his fingers through his tangled hair, he wondered if he looked presentable, then decided he didn't care. When he opened the door, he was surprised to see two identical elderly ladies. One carried a man's hat on her outstretched hands.

"We watched you ride into town and noticed your hat appears to be quite old. This one is a new design we're trying out to see if men prefer it to their old round hats. You see the crown is flatter, the brim wider. What do you think?"

"It's very nice," John said. "Who are you?"

"They've been calling us the hat-shop ladies," one lady said with a giggle. "They can't tell us apart."

The other lady put her hand to one side of her mouth as though to whisper a secret so passersby could not hear. "No one tries very hard. Besides, we're always together. One doesn't need to know which one of us is which." She put her hand down and resumed speaking in a normal voice. "Do you like the hat? It's for you. A gift."

"That's very kind," John said. "But why?"

"Annie Gray announced you're no longer a preacher and that you're thinking only of yourself and you won't pray with us. Such independence should be rewarded, not attacked by the likes of a crotchety old biddy who scares the wits out of everyone in town. Look, I even have a feather I can sew on the brim if you like." The lady who'd carried the hat reached in her bag and pulled out a cock pheasant tail feather.

John took the hat and placed it on his

head. "It fits. But I don't think the feather is needed. The hat is perfect just the way it is."

"Well then, we'll be on our way." The hat-shop ladies walked off at a fast pace.

Musing that he'd not learned the ladies' names or anything about them except they had a hat-shop business, John pulled out his pocket watch to see the time. His nap had lasted longer than he thought — almost an hour. He sat at the table and explored the contents of Annie Gray's basket for his lunch. Tearing off a hunk of bread, he used the spoon to spread preserves. *Delicious!* Perhaps he would offer Annie Gray a private prayer session when he returned her basket and spoon. If she would allow it, of course. The "crotchety old biddy" comment from the hat-shop ladies suggested Annie Gray's temperament had not mellowed in the time he'd been away.

Tempted to pull off his boots and try the nap one more time, John instead ate another hunk of bread with preserves and considered where he might go for a cold glass of lemonade and a meal. Accustomed to invitations from the townsfolk in the past, he might not earn their consideration this time. He decided to take care of his primary mission first, that of delivering the two letters to Mary Proud. He pulled a wide-tooth comb through his hair, withdrew the letters from his saddlebags and placed them in his pocket. Tugging the brim of his new hat low enough to shade his eyes from the bright overhead sun, John walked to the school.

Children sat at desks in the one-room schoolhouse, but no Mary Proud. Sarah stood at the front of the room, a book in one hand and a piece of white chalk in the other. He remembered her as a frail young woman who cried through his sermons and prayers but had never opened her heart, at least not to him. A chance meeting long ago left him thinking she smelled of whiskey, but she had scurried away as if to avoid a prolonged conversation.

John remained at the rear of the classroom until Sarah acknowledged his presence and waved him forward. He asked about Mary. Sarah told him Mrs. Proud was assisting Doc Hemmer and pointed toward the south of town, then promptly dismissed him and turned to her students. She seemed to be stronger than he remembered, her voice confident and authoritative. No longer weepy and reclusive, as she'd been in the past.

Recalling days when he'd been a popular visitor to the town, sought out for counseling and conversation, John felt that weight of rejection again. He ambled along the road with his hands in his pockets and continued toward the doctor's office. As he approached the building with the sign out front, he studied the cluster of small buildings. Most of the underpaid physicians he knew from other towns rarely received cash for their services. More likely, payment came in the form of chickens, eggs, labor, or empty promises. The nicer accommodations for Doctor Ernest Hemmer indicated a wealthy background.

Assuming the office door would be unlatched, John knocked and then tried to enter. The door did not budge. He knocked again. He heard sounds — the bustle of someone crossing the room, the scraping of a wood bar sliding in its metal frame, the creaking hinges. Mary Proud opened the door a crack and peered around the edge — but what a different Mary from the last time he'd come to Sangamon. This Mary stood tall, wore a clean blue dress with a white lace collar, and studied his face as though to determine his intentions. Then her eyes widened in recognition.

"I know you," she said. "You're the preacher." She raised both hands to smooth her hair and tuck the loose strands behind her ears.

"Yes. May I come in?"

"The doctor is not here."

"I have something for you, Mrs. Proud."

"Me?" Mary stayed silent for a moment. "What would that be, Preacher?"

She opened the door a little wider, enough for the preacher to see into the shadows where a young woman sat in a rocking chair. A quilt covered her shoulders and body to the waist. A large pillow cushioned her left side. The woman glanced up for a moment, made eye contact, then looked at her lap. John stared. She had the most beautiful eyes he had ever seen in his life, dark as night with long black eyelashes. Yet he had seen pain in those eyes.

Another movement caught his attention as a young black boy ran into the doctor's office from a separate room and then ran out another door.

Mary cleared her throat. "Preacher?"

Startled, John looked at her, recalling his original mission. "Uh, yes, letters. I have two letters for you. Who is that woman in the rocking chair?"

"She's a patient. What letters? From whom?"

"Who was that boy? Surely the doctor does not keep a slave."

"No, of course not. The child is free. He came here with the woman. Preacher, what about the letters?"

"I'm sorry. I'm being too forward." He pulled the letters from his pocket and handed them to Mary. "I'd like to meet Doctor Hemmer while I'm here. Is he expected soon?"

"Won't be long. He went to the general store. Would you like to wait? I have stew and biscuits warming over the fire if you're hungry."

"You're very kind. I'd be much obliged for a good meal and something cool to drink."

Mary ushered John through the office and out the door that led to a cookhouse. He tried to avert his gaze from the young woman on the way but noted she had closed her eyes and leaned into the pillow.

In the cookhouse, he sat on a bench at the table as Mary served him a plate of food and a tin cup of water. Then she sat in a rocking chair by the fire, the two letters side by side in her lap.

CHAPTER ELEVEN:
MESSAGES FROM MARY'S PAST

Letters! Mary had not received a letter since her days in the Illinois army camp. After her soldier husband died in an Indian raid, leaving her alone with a baby, she'd appealed to her father for help. His return letter from Philadelphia had denied her plea. His own circumstances had changed, his wealth confiscated. Months later an old beau brought her news of the troubles her father experienced after accusations of spying for the British destroyed his life.

One of the two new letters the preacher handed her was addressed in that fine script she recognized as her father's. Years after he'd left Philadelphia, Mary's father had found her in Sangamon. He announced that he planned to start a sawmill and lumber business closer to St. Louis. When he returned a second time, he promised to build her a new home of real lumber instead of pine logs, but only if she would change into a productive member of the community. She had not heard from him in more than three years.

She opened her father's message first, hoping it would announce his arrival date in Sangamon. After all, he had promised.

Dear Mary,

I apologize for not writing sooner but I had hoped to solve my business problems and get back to you with the building materials as I promised. Unfortunately, several bad debts left me without the resources to continue with this venture. I am now in St. Louis and am engaged in discussions with men of adventurous spirit who plan to lead a migration into new territories. If these dreams become a reality, I want you to go with me. I still have enough in assets to finance our journey.

When I have more information and a firm commitment for a large group to travel together for convenience and safety, I will return to Sangamon for you and your possessions. I trust you will be prepared to travel.

Father

Mary placed her father's letter to one side, her thoughts a-jumble. Her heartbeat sounded in her ears and one eyelid twitched. She couldn't distinguish between anxiety and excitement at that moment, but one or the other had taken possession of her body. She took a deep breath, but it didn't seem to help calm her nerves.

An animal skin pouch decorated with beads and feathers held the other letter. Mary's name was printed on the outside. To get her mind off her father's plan, Mary peeled open the rawhide pouch where it had been sealed. Inside were three pages of paper. One side was printed with English lessons from a school primer. The other side of each page contained a letter printed in ink by a childish hand.

Dear Mama,

This mountain man named Henri is a friend to the Indian named Fish. He came to see us on the Kickapoo reservation and told me he is my father. I am happy to know this. He said he would take my letter. Little Annie and I are safe for now. Fish is getting older and has been sick. If he dies, his tribe may not want us to remain on the reservation. Henri, my father, said he would take us to the soldiers' fort if that happens. Perhaps you and I can meet again someday, and you can get to know your granddaughter. My father helped me write this letter.

Jo Mae Proud

For Mary, receiving the two letters in one day was almost more than she could bear. Her guilt and sadness overwhelmed the reserved demeanor she wanted to show the preacher. She covered her face with her hands as she burst into tears.

She felt a hand on her shoulder and looked up. The preacher had risen from the table with his meal unfinished and now stood beside her.

"Is there anything I can do?" the preacher asked.

Mary shook her head. "This is unexpected. I don't know what to think."

"The letters?"

"Yes."

"Bad news?"

"No, just disturbing. See for yourself."

Mary handed both letters to the preacher. He took them and returned to the table. His meal grew cold as he gave his full attention to the two communications. Rocking didn't help calm Mary's nerves, so she got up and removed the preacher's plate to dump the cold, untouched food into the pot to reheat. She ladled a new serving of hot stew and placed it on the table. "Eat now," she said. "We can talk when you finish." She sat across from him as he laid the letters aside and picked up his spoon.

Can the preacher help? For that matter, would he want to help? Mary remembered the time she'd scoffed at his promise to pray for her and her family. But she was a different person then. Self-centered, greedy, stubborn, and angry. So very angry. She recalled the words she'd shouted at him when he offered to pray for Caswell after his accident. "Fat lot of good that'll do. You can't eat prayers or burn them for firewood. Worth about as much as a daydream."

Now instead of anger, she felt guilt. She'd resented her father's misfortunes instead of showing compassion. She'd hated and shunned her daughter instead of helping. She'd despised the son she'd once adored as soon as he became difficult to care for. Not that she did much of the caring. Who was she in those days? A shrill, hateful harridan.

An even bigger question, one that had no answer, sent her thoughts reeling to the day she'd sat on the edge of her bed in her dirty cabin with the almost full bottle of laudanum in her hand. The drug would have ended her suffering. Why didn't she kill herself that day? What had made her pour the laudanum into the outhouse pit? Instead, she had cleaned herself up, used the money Henri and her father had given her to buy eyeglasses and books, and sought work tutoring the farm kids who missed so much school every fall. Her life became even better after Doc Hemmer moved to Sangamon.

All this time Mary had worked to better her life, she'd avoided guilt over her past. She had not examined the changes in her heart. Now, because of two short letters, a weight pressed down on her shoulders. She could not throw it off.

"Preacher, I don't talk to anyone about the things I've done or the way I lived before. You know I wasn't a good person. You saw that for yourself. Can you help me?"

"To do what? Understand these letters? Decide what to do?"

"No, not that. I don't know." Tears welled in Mary's eyes again. "I can't explain. Oh, I'm being foolish. Never mind."

Mary rose from the table and put the preacher's empty plate on the sideboard. As she started to tell the preacher she needed to return to the doctor's office, Doc Hemmer strode into the cookhouse and stopped short at the sight of a strange man sitting at the table. Mary introduced the preacher, then slipped out the door and went to check on Delia.

CHAPTER TWELVE:
THE PREACHER LEARNS MORE

John explained his presence to the doctor and agreed to sit and talk, although declining Doc Hemmer's invitation to the evening meal. The doctor had the smell of whiskey on his breath. There had once been a day when John would have admonished a man like the doctor for indulging in drink, perhaps even spending time inside the saloon. No longer did the preacher consider it his business.

The doctor noticed the letters Mary had left on the table and reached for them. "What's this?" he asked.

"The letters I delivered to Mrs. Proud. Perhaps she would not want —"

"She seemed distressed. I might be able to help." A quick glance at the note from Mary's father brought a deep frown to his forehead. Then he read Jo Mae's letter. "Do you know anything about this?" Doc asked.

"I delivered the letters."

"Where did you get them?"

John explained how he'd come by the messages and why he had returned to Sangamon this one last time. "Who knows," he mused. "I may one day end up on the same wagon train as Mary and her father."

"I would hate to lose her expert assistance," Doc said. "She's a fine woman."

"Yes, she seems to be doing well."

"This Jo Mae. She addressed Mary as Mama."

John nodded.

"Why does she live on an Indian reservation?"

"It's a very long story, Doctor. Perhaps Mary will tell you about that someday."

"Mary doesn't talk much about her past life and her family."

"It's not my story to tell." John pulled his pocket watch out and made a show of checking the time. "I'm afraid I must go," he said. "It has been a pleasure to meet you. It seems the folks here are in good hands." John stood and picked up his new hat, started toward the door, then glanced back. "Doc, forgive me if I'm too inquisitive, but the lady in the rocking chair in your office. Who is she?"

"She's a patient. Recovering from surgery. She'll be on her way soon."

"She doesn't live in Sangamon, then."

"Well," the doctor said with a smile. "Her story is also not mine to tell."

John left the cookhouse, taking the shortcut through the doctor's office to reach the road. The young woman had her eyes closed and sat very still, so he crept through the room, opening and shutting the front door as quietly as he could. Once outside, John pondered whether to walk farther along the road toward Annie Gray's farm or return to Pritchard's room behind the stable to try one more time for that nap.

Miss Gray's farm won, although John could not say why. Now that he had delivered those two letters, he had no reason to linger in Sangamon. No reason to complete any of his old circuit, for that matter. But there it was. He needed to make amends.

Annie waited in front of her barn and watched him approach. Her hands on her hips and a scowl conveyed everything he needed to know about her feelings. John kept on anyway, walking straight to the woman and extending his hand. "I've come to apologize."

"Where is my basket?"

"I still have much of your delicious bread and preserves to eat later. I'll return the basket before I go."

Annie sniffed, staring at his new hat. "When will you be leaving?"

"I haven't decided," he said, directly contradicting his own resolve to leave first thing in the morning.

Without warning, Annie dipped her chin, smiled, and motioned him to step inside her cabin. "Would you care for a cup of tea?" she asked.

Startled by the sudden change, John nodded. "That would be kind of you, Miss Gray."

She led the way inside and waved John into a chair at her table. By the time she served tea and johnnycake, Annie had worked up a sweat. She dropped into the other chair and used her apron to wipe her forehead and dab at her neck. "It's very warm for September," she said. "Perhaps our winter won't be quite so cold this year."

"Miss Gray, do you know anything about Doc Hemmer's patient? He said she's recovering from surgery but he seemed reluctant to say more."

Annie huffed, raised her eyebrows, and pursed her lips. "I most certainly do. That woman rode into town with a bullet in her shoulder, thinking her brother would take care of her. He made short work of that notion, sending her off to the doctor and telling everyone that he'd see her gone as soon as she could travel."

"Who is her brother?"

"Why, that Pritchard boy, of course. Don't you know the story about that family?"

"I do not."

Annie launched into the Pritchard saga, ending at the sudden return of Delia to Sangamon. "She brought a little boy with her." Annie leaned forward and whispered, "A black child." She sipped her tea, then felt the teapot with her hand. "The tea has gone cold. Would you care for more? Can you imagine that? A black child in Sangamon. But the Pritchard boy promises they'll be gone soon."

"No, no more tea, thank you. I'd best be on my way to the stable before it gets dark."

John quickly escaped Annie's cabin and walked at a fast clip toward Doc Hemmer's office. With no good reason to stop there again so soon, he continued to the main road through town and on to the little room behind the stable. Too full of johnnycake to eat another piece of Annie's homemade bread, John set his hat on the table, removed his boots and belt, then stripped to his long johns. He fell asleep in minutes.

The first thing John thought about when he woke the next morning was the girl with the beautiful eyes. He dressed and walked to the general store to buy jerky, but mostly to see if Jeremiah Frost would elaborate on Delia's past life. Jeremiah had none of Doc's reluctance.

"That girl proved a trial to her parents from the moment she grew old enough to talk. Sass all day long. The schoolmaster used a willow switch on that girl more than once. And then, after she ran off, her reputation included thieving, running from the law, and even a killing or two."

By the time John left the store and headed to Pritchard's stable, he knew more about Delia Pritchard than he had bargained for and far more than he cared to believe. It took time and an invitation to prayer to wear Colin down and get him talking. There turned out to be even more to Delia's story, and it shocked John to the core.

"Preacher, Delia and our mother suffered at the hands of our father. Too young to understand my father's violence, I believed his claims that my mother deserved her fate. I ran off to the stable to muck out stalls instead of standing up to that man. The day my sister ran away, she didn't tell me anything except that I needed to stay at the stable until someone came to get me. When the story went around about her murdering both our parents and burning the cabin, I knew the facts about my father might explain what happened and bring a greater kindness Delia's way. But talking about his cruelty was impossible. The shame I felt at not helping my mother and sister overwhelmed my good sense. I let everyone believe the worst. Later, when the law came to talk to me and said Delia consorted with thieves and killers and had a price on her head, I convinced myself she was a bad person and wouldn't ever come back."

"But now she's here."

Colin looked away, unable to meet the preacher's gaze. "Not for long. I don't want her anywhere near me. I have nothing else to say in defense of Delia."

"But if the rest of her story were known, she would get the sympathy she deserves."

"No, Preacher, she would not. You don't know the people in this town like I do. She's an outcast and she lived with outlaws. If she stays here, that bad lot might be along to join her . . . or hunt her down. And if the law comes looking for her, I don't want to be accused of hiding her. We don't want her here."

Colin moved into the stalls, turning his back on the preacher. *Dismissed.*

John returned to his room and finished

Annie's bread and preserves, then sampled the jerky. He tried not to think too much about Delia's past or wonder what her future might be like. As much as he wanted to feel sorry for her and get to know her better, the knowledge that she had made bad choices over and over gave him pause. He put Delia out of his mind and concentrated on what else he needed to do in Sangamon. Annie Gray's basket and the spoon had to be returned. Might as well do that before he forgot.

Then, perhaps, he'd visit Doc Hemmer's office and ask to speak to Delia Pritchard. He shook his head. He could not keep his mind off the woman with the beautiful eyes.

CHAPTER THIRTEEN:
COLIN PRITCHARD'S STORY

When Colin Pritchard was a boy, he spent more time in the stable than he spent in his parents' home. As soon as he understood the beatings his mother and sister endured and realized his mother would not defend herself or her children, his world turned into an ugly place. He needed to escape. Spared his father's rage so far, he feared the consequences of interfering. He scurried out of sight and hid from his father whenever possible. Even at fourteen, he dared not speak out. He was sure his father would whip him mercilessly. No one would believe his story, so he never told anyone. He rose early and went to the stable, tended to the farmers and townsfolk who brought their horses for shoeing, and watered and fed the stabled animals.

In school, Colin behaved himself and strove to be like the good children. The old teacher often raised his cane against other boys, especially the older ones, but never against Colin. The others said he was the teacher's favorite and chased after him in gangs with every intention of beating him up. He ran faster than they did to escape, although he doubted even a gang of boys could make his pain worse.

Until he discovered the truth, Colin hadn't understood why Delia always looked so sad and why she rarely left the cabin unless accompanying their mother.

One day that would stay in his mind forever, he had walked into their home and discovered Delia yanking on their father's arm while their mother cringed in her rocking chair, blood streaming from her nose. Father pushed Delia away, knocking her to the floor. Colin reacted by running away.

Delia found him huddled in a corner of the stable, trembling as tears ran down his cheeks. "I'm sorry, I'm sorry," he whispered.

"No, you did the right thing," Delia said, patting his shoulder and ruffling his hair. "If you try to help, he'll hurt you."

When Delia left Sangamon, he knew in his heart his sister had saved his life while giving up her own. He could never share what he knew with anyone, because telling the truth about Delia would be telling the truth about his parents and his own cowardice. The shame consumed his heart, shame of himself more than shame of his father. He would take that secret to the grave.

For years, Colin had stayed good in his heart and actions, his desire to be a better man than his father foremost in his mind. He married, and not long after, he and his wife announced a baby on the way.

Colin's wife, even though strong and healthy, suffered from severe morning sickness from the beginning. She lost weight, retired to her bed, and kindly but firmly refused Colin's attentions.

Colin's resolve to be a better man than his father dissolved.

When he learned that Caswell Proud sold his young half-sister's body for a pittance to a few of the men in Sangamon, Colin paid. Later, his fear of discovery overcame his desire and he left Jo Mae alone. Now that Delia had returned to Sangamon, that fear of discovery had returned. What if she learned what he did with that little girl? As far as he knew, Delia still thought him a good man, even if he didn't welcome her home. He couldn't bear the thought his secret might be exposed. Only one person in Sangamon knew what he had done. Jeremiah Frost. The older man had never spoken to Colin about the girl after she'd disappeared, but what if, in a moment of anger at Delia, Jeremiah blurted out the truth?

Getting his sister to leave Sangamon now consumed Colin's thinking every minute of every day. If she stayed, he would never have peace of mind again.

Chapter Fourteen:
The Day Delia
Left Sangamon

At sixteen years old in 1825, Delia rose before dawn each day, shortly after Colin left the cabin to work in their father's stable. She had already opened her eyes the morning her mother screamed, a horrifying sound that ended abruptly. Jumping out of bed in her shift, Delia rushed into the cabin's small bedroom where her parents slept. Her father stood by the bed, fully clothed. Her mother lay on the feather mattress, her head lolling to one side, her mouth hanging open, her eyes wide but lifeless.

Delia rushed to her mother's side, knelt by the bed and shook her arm, then jerked away when her mother's head wobbled back and forth. Hands clenched at her side, Delia jumped to her feet and turned toward her father, hatred winning out over fear.

"What did you do?" Delia yelled.

Delia's father lunged in her direction and grabbed her by the shoulders.

She twisted out of his sweaty grasp and ran toward the fireplace where her mother kept her cooking tools and a gutting knife. Delia grabbed the knife from its sheath and crouched as she eased around to face the monster. Instead of chasing her, he'd gone to the front door to fasten the latch. Delia ran toward him and drove the blade into his back all the way to the hilt. He crumpled to the floor facedown, writhing and twisting, then went limp, his head turned so one weeping eye watched her double over, her hands shaking, to pull the knife from his back and wipe it on his shirt. He aimed a glob of pink-tinged foam in her direction, but it dribbled down his cheek and fell to the floor.

Breathing hard, swallowing to quell an urge to vomit, Delia placed the knife on the table.

What now? I can't stay here.

She had to think. She ignored her father's eye as it seemed to track her every move. Without much more than reflex action, she pulled the bandanna from his back pocket and spread it over his face.

Out of sight, out of mind.

Delia could not wear her own dress and shoes to ride away from Sangamon on horseback. Dragging her brother's box of clothes from under his bed, she tossed aside her shift and pulled on a pair of pants and a shirt. The new boots Colin never wore to the stable sat by the door. They fit perfectly. She retrieved the leather strap and sheath from the fireplace and fastened it around her waist, securing the knife at her side. Her father's hat hung on a peg. It smelled like him, which almost put her off, but it was the only man's hat in the cabin big enough to stuff her hair inside. Taking a moment to hold her mother's hand and kiss her forehead, Delia then retrieved the musket and powder from under her parents' bed and set the long gun against the wall next to the door.

Now what? I can't leave the bodies like this for Colin to find.

Delia's gaze lingered at the fireplace. Her mother had laid the makings of a fire the night before. It took only a minute to light the kindling and another minute to see the larger sticks take hold. Once the flames burned high and hot, Delia used the poker to spread the coals and logs onto the floor, using a trail of bedding and clothes to speed the fire's path. A quick glance out the front door confirmed no one in sight. She slipped out with the musket and her father's saddlebags and ran all the way to the stable, trusting the morning haze to hide her identity if anyone should see. She stopped just inside, letting her eyes grow accustomed to the darkness.

"Colin, where are you?"

He wandered from one of the stalls, his hair mussed and his eyes bleary.

"Have you been sleeping?" she said.

"What's wrong? Why are you wearing my clothes? Those are my new boots!"

"Don't go home! Stay here until someone comes to get you. Look like you're working. Dirty your pants."

Colin rubbed his eyes. His brow creased with confusion. "Don't tell Pa I was sleeping in here. He'll kill me."

"You don't have to worry about Pa anymore. I need his horse and saddle."

"You're leaving?"

"Yes, Colin, I'm leaving. But you've got to promise you'll stay right here until someone comes to get you."

His expression began to clear as he realized something bad had happened and Delia caused it. "What did you do?" he said. "Is this going to get me in trouble?"

"No, you'll be fine."

"I should go with you."

"I'd bring nothing but hard times to you, Colin. You're safer here."

Colin watched as Delia saddled the horse, shoved their father's musket into its leather straps, and mounted. "Remember, stay here," she said. She rode out of the stable, turning toward the river road.

As she passed the general store, Jeremiah stepped into the doorway, his dark shape barely noticeable from the corner of her eye. She turned her face away, hoping he'd pay no attention. As she reached the river, Jeremiah yelled. "Fire! We got a fire!"

Delia prodded the horse with her heels, urging him into a gallop. She did not look back.

As far as she knew, Jeremiah had seen her last. Once he put all the pieces together, he'd tell everyone she killed her ma and pa and set the cabin afire. He'd also tell folks, and the law, that she'd been nothing but trouble since the day she made her entrance into the world. That was the story her father told around town in case anyone noticed the bruises on Delia's face and arms.

Lots of bad things happened to Delia after she left Sangamon, and she'd done her share of crimes, often from necessity or self-defense. Most of the stories likely got to the town and to her brother over the thirteen years she'd been gone. She felt sad that Colin didn't know the whole story, but she couldn't bring herself to tell him the gritty details. He'd have to go on thinking bad of her without knowing the worst.

Delia opened her eyes and realized she sat askew in the rocking chair in the doctor's office, her shoulder throbbing so bad when she tried to shift her position that it brought tears to her eyes. With all those old thoughts racing through her mind, Delia wondered if she'd been close to dying. *Might be just as well.* She struggled to her feet, wobbled on rubbery legs, then slid one foot forward and shifted her weight.

Tempted to sit again, she waited to see if her legs would stop trembling. She wondered if anyone in Sangamon had gone to fetch the law. They'd lock her up for sure. And hang her, most likely. She straightened her back and stretched her neck from side to side, working out the aches and pains. Another step, then one more.

Doc Hemmer's voice startled her. "Where do you think you're going?"

"I need the chamber pot," she said.

"Mary," he called.

Clearly, Doc Hemmer was not a man to take liberties. Mary came into the room carrying a bowl of soup and a plate of biscuits. She set them on the three-legged stool and helped Delia use the pot, then carried the pot outside to empty. Doc helped position Delia in the rocking chair again and covered her with the shawl and quilt.

Even though her shoulder ached like the devil with every movement, Delia felt better everywhere else. "Is my fever gone?" she asked. "I'd sure like that bath as soon as you think I'm ready."

Doc Hemmer came closer and put his hand on her forehead, then the back of her neck. "Not yet," he said. "We'll know more when I change your bandage. Eat first. I'll talk to Mary about setting up the washtub."

Delia glanced around the room as Mary returned. "Where's the young'un?"

"Feeding the chickens," Mary said. "I told him to come inside as soon as he finished."

Moments later, the sounds of laughter came from outside. It didn't sound like Jackson.

"I'll look," Mary said. As she went to the door of the cabin, the laughter turned into giggling. Two voices.

When Mary walked inside, Jackson held one of her hands and the girl with the yellow parasol held the other. "We have a visitor," said Mary. "This is Elizabeth Frost, Jeremiah's little girl. Jeremiah, the storekeeper? Close your parasol, dear."

Elizabeth executed a perfect curtsey and twirled her parasol before closing it with a snap. "Papa gave it to me for my birthday present," she said.

"It's lovely," Delia murmured. "Does your father know you're here?"

"Oh, no. He would be very angry. He told me not to have anything to do with you, that you were trouble and would bring bad people to Sangamon."

"Then why are you here?" Mary asked.

"He didn't say I shouldn't call on you and Doctor Hemmer to show you my beautiful parasol."

Mary raised her eyebrows. "I see. Well, you'd best run on home before he finds out."

Elizabeth looked very serious. "Yes, I will. But first, might I ask a question?"

"Of course. What do you want to know?"

"This boy. He said his name is Jackson. Is that a fact?"

"Yes, it is."

"But he doesn't look like the rest of us. What's wrong with him?"

"Nothing, Elizabeth. His skin is a different color because he's from a different land. That's all."

"What land is he from?"

"Why, I suppose he's —"

135

"From Kentucky," Delia said. "Jackson came from Kentucky."

"Oh. I guess that's okay then. But Papa said he wasn't like us and that we couldn't tolerate his kind being in our town. Why did he say that?"

"Your father is a —"

"It's hard to explain," said Mary. "Isn't that right, Ernest?"

Doc Hemmer cleared his throat and stepped to Mary's side. "Very hard to explain," he said. "Shall I escort you to the store, Miss Elizabeth?"

Elizabeth, preening at the unexpected attention from Doc, opened her parasol and ran to his side. She turned for a moment to glance at Jackson, then followed Doc out the front door of the cabin.

Mary let out the breath she'd been holding. "I feared you'd say something she would repeat to her father."

"I almost did that very thing," Delia whispered. "Jeremiah Frost was always a hard man. It would be difficult for me to pretend otherwise."

"Yes, I know. The girl seems to be doing quite well, however. I think Jeremiah takes out his bad nature on Sarah. I wish she had never married him. Annie Gray did her best to intervene before the wedding, but Sarah wouldn't listen."

"I know he could be a mean one. I guess I left town long before this schoolteacher arrived. This Sarah, I mean."

"Yes."

Delia noted the shadows from the partially closed window slats and wondered if more time had passed than she realized. "Is it evening?" she asked. "Did I sleep all day?"

Mary smoothed her dress with her hands and smiled. "Two days have passed since you walked in the door and Doc tended to your wound. When we get you into bed this evening, Doc will give you more medicine. You'll most likely sleep the whole night and into another day."

"When I wake, four days will have passed?"

"Yes, indeed. After you eat, we'll move you to the bed in that other room. If you're enough improved tomorrow, you'll be able to sit and stand on your own. There's another rocking chair with pillows. Doc says it will be at least another week before you should get on horseback."

"Are you sure it's safe for me to be here? Safe for you and Doc, I mean."

"I depend on Doc to make that decision. I don't know of anyone else who'll have you, Delia. Doc could ask your brother, but I believe he'd say no. Colin will do what Jeremiah tells him, I am sure of that."

"I honestly thought Colin would take me in," Delia said. "When I left Sangamon, he was fourteen. We were best of friends until the day I left. I reckon he thinks the worst of me. Especially if he believes all the stories."

"Aren't the stories about you true?"

"Not all of them. I'm turning into a real frontier legend. Delia Pritchard, the woman who shot a federal marshal in Shawneetown. That one never happened. I never shot a lawman."

"Did you kill a man in Indiana?"

"That one is true. It's a long story, but I can tell you he deserved to die."

"But the law —"

"There was no law in those parts, at least no law that looked out for people like me."

Mary tightened her mouth, seeming to signal a mixture of disbelief and disapproval. "I reckon we'll be reading about your adventures in books someday. The real ones and the made-up ones."

"That's not something I ever wanted."

"And the stories about your parents?"

Delia shook her head. "I can't . . ."

Mary waited a moment to see if Delia would say more, then gave up. "Let me get you more soup," Mary said. "I'll be right back."

As Mary returned from the cookhouse, Doc Hemmer strode in the front door. He placed the bar across the latch, then retrieved Delia's gun from his worktable. "Do you have shot for this thing? I've never seen one like it before."

"Yes, in my saddlebags. Why? Am I going to need it?"

"I'm not sure. When I escorted Elizabeth into the store, there was a lot of talk going on. I listened while Sarah filled our flour bag. Appears two men rode into town today and asked if anyone had seen a woman riding a big Palouse stallion and leading a packhorse. Jeremiah said he'd seen such a rider about four days ago, but she'd passed on through Sangamon and he hadn't seen her since. They stopped at the saloon and had a meal, then rode out of town an hour or so later."

"They didn't go inside the stable?"

"Guess not."

"Jeremiah must have thought they looked dangerous for the town," Delia said. "I'm sure he wouldn't lie to protect me."

"He might be willing to give Doc and me protection, though," Mary said. "We don't cause the town any problems and we help

139

everywhere we can."

"The two men — did Jeremiah say what they looked like?"

"One was short and broad through the shoulders. He had a long feather in his hat. The other was tall and had long black hair. His nose crooked to the side, like he'd been beat about the face."

"I think I know who they are. Jeremiah did right to send them away with a lie. If those two got full of whiskey, they'd shoot up the town for fun."

"Friends of yours?" asked Mary.

Delia glanced at Mary to see if she joshed or wanted to make a point. Mary returned her gaze with a straight face. "I'm not certain," said Delia. "We might never know unless they return."

Chapter Fifteen: During the Night

It took the next hour to get Delia bathed and dressed in one of Doc's nightshirts and moved into the bedroom, a clean chamber pot slid under her bed, and the pillows plumped and arranged to cushion her shoulder. Delia already had less pain and was able to move her arm in a careful arc. The terrible throbbing had eased, so the ordeal of stepping into the tub in the cookhouse with Mary's assistance was easier than Delia expected. She didn't want more of the pain-killing medicine. It knocked her out and made her feel woozy when she woke. Even though Delia thought she'd rest quite well after her trip to the cookhouse and back, Doc insisted on one more dose of the drug, determined she sleep again to help speed her recovery.

Delia, who wasn't one to pray very often, muttered a quick request to God to keep Doc Hemmer, Mary, and Jackson safe for another day. A whole posse of men, good or bad, could come in the front door and haul her away before she knew what happened. The two oddball scoundrels that might have shown up so far were nothing compared to the Biedler gang, the Cave-in-Rock outlaws she'd robbed. They'd never give up. More than likely, Jack Biedler planned to kill Delia on the spot, just for running away with a horse and gun that didn't belong to her. It didn't take much to trigger their killing side. The fact that she'd also stolen a bag of gold coins made their pursuit inevitable.

The two who had apparently followed her to Sangamon, Moose and Beak, were dumb as all get-out. How had they managed to track her? Didn't they realize the Biedlers knew she once rode with the two old fools and were most likely following them in the hope they'd lead the gang to Delia?

Finally settled onto the bed, Delia had the gun at her right side and her saddlebags within easy reach. Doc Hemmer had seen to that while Mary looked on with her passive expression. Mary clearly disapproved of Delia's presence as well as her guns but did not challenge Doc's decision. Delia insisted she was comfortable, hoping Mary would stop watching her as though she might fall out of bed or scream in pain at any moment.

It worked. Mary retired to the cookhouse, saying she would check on Jackson, who had formed a special relationship with the chickens and preferred their company to the adults in the cabin. He had even protested, Mary reported, when she went to select a victim destined for the cooking pot. Doc Hemmer had to distract the youngster with a walk to view a gaggle of geese while Mary handled the execution and cleaning of the young hen.

After Doc and Jackson returned, the doctor went to work in his office, apparently straightening the implements on his worktable, judging by the sounds. He brought Delia a bundle of clean rags and asked if she would fold them into neat bandages when she felt like it. When she agreed, he placed the bundle on the three-legged stool and set it beside the rocking chair.

Delia lay back and let herself relax as the medicine began to work. She thought about Moose and Beak, wondering if they had moved on. They could be camping outside of town, waiting to see if the Palouse made an appearance. Or perhaps one of them had already sneaked inside the stable, saw McAllister, and now waited for Delia herself to ride out where they could meet with her unseen by the townsfolk.

The short one called himself Moose because of his hefty shape and his cantankerous nature. The first thing anyone noticed about the other man, known as Beak, was his long nose bent to the side. Delia had met them the day after she ran away from Cave-in-Rock. Even though she moved as fast as she could, they'd caught up with her on the road.

Moose and Beak rode along behind her, even camped nearby that first evening, talking constantly even though she never answered their questions or asked any of her own.

"We know you done stole from Jack Biedler," Moose said. "If we know it, then they know, too. They'll be after you afore long. How you going to get away?"

Delia ignored their babbling as much as possible, but their relentless questioning wore her down.

"They'll string you up like any other horse thief. Won't matter to the Biedlers that you're a woman. There's five of them and one of you. You got a plan?"

After they gave up trying to scare her to death and find out where she intended to go or who would help her, both men tried to woo her, after a fashion. They admitted defeat when she pointed her rifle at Moose and threatened to blow his wooing parts away with one shot.

She'd left them behind while they were busy drinking in a saloon a good day's ride west of Shawneetown. As far as she knew, they'd only spotted her once since then, could be a month or two ago. She'd already acquired the Palouse by that time and outran their scrawny horses in minutes.

How had they found her again? Could be a coincidence they'd come to Sangamon. Or perhaps the Biedlers were getting close and Moose and Beak wanted to warn her and earn her gratitude.

Unless the price on her head had increased. She doubted they liked her enough to give up a hefty bounty. Her heart sank, and a wave of nausea threatened to bring her soup up from her stomach. She *had* killed a man. Two if truth be told. What if there was another witness she didn't know about? What if the reward offered by the law tempted more and more bounty hunters to the chase? Maybe the law now wanted her dead or alive. If the two men showed and found McAllister in the stable and figured out Jeremiah had lied to them, then Jeremiah was in trouble, too.

"Doc!"

Doc Hemmer came to the doorway.

"I need Mary to help me with my clothes."

"Why is that? You'll be asleep in a few minutes. No one will see you in that nightshirt. I won't let anyone inside."

"I think it's best I leave town now."

"Why is that, Delia?"

"I don't want to say. It's just, staying here is bad for everyone. Those two men, they're dangerous. They might not have moved on. If they find the Palouse, they'll kill Jeremiah for lying. They might destroy the whole town looking for me." Her exaggeration about Moose and Beak seemed to get Doc's attention. He studied her for a moment as if weighing her request.

"How about I move the Palouse to Miss Gray's farm? I'll tell her I bought McAllister and need a place to keep him because there's no room at the stable."

"You'd tell an untruth like that?"

Doc raised his eyebrows. "An untruth for a good cause is noble. I'm sure God will approve."

"I don't think Mary will approve."

"Perhaps not, but she won't object when she knows it's for the good of the town."

"You'll take McAllister to the farm tonight?"

"That would be best, don't you think? I'll throw a dark blanket over his back. He'll be near invisible."

Delia did not protest, acting as though she agreed to everything Doc said. "Miss Gray's place is by the river, if I remember right. That's a fair walk, first to the stable and then to the farm."

"Not too far. Her land is situated near the bend of the river. Her barn is new and sits a bit back from the road. With the mule and the goat, no strangers will come close without her knowing. In spite of her strange ways of late, she's good with her weapons and can raise an alarm with her bell as well as the musket."

"Then I agree," Delia said. To herself, she imagined the layout of Sangamon and the farm. She vaguely remembered the woman who owned that land, knew she inherited the farm from her parents. When Delia left Sangamon, the farm buildings consisted only of a lean-to shelter for a goat, a mule, and an old milk cow. The whole town must have come together to help Annie Gray build a barn.

The story Doc planned to tell would likely hold if strangers saw the horse grazing and asked after its owner. They would ask, Miss Gray would send them to Doc Hemmer, and he would tell his noble untruth once again. How would he explain what happened to Delia Pritchard after she sold her horse? She wondered if Doc's noble untruth could include pointing out a fresh-dug burial plot outside the cemetery.

She decided not to ask. Instead, she would wait until she knew McAllister was safe on the farm, then find clothes for herself, recover the Palouse, and sneak away in the middle of the night. She'd leave a note telling Doc he now owned the sorrel mare in payment of services rendered.

And the boy. What about the boy? *I might have to leave him behind.* The thought caused her pain. *I'm getting soft. One thing I don't need is getting attached to that young'un.*

Delia didn't know where Doc slept. It might be difficult to get away without him hearing unless he bunked in a separate cabin. She tried to remember the layout from the day she arrived with her bad shoulder but couldn't recall. The only thing on her mind that day was her pain.

If Moose and Beak returned to Sangamon before nightfall and told folks why they hunted her, showed around a wanted poster, there might be more than one person ready to hand her over for the reward. Maybe hand her corpse over to make it nice and easy. Would her brother come to her aid?

Doubtful. Doc Hemmer might, but at the risk of his own life. Mary? Would she help Delia? Probably not.

What would happen to poor little Jackson then? She had no choice but to take him away with her. The more she thought about it, waiting until after Doc moved the Palouse to Miss Gray's farm seemed foolhardy.

Delia placed her right hand on the rifle and closed her eyes. She needed to rest for a few minutes. Then she'd get out of bed, find her clothes, and walk to the stable.

CHAPTER SIXTEEN: MOOSE AND BEAK

Moose and Beak had circled around the north side of Sangamon and camped in the woods on the west side of town by the river. Remnants of an old Indian hut sat next to a small clearing. A few cornstalks and a wandering pumpkin vine showed where a garden once grew. Most of the space was overgrown with weeds and tallgrass, but the fire pit in the center remained clear. Logs sat on one side of the pit, though much of the wood had crumbled under an assault by huge black ants.

Beak found a section of log that seemed sturdy enough to hold his weight. He didn't worry about what Moose did and when he did it. They'd been traveling together long enough that they'd worked out a routine, each performing his own tasks, each carrying his share of the load.

Moose wandered the edge of the clearing, looking for dried brush and twigs. He brought an armful and dumped the lot into the pit. When Moose walked away, Beak bent over the pit with his hunting knife and the piece of flint he had dug from his pants pocket.

By the time Beak started a fire, Moose had found a few larger branches. Planting one foot near the center of each branch, he pulled the end until the wood snapped. Minutes later they had a good flame going, one fit for cooking or for scaring away animals that might roam at night.

"I still don't understand why you want to hang around this little town," Moose said. "The food weren't that great, and I'd swear the whiskey was half water and half mule piss."

"I got a feeling about that gal Delia," Beak answered. "Her and me hit it off fine until you got all lovesick and tried to touch her where she didn't want touching." He gave Moose a look meant to send a message. That Delia gal belonged to Beak if she belonged to anyone.

"Ah, hell, I was funning her and you. She don't smell good enough to cuddle with for more than a minute."

"She smells fine."

Moose stared at Beak's face for a second, then bust out laughing. "How would you know? With that nose, you couldn't smell horse manure covered with skunk squirt."

Whenever Beak thought about the way he looked with his broken-up nose, it rankled at his mood. He got madder than a she-bear with cubs when Moose made fun of him. After all, there had been a day when Beak, then known as Baxter, was popular with the ladies. It hurt his feelings to see how women looked at him now, then looked away. They usually walked away, too. His heart broke a little more every time that happened.

Beak rubbed his hand across his nose as he peered across the fire at Moose from under half-closed eyelids. "I can smell you from here, you ornery bastard. When was the last time you had a bath?"

"Same as you! A month, maybe two."

They laughed, although Beak didn't feel as much like laughing as Moose obviously did. Still, what's a little laugh to keep the peace? He didn't want to ride away from Moose yet, especially now they had such a good camping routine.

"I think I remember that bath," said Beak. "Ain't that the day the little redheaded whore from out east rode into Shawneetown with nothing but that raggedy green dress and shoes packed with paper to cover the holes? They put her in the back room to tote buckets of hot water to the tubs."

"That's right," said Moose. "You pulled the girl inside the tub with you, in that dirty old water, and you as naked as the day you was born. She started screeching and scrambling to get loose, and you were feeling every part of that gal like you had ten hands, all of them busy at the same time."

Beak looked at his hands and wiggled his fingers, setting Moose to laughing so hard he bent over, his arms gripping his stomach like it hurt. Beak wished Moose would stop now, but that never happened. His friend always had to hit him with the rest of the story, add that one more little twist of the knife. For a second, Beak wondered what would happen if he drew his gun and aimed it at Moose's head.

"You remember what happened, then, don't you, Beak? That little gal still had ahold of the handle of the bucket, and she swung it hard enough to knock your brain into mush. I think she might of even smashed your nose a little flatter than it was before."

Beak grimaced as he pushed away his vision of Moose's untimely end. "I was having a fine time until she did that. I could of drowned if the water in the tub was deep enough."

"You shouldn't have shot her, though."

"I know. I got so mad there for a minute I wasn't thinking straight."

Thank the Lord, thought Beak. He had been dragged through the tale again and still hadn't gunned Moose down or stuck a knife in his gullet.

They fell silent, as though thinking on good times. Moose stood and wandered closer to the trees, gathering an armload of firewood. Beak thoughtfully poked at the fire with a stick until it flared and burned hotter. After a few minutes, he got up and pulled the saddle and blanket, bedroll, and supplies off his horse and dropped everything a short way from the flames. He led his horse to the river to drink, then tied her reins to a sturdy bush. He fed her the few oats he had left in the feed bag.

When he returned to the campfire, Beak opened his bedroll and grabbed the fry pan and his long fork, then threw in a piece of fatback and a handful of soft beans kept moist in a buckskin pouch. When the meat began to sizzle, he flipped it over and let it get crisp on the other side. He added a little water from his canteen and a bit of cornmeal from their dwindling supply, cooking the mush until it set into something that looked almost like real cornbread. Wouldn't taste like much, Beak knew, but it was all they had. Without salt and sugar, this food wouldn't suit nobody except down-on-their-luck men like them.

Moose carried in another armload of wood and piled it near the fire. After tending to his own horse, he untied his bedroll and unwrapped a blackened pot they used to heat water and make coffee. He shook his water bag, listening for how much sloshed around inside, and left it with his saddlebags. The water in the river flowed fast enough to swirl eddies near the muddy bank, but the water near the middle looked clear. Beak watched as Moose slipped off his boots and socks and waded in. He dipped his pot into the clearest spot he could find, then toted it to the pit and set it into the fire. He retrieved his boots and socks, then sat on one of the sturdy spots near Beak and dried his feet near the flames.

Beak had paid close attention to Moose's efforts while he thought of more ways to end the man's endless yakking. If he ran to the river, knocked Moose into the water, and held his head under, he'd never have to hear about the redheaded whore in the bathhouse again. He was mighty tempted to do exactly that. Satan had a powerful hold on men like him and Moose. Beak worried about that a lot. His life had been nothing but one bad deed after another. If Satan didn't loosen his hold soon, Beak was headed for an eternity of fire and brimstone.

"You think we might be moving on tomorrow?" Moose asked. He wiggled his toes, then pulled on his socks and boots.

"Could be. Depends."

"You think we might go into town, get supplies at that general store?"

"You find a pile of gold nuggets by that river? We can use them to buy all the goods you want."

Moose tossed a few twigs in the pit. "We need a hotter fire if we want this water to boil."

Beak scrambled to his feet and moseyed to the few supplies remaining on his bedroll. "I got just enough coffee to throw in the pot for one more meal. You want it tonight or in the morning?"

"In the morning, I guess. We leaving early?"

"Maybe. Maybe not."

"Shit-in-the-woods, Beak, how am I going to know what to do if you keep saying 'maybe' to every question I ask?"

"I ain't made a plan yet. I'm thinking on it. What if we sneak into town after everyone is asleep and borrow whatever we need from the general store, go on to the saloon and borrow a bottle of whiskey, and then slip into the stable and borrow us an extra horse and saddle?"

Moose nodded, his expression thoughtful and dead serious. "That might work. When would we pay back all this borrowing?"

Beak looked at Moose, wondering if the man was pulling his leg or if he really thought "borrowing" meant they'd be "paying back" someday. "I don't know, Moose. Whenever we can, I reckon."

"Okay, I'll do it. You just say the word."

Beak poked at the fire again, then grabbed their metal plates and divided the cornmeal mess. After they ate what they had, Beak poured some of the boiled water into another pot to cool for the water bags. Beak emptied the coffee into the water pot and set it aside so the coffee could flavor the liquid overnight. They could reheat it in the morning, and it might even taste like coffee instead of colored water. Using handfuls of dried leaves, they cleaned their plates and the fry pan at the river and set them near the bedrolls.

Beak stretched out on his bedding near the fire and pulled his hat lower to cover his eyes. "I'm going to get a little shut-eye before we go into town. Your turn to keep lookout." He figured he got an ornery look from Moose for that, but he didn't give a hoot. After bringing up that story again about the face-smashing Beak got from that redheaded gal, Moose didn't deserve any special favors.

CHAPTER SEVENTEEN: DELIA, EIGHTEEN HOURS LATER

Delia's plan to slip away from Doc Hemmer's office and disappear with Jackson didn't go as she planned. After a few minutes of fighting off sleep, once even struggling to sit on the edge of the bed and look around for the clothes Mary had promised to bring, Delia relaxed and gave in to the medicine.

The next time she opened her eyes, her whole body ached from lying still so long, but the deep throbbing in her shoulder had not returned. Her gun lay at her right side, the saddlebags nearby.

The bright sun filtering through the still-closed shutters told her she'd slept through the night and more. The sun had already passed high noon and now shone from the west. Delia eased up to sit on the edge of the bed, planted her bare feet on the rug of fox fur, and tried to stand. Wobbly at first, she didn't move until she felt steady, then took a step. Then another. By the time she reached the window, she felt achy, sleepy, and hungry. Thankfully, she had not felt dizzy or confused.

Unlatching the shutters, she pushed them open to let more sun into the room. The rear of the cabin looked out on a large garden and a building she identified as the cookhouse by its chimney. Beyond, close to a wooded lot and slightly downhill from the cabin, was the outhouse. A bit closer to the cookhouse, by the garden, someone had built a chicken coop. Hens of various colors roamed the garden and the yard. A white rooster stalked among the hens as though giving orders for the day.

Set to the side and between the cookhouse and the doctor's office, Delia saw another cabin she assumed was Doc's home. Stepping-stones connected the buildings.

She'd slept soundly, for she had not heard the rooster crow in the early morning. If the doctor slept in his own cabin, Delia had been left alone for hours. She wondered where Jackson had spent the night.

A man's voice called out for the doctor from the office. Delia glanced over her shoulder and saw the man standing near her door. He seemed vaguely familiar, but way too interested in watching her. Grabbing her handgun, almost as a reflex, she pointed it at him, then realized she'd over-reacted. She crossed to the bedroom door and slammed it shut. A murmur of voices followed. A few minutes later, Mary brought Jackson in.

"The preacher has come to call," Mary said. "He wants to know if you'll talk to him."

"Why?"

"He said he comforts the sick and injured as part of his ministry."

Delia grimaced. "No, I've no interest in being preached at today."

Mary relayed the message to the preacher, then returned to get Jackson, leaving Delia to herself.

As Delia headed for the rocking chair, she noticed the rags Doc Hemmer had left on the stool. She folded while she rocked, both actions calming. Once that chore was finished, Delia considered trying to use the chamber pot by herself, or even walking to the outhouse, but decided it would be safer to have Mary's help. She went to the door, listened for a moment, then opened it and looked into the office. It was empty.

Uneasy about leaving the cabin without her weapon, she returned to the bed for her gun and wrapped the quilt about her shoulders. She kept the gun hidden under the quilt at her waist as she passed through the doctor's office to the other back door, the one she assumed led to the cookhouse. When she pulled it open, she found Jackson sitting on a bench, whittling a stick with a bone-handled knife.

He grinned at her, his eyes sparkling in a happy way she hadn't seen before. "Doc Hemmer showed me how to whittle," he said. "Lookit this, Miss Delia. I ain't never had a whittling knife."

"You won't cut yourself, now, will you?"

"No, ma'am. Doc showed me. I'm being mighty careful."

"Where's Mary?" Delia asked.

"She's cooking in there." Jackson pointed to the nearest building.

"Where's Doc?"

Jackson waved toward his right where the other cabin sat a few feet from the doctor's office. "That's where he lives when he's not here. He said to tell you he did what he said with McAllister and that he was going to the general store for a bag of cracked corn for the chickens and then he was going to Miss Gray's farm to deliver medicine."

"You remembered all that?"

"I sure did. Doc Hemmer told me, and then he had me tell him what he said, and then he said if I minded my manners, he'd bring me rock candy from the store."

"Have you ever had rock candy before?"

"I sure have. My mama made rock candy for me and my brother . . ." Jackson bent his head and began whittling with a fierce stroke.

"Careful, young'un. You won't have anything left of that stick."

Jackson slowed the blade's motion but didn't stop.

"I didn't know you had a brother. Why wasn't he with you that day in the woods?"

"John Quincy ran away a long time ago." Jackson stood and put the stick and knife on the bench. "Did you see the chickens, Miss Delia? They like me. If I go sit on the ground by the garden, that one brown chicken comes right up and lets me pet her."

Delia had thoughts about that. *They're not meant to be your friends, young'un. They're meant to lay eggs, hatch baby chicks, or end their lives in the soup pot.* After seeing him turn his sweet smile on the little brown hen, Delia decided not to say anything, especially that part about the soup. He'd find out soon enough. Meanwhile, she'd ask Mary to let the brown chicken live until they were gone.

"Land sakes," Delia said. "A chicken for a

friend. I never heard of such a thing."

Jackson, who appeared to put thoughts of his mama and his brother away from his mind, returned to the bench and picked up the stick and knife.

Delia let him be and walked toward the cookhouse. She lingered in the doorway for a moment, letting her eyes adjust to the semidarkness inside. By the fireplace, Mary stirred the contents of a pot that hung from a long hook she'd swung away from the red-hot logs.

Delia spoke before she entered the room, so she wouldn't startle Mary. "Something smells good." She stopped just inside the door.

Mary looked up. "I didn't think you'd be out of bed yet. I forgot to put clothes on the chair for you. How do you feel?"

"Much better," Delia said. She decided not to mention the aching and fatigue. The doctor would want her tucked in bed if she voiced a complaint. "If I had something to wear, I think I could manage the outhouse on my own. Where are my clothes and boots?"

"Your boots are still in Doc's office. I think they got pushed under the worktable. I'll get a shirt for you."

Delia started to ask about her pants, then

saw them draped over a chair near the fire. "You washed my drawers."

Mary leaned over and felt about the legs and pockets. "They're dry," she said. "Don't you have any other clothes?"

"I did. I dropped my things when I ran into the problem with Jackson and his ma and pa. After that, I figured we'd best move on. I couldn't leave him out there on his own, and I sure couldn't take him back with no folks to look out for him."

Mary turned to her pot and stirred its contents. "Where did that happen?" she asked. "Where did you come from?"

My, that gal won't stop asking questions. "South of here. I'm going to take these britches and my socks and try to pull on my boots. I want to go out. Do you have that shirt close by?"

"Inside Doc's cabin," Mary said. She swung the pot over the fire and set her long-handled ladle on the table. "I'll get it."

After Delia returned to the bedroom in Doc's office, she dropped the quilt and set her gun on the chair while she changed into her pants and socks. As soon as Mary brought the shirt, Delia slipped it on, folded up the sleeves, and tucked in the shirttail that hung past her hips. She folded the quilt and slipped the gun inside the folds, then went outside to check on Jackson. He was busy whittling, so she left him alone and returned to the doctor's office. After setting the quilt at the end of the bed where she'd slept, Delia found her boots and sat on the bed to put them on. Then she stood, shoved the gun into her waistband, pulling out a section of her shirttail to let it hang.

By the time Delia was fully dressed, she felt exhausted. She worked on her hair with the brush Mary gave her but couldn't keep her left arm raised long enough to braid it. She sat in the rocking chair until she felt she could make the trip to the outhouse. Once that big excursion had been accomplished, she stopped at the door of the cookhouse to ask for food. Mary was a step ahead of her. A cup of steaming coffee and a plate of beans and cornbread sat on the table. Delia thought beans might never have tasted so good. And she declared the cornbread the best she'd ever eaten. Mary had even spread butter on the hot bread.

"That butter's from Miss Gray," Mary said. "Doc gets it in pay for her medicine."

Delia's mouth was full. She managed a "moof" of acknowledgement but kept on eating until she cleaned her plate. "Did Jackson get something to eat?" she asked.

"My, goodness, yes. He had eggs, side

meat, and biscuits for breakfast and corn-bread and beans at midday. Jackson has a big appetite."

"You or the doctor said you've been teaching school. How have you done that with me and Jackson here? Seems like you've been around all the time I'm awake."

"I've been at the school while you slept and Doc could be here. Other times, I sent the children home early or had Sarah Frost sit at the desk while the children did studies. This time of year, attendance is not too good anyway. All the farm children stay home to work in the fields, especially the boys. We won't get everyone at school until harvest is over."

Mary paused, then faced Delia and cleared her throat. "The preacher said he'd stop by tomorrow to see you." She looked at Delia's hair, frowned, and reached for the blue ribbon she'd placed on the table. "Let me tie back your hair."

Before Delia could respond, a noise came from the front of the doctor's office. "That's sure to be Doc," Mary said. They waited for more sounds. When Doc spoke aloud, Mary wiped her brow.

"You've been whittling a real pile of shavings, Jackson."

"Yes, sir."

Doc appeared at the door and nodded as though in approval that Delia was up and dressed. He acknowledged Mary who toiled at the fireplace, then he walked inside and sat at the table.

Within minutes, Mary handed the doctor a plate of food and brought him a cup of coffee. "You were gone a long time," Mary said. "Is everything okay?"

Doc chewed and swallowed. "A lot has happened." He turned to Delia who sat across the table from him, now sipping at the coffee. "I was not the only one creeping around town in the middle of the night."

Chapter Eighteen:
Doc Hemmer's
Night Adventure

Doc had sat up late the previous night, reading by an oil lamp, and remained alert long after Jackson fell asleep in a makeshift bed on the floor of his cabin. He assumed Delia would be under the spell of laudanum through the night, so he barricaded the front door of his office from the inside and secured the other door with a lock.

The town grew quiet later than usual on warm September evenings. Children hated to go inside before dark, knowing days would soon be too short. Eventually, after the meal ended and bedtime enforced, the residents of Sangamon closed and latched their shutters and barricaded doors. Doc had been told that years in the past, when everyone in town knew everyone else, no such precautions had seemed necessary. But during the time when Caswell Proud roamed at night, stalking folks and peering in windows, lives profoundly changed. Folks formed new habits for self-protection and now clung to them as though any new visitor to the town could bring unspeakable evil.

Once innocence is exposed to the dark underbelly of life, there's no way to shove that darkness back where it belongs. Such were Doc Hemmer's thoughts as he set the protections in place for his office. He was confident Mary had done the same in her own room behind the schoolhouse. He worried about her, as he would worry about an aunt or older sister. The schoolhouse was closer to the main part of Sangamon. Trouble near the saloon would be nearer her door than his.

Doc's plan to slip out of his cabin and use the woods behind his property to hide his secret foray into the village would leave his cabin unsecured for the hour or so he'd be gone. His only lock protected his office and Delia. He considered moving Jackson into his office, but the boy was sound asleep and unlikely to wake in the next hour. He decided to leave him be.

If not for the two strangers who had passed through town that week, his concern might not have surfaced at all. But strangers worried him, especially two who appeared to Jeremiah as rough and fearsome and wore their grim expressions like warnings. Doc would move as fast as he could on his mission, making every effort to carry out the plan as quietly as possible.

The path across the tallgrass field to the woods was lit only by a sliver of moonlight. Once in the woods, Doc found it hard to see at first. Gradually his eyes adjusted to the darkness. No breeze stirred. No sounds except the rustling of his own boots through the fallen leaves.

The north edge of the woods opened onto the road that came from the Sangamon River and moved past the general store, the blacksmith shop and stable, and the saloon.

Moving slowly from building to building, slipping through the shadows next to each business, Doc Hemmer finally reached the stable. He crept about the building to make sure Colin Pritchard did not stand guard, then lifted the bar from the door and eased it to hang free. Opening the barn door barely more than a crack, he went inside and approached the stall where the Palouse stood with ears perked as though expecting company any minute. He showed no alarm at seeing the doctor, thanks to their acquaintance the day Delia arrived in Sangamon.

Doc entered the stall and pulled the Palouse's bridle and reins off the hook on the wall. Once tacked up except for a saddle, the Palouse seemed ready to leave, dancing about with more energy than Doc hoped he would show once outside. He guided the horse through the door, held onto the reins while he replaced the bar on the front of the barn, then led the animal straight along the road past the saloon. At the crossing, they turned toward the doctor's home and office, then continued to Annie Gray's farm. Doc figured the whole trip lasted about thirty minutes.

The Palouse behaved perfectly without whinny or undue struggling until Doc tried to get him into the rear stall. There was one complication. A mule had taken possession of the space, and McAllister had no intention of sharing quarters. Annie Gray had neglected to mention that the mule roamed freely in the barn and might choose the back stall that night.

The cow rested comfortably on a bed of straw in its own stall. The Palouse backed away, not willing to share that one either.

That left only the front stall available for McAllister, a spot visible from the road when the barn door stood open. He'd have to return the next day to help Miss Gray reposition the animals. He removed the horse's tack and hung it on the wall, added a little hay at the front of the stall, then closed the gate and left the barn. Miss Gray's house remained dark. Either she hadn't heard him deliver the horse or she lurked inside her door with her musket. The thought made him nervous. He picked up his pace, anxious now to reach home.

A sound like the crunching of boots on small rocks brought him to a halt as he rounded Miss Gray's cabin. He peered about, looking for signs of movement. Another sound. Doc scanned the darkness, then tried to see across the tallgrass and into the woods. A shadow? A dark form moving slowly. Two shadows. Men creeping along the edge of the trees that bordered the field behind Doc's property. Had they been prowling around Sangamon's main street? Had they seen him bring out the stallion and walk it along the road?

Doc crouched as low as he could and remained still. Barely visible now, two men disappeared into the cover of willows that hung over the river's edge. Doc contemplated returning to his cabin, waking Jackson, and then moving into the office and barricading the door. He thought about the two men who had come through town, asking questions about Delia. They were the reason he stole through the night to hide the Palouse. If they had gone to the stable and not found McAllister, would they return and search the whole town? Perhaps go to Miss Gray's farm? It seemed they might be headed that way now. He needed to do something.

He wished he'd brought his musket along on this midnight excursion. If he did confront the two men, what would he say? Ask what no-good business they were up to, sneaking through the woods at night? He doubted that would scare them away. They had been armed when they rode into town. Stopping by his office for a weapon would be wise. He could use Delia's rifle, which was more up to date than his own.

Delia's new handgun would be even more useful, but he might wake her if he tried to remove the Colt from her side. Her long gun still rested against the wall near the front door. Doc set out for his office, staying on the road instead of following the two men into the woods.

His stealthy entry through the back door and across his office did not wake Delia. She didn't utter a sound or even rustle the sheet on her bed. He escaped with the long gun and a pocketful of shot, secured the lock, crept past the cookhouse and cabin, and hurried toward the weeping willows.

Hoping to intersect the two men's path before they reached Annie's farm, Doc moved as fast as he dared while trying to avoid noises that might attract their attention.

Even with the trees showing their late summer foliage, small clearings allowed the moonlight to shine through. He entered the woods and slowed his pace, listening for steps or voices. A twig snapped, followed by the rustle of leaves from a downed tree. A gasp, followed by a string of cuss words. Doc crouched behind a bush as he detected the two intruders lurking near the river, their backs hunched and heads together as they talked softly. *Now what to do?*

Doc decided to take a chance.

"Halt!" Doc cried. He stayed in his crouched position, hoping to remain invisible as the two tried to see into the darkness. "You're surrounded. It's you two against seven armed men." He felt around the ground until he found a rock small enough to fit in his hand but large enough to create a diversion. He tossed the stone as far into the woods as he could. It made a satisfying *thunk* as it landed.

Doc called out again. "You two men. What are you doing here?"

"We're lost," one man's voice answered.

"We was out walking and got turned around."

"How could you get lost? Follow the river back where you came from."

"We was looking for firewood and figured these trees was best for that. When we got in here, that's when we got lost."

"That's hogwash, gentlemen. How about you collect your horses and gear and move on. We'll keep watch and make sure you don't come back."

"I hear one man talking," the voice said. "It's just one of you, ain't it? There's no seven men out here in the middle of the night."

Doc felt around for another rock and tossed it into the woods closer to the road. "You want to find out?" he yelled.

"Nope. We're going. Hold on to your britches and let us figure which way to go." A few seconds later, the two shadows moved quickly through one of the clearings. Doc straightened and followed, no longer concerned. They could not be sure whether he'd brought an army or wandered alone. Once he confirmed the two shadows had reversed their course and made a beeline for Sangamon's main street, he turned toward his office. He could only pray the two did not return. He did not feel comfortable hiding in the dark and standing alone against intruders. He often mused about why he'd abandoned civilization in the East, where he'd gone to school. And why he'd come to this backwater town. The notion he'd help more folks than in a city crowded with doctors? The foolish desire to experience danger and adventure? Be a man?

For the moment, this man was mighty happy to return Delia's rifle to his office, hurry to his own cabin, slip inside, and bar the door.

Doc tiptoed past Jackson and climbed into his own bed. He had no trouble falling asleep, confident he'd routed the prowlers.

A loud blast in the distance jolted him awake. He waited, frozen, to see if the sound came again. Seconds later, a yard bell clanged. The schoolhouse? No, the noise came from Annie Gray's bell, he thought. He pulled on his boots, crossed to his office to retrieve Delia's rifle, and went out into the early dawn.

Not the only man raised from his slumbers, he met two of the townsfolk on horseback in front of his office, the morning sun now sitting in a bed of orange clouds above the horizon. He alerted them to the men he'd found wandering the woods during the night. Colin Pritchard soon joined the others, and they rode to Miss Gray's farm to check on her safety. The men told Doc they would work their way toward town along the river to look for the strangers' campsite and confirm they'd skedaddled.

After checking on Delia and Jackson, both still asleep, Doc walked to Miss Gray's cabin.

Annie stood in her doorway, her musket ready to lift and fire. "A varmint tried to get in my barn," she said. "Mule raised a terrible racket."

Doc went to the barn and checked inside. All was as he had left it the night before. He motioned Annie to give him a hand in moving the animals about, then cautioned her to be on the lookout for strangers.

The sun beat hot and dry on his shoulders as he finally returned to his office. He found Jackson outside on the bench. Mary and Delia were in the cookhouse. He described his confrontation with the men, the gunshot, the bell.

Mary gasped. "I did not hear one sound."
"Nor did I," said Delia.

That revelation alarmed Delia. If the two men had broken into the doctor's office, Delia could very well be dead by now, or dragged away into the night without her clothes or weapons. That sounded worse in her mind than being dead.

"I borrowed your rifle," Doc said. "I returned it to its place behind the office door. Perhaps you should move it into the other room and hide it under the bed."

"That I will," Delia said. A hollow promise beat a long argument with Doc as far as she was concerned. She needed to leave this town as soon as possible. But what would she do about the young'un? Would he be safer if she left him behind? Back and forth, she argued with herself, unable to decide what was best.

How could she abandon him now? As hard as she'd tried to hold the boy at a distance, avoid learning too much about his fears and dreams, even resisting the use of his name, Delia knew she would feel empty and mean if she left without the boy at her side.

She went out to the bench and sat by Jackson. "You give up on your whittling?"

"No, just thinking about what you and Doc said."

She patted him on the knee. "A little disturbance during the night. Nothing for you to worry about. Let's go in the cookhouse and see if Mary has a biscuit for you."

CHAPTER NINETEEN: THE DAY THE PREACHER MET DELIA

The day the preacher had returned the basket to Annie Gray's cabin, he left it sitting outside her door, relieved that she had not answered his knock. He had no more questions to ask and nothing else to say. When he heard her voice chattering away in the barn, however, he could not resist the temptation to see who else she entertained. He moved closer to the open barn door and looked inside. Annie sat on a three-legged stool, talking to her goat. Unable to hear her words and not willing to enter the barn where she could see him, John had backed away and headed for Doc Hemmer's office.

There he had found the office door unbarred, so he went inside without knocking. No one was in the front office, and the door into the bedroom was partway open. Delia Pritchard stood at the window, looking out. The quilt that had covered her while she sat in the rocker now lay in a heap on the floor.

Delia wore a man's nightshirt, but her left shoulder and arm remained free of the sleeve. A large bandage covered the back of her shoulder.

John had pushed the office front door shut with a bang as he called the doctor's name. "Anyone here? It's John Claymore." Delia turned and lunged toward her cot.

"Sorry, I didn't see you," John said. "I mean no harm. Is the doctor around?"

Delia straightened with her handgun pointed in his direction.

"I'm the preacher . . . or at least, I used to be the preacher. You can put the gun down. I won't hurt you."

Delia stepped closer to the bedroom door and slammed it closed. At the same time, Mary hurried in from outside. "Preacher. You frightened me. I didn't expect to see you again."

"I intended to leave this morning, but I have learned that Doc's patient is Miss Delia Pritchard. I hoped to have a word with her before I go."

"She is ill and in pain. She has no desire to talk to anyone."

"Even a preacher?"

"I would be quite shocked to find Delia wanting to talk to a preacher."

Jackson slipped into the office and looked

181

at John intently, studying his face, clothes, and boots. "I'd want to talk to a preacher."

"Jackson, go outside."

"But Miss Mary . . . my ma and pa said it was good to talk to the Lord and the best way to do that was by praying. Preacher, are you fixing to pray today?"

"Why, I suppose I could. What would you want to pray about?"

Jackson had rattled off a whole list, including prayers for his ma and pa to be in Heaven and one to make Miss Delia all better so they could get out of this town.

Mary moved quickly toward the bedroom, tapped on the door, and then slid inside, beckoning Jackson to come with her.

John stayed in Doc's office, holding his hat in his hand and shifting from one foot to the other. Knowing Delia Pritchard had a gun made him nervous, but he still wanted the chance to talk to her. As the very last action of his ministry, he could offer Delia the opportunity to plead for God's forgiveness with John as her witness.

Once again, he had pretended to be a preacher who could bring a soul to salvation. *Old habits are hard to break. Who am I fooling? Don't I wish only to look into Delia's eyes again before I go?*

When Mary returned, she had shut the

bedroom door, leaving Jackson with Delia. "She doesn't care to talk to you."

"What about the boy?"

"He changed his mind."

"I'll return tomorrow to see if Miss Pritchard feels more like talking."

"I thought you planned to leave town!" Mary herded John toward the front door of the office.

"I have changed my plans," he said.

Heading toward his room behind the stable, he made it as far as the junction by the saloon when two scruffy men stopped their horses at the eastern edge of town. They appeared to be arguing, one guiding his horse toward the saloon while the other man refused to budge. Finally, both turned and rode away. Neither seemed to notice John.

At the stable, John once again tried to engage Colin Pritchard in conversation. Pritchard did not respond. He broke apart a bale of straw and used a pitchfork to spread fresh bedding. John entered his horse's stall with a curry comb and cleared the tangles from its mane. Pritchard disappeared, clearly unwilling to talk. Alone with his horse, John leaned against the wall and thought about his options. The desire to learn more about Delia, to see if he could help ease her future path, was an old pattern he recognized but seemed unable to fight. Always the preacher, always the arrogant conviction that God had chosen him as emissary.

There was nothing for it. He would stay another night and see what happened. Jeremiah had told him the saloon served an evening meal, so even though he advocated sobriety, John had walked from Doc's office to the saloon. He attracted a few curious glances from those sober enough to notice his presence, but most appeared too drunk to care.

Chapter Twenty: A Change of Heart

During the night, John had jerked awake when scuffling noises from outside and a whispered conversation drifted through his open window. Then silence. A horse whinnied. More silence. Soft voices. Then nothing. He decided it must have been Colin, checking on the horses. John went back to sleep.

By the time he left his room early the next morning, the townsfolk had gathered on the main road, gesturing toward the general store and pointing at Colin and two other men on horseback approaching from the junction.

"What's going on?" John had asked a nearby fellow.

"Strangers creeping around in the night. Stole food and tobacco from Jeremiah's place. Seems Doc was out and saw 'em in the woods, tried to scare 'em off. Then Miss Gray caught one of 'em sneaking around her barn. Fired that old blunderbuss of hers and rang her bell. Near scared the pants off half the town."

John pointed toward Colin and the other two riders. "They already been to the farm?"

"Yes, sir. Fancied themselves to be a posse. They're coming from a second trip out to make sure those scoundrels are gone for good."

John now understood the scuffling and voices he had heard during the night. Because most of the businesses closed by dinnertime, and families lived in their own cabins away from the main road, John may have been the only person close enough to Jeremiah's store to hear the thieves. He could have stopped them. Or died trying. He headed for the stable to make sure his horse was still there. Colin Pritchard was just ahead of him and dismounted at the front of the stable. He secured the horse to the hitching post by the fire pit and hurried inside. As John followed, he spotted Colin hightailing it out the back door.

"Colin. Hey, Colin!"

When the smithy failed to answer or return, John walked on past the general store and strolled along the river road. The woods and slow-moving waters stirred up

186

memories, many of them so bad he tried to push them away and replace them with more pleasant thoughts.

The young Jo Mae Proud wading near the muddy banks with the old Indian's crippled dog at her side.

The Indian's dwelling and garden close to the water, hidden from the road by the woods.

The day he stopped at the Indian's camp with Annie Gray to see Jo Mae and her baby and offer a baptism. But then, the horrors that followed. Caswell Proud's sudden appearance and attempt to grab the child. The blood pouring from Caswell's throat as Annie wiped her hunting knife clean.

John shook off the vivid pictures and tried to concentrate on the white clouds against the brilliant blue sky and their reflections in the sluggish Sangamon River. He avoided the woods and the Indian's camp. When he reached the junction where the main road crossed the river over a wide wooden bridge, he followed the river toward Annie Gray's farm. Before he reached her place, he ventured into the tallgrass meadow that ran between the woods and Doc's buildings. By approaching Doc's place from the field, he reached the chicken house first, then the cookhouse. Sounds from inside prompted

John to call out and warn Mary of his presence. When he reached the door and looked inside, instead of Mary, he found Delia and the boy seated at the table.

John looked at Delia in surprise. She turned away, but the boy jumped from the bench and ran to the door. "I'm Andrew Jackson, just like the president, but everybody here calls me Jackson. Did you decide to stay and have a prayer meeting?"

"No, Jackson, I'm not a preacher any longer."

"Why not?"

What would be a good excuse to give a child? "I wasn't a very good preacher. I've decided to explore the new country instead. Perhaps I'll be a farmer."

"My ma and pa were farmers."

"Where are they now?"

"They got kilt."

"Killed," Delia said. "Not kilt." She glanced at John then looked away. "The boy's ma and pa got murdered by slave hunters who didn't set any store by Negroes being set free. When they found freed slaves that wouldn't return a good reward, they hanged them. Jackson's ma told him to run like the wind. I found him in the woods, scared out of his wits."

"You saved his life?"

Delia gave John another side glance. "I did. Now I don't know what to do with him."

Jackson put his hands on his hips and ignored Delia. "Preacher, she says words like that, but she doesn't mean them. Miss Delia is a good person."

"Young'un, you don't know what you're talking about," Delia said.

John's thoughts stayed with Jackson's words and his defense of Delia.

Jackson tugged at Delia's sleeve. "Miss Delia, can I go back to my whittling now?"

"Yes, go on. And call me Delia."

"I will, if you call me Jackson instead of young'un. Preacher, if you want to come sit with me while I whittle, that would be a fine thing."

"I'll do that, Jackson. I need to talk to Miss Pritchard first."

Jackson dashed out the door. John gestured toward Delia for permission to sit at the table. He chose the bench across from her, hoping she would stay, even though she was clearly uncomfortable.

"I've learned a great deal about your life up to now," he said.

"From Annie Gray, that nasty gossip. She gets a lot wrong."

"I know. I also talked to Jeremiah Frost."

"Puh!"

"He gets it wrong too?"

"I wouldn't trust Jeremiah for one minute. He made it quite clear that first day he wanted us gone, before I caused trouble for the town."

"Did he have good reason?"

Delia didn't answer.

"I also spoke to your brother."

Delia finally met John's gaze. "You should leave Colin alone. He doesn't understand everything that happened. Doc says he has a good life here with his wife and kids. I don't blame him for wanting to be rid of me. Bad memories make for sleepless nights."

"I believe Colin understands more than you think. Guilt has a way of eating at a man. You being in town keeps that guilt in his mind, so he can't be rid of the past."

"I know. It was foolish to come here, but when I got shot so close to Sangamon, it felt like I had no other choice. I'll be leaving soon. Doc fixed my shoulder good. Another couple of days and I'll be strong enough to ride."

"Are you taking the boy with you?"

Delia shook her head. "If he stays here, he can get schooled. Doc will take good care of him. With me, he'd be on the run."

"What do you mean, on the run? From the law?"

"The law and worse. That bullet in my shoulder didn't get there by accident."

"What happened to you, Miss Pritchard?"

Delia got up and moved toward the cookhouse door. "I'm tired now. I need to rest." She left without even a backward glance. By the time John reached the door, she was gone.

Jackson sat on the bench outside the doctor's office, attacking a piece of tree branch with enthusiasm. John watched for a moment, wondering how dangerous it might be to sit next to the child as he wielded the knife with big strokes. "What are you making?"

"Nothing. I'm just whittling."

John watched a moment longer, then started to walk around the doctor's office toward the road. Before he rounded the corner, Jackson called out to him.

"I heard what Miss Delia said."

John took a deep breath and waited.

"I'm not staying here with Doc," Jackson said. "I don't like it here."

"The doctor is a good person, isn't he?"

"He is. But I'm going with Miss Delia."

"You better tell that to Miss Pritchard."

"I will. You can pray for us if you want."

"I will do that, Jackson. For both of you. Every day, forever." He did not look at the boy as he rounded the corner. When he passed the window of the bedroom, the curtain twitched. No doubt Delia had been watching. He wondered if she overheard his exchange with Jackson. If she did, so be it. At least she would know that John's prayers, useless as they were, included her.

CHAPTER TWENTY-ONE: JACKSON'S STORY

Andrew Jackson could shut out most of the world if he had a book in his hands. But in the split second his mind wandered from the page, he heard his mother scream, saw his father hanging from a tree. Then the terror would wash over him again, the urge to do as his mother said and run and run until he couldn't take another step. Shoving those pictures away used every ounce of energy he had left.

Sometimes he set the rocking chair to moving back and forth to calm his mind and body. Sometimes he put himself to sleep that way.

Remembering how Miss Delia had chased him and grabbed him in her arms, turning his fear into comfort, did the most good of all. At first, he had tried to back away. Truthfully, she didn't smell so good. And with her hair all messy and her eyes full of tears, Jackson imagined her to be a wild woman, a monster.

"It's fine. You're going to be fine," she had said, trying to quiet his struggling body, trying to hold him tight so he couldn't get away.

Jackson yelled and hollered and kicked and wiggled, but it didn't do any good.

"Shhh," she had said, over and over. "You're safe now. I won't let anyone hurt you."

Eventually, Jackson gave up, worn to a frazzle. His terror had been trampled to dust. There was nothing left but an exhausted sleep that lasted until the next morning. He woke to an early dawn, birds raising a ruckus overhead. Miss Delia sat by a campfire, roasting a bird on a spit. Her big spotted horse and the smaller brown mare grazed nearby.

"You hungry?" she asked.

"Yes, ma'am."

She had reached in her pocket and pulled out a chunk of hardtack wrapped in cloth. "You can start with this. Meat will be done soon. Water's boiling. Do you drink coffee?"

"No, ma'am." He pried a corner off the biscuit and chewed until he could swallow. "Maybe a little coffee," he said.

"Good. You can head over there to those bushes if you need to pee or anything. Don't take off now. I won't hurt you."

Jackson had put the rest of his biscuit on a tree stump and walked into the bushes. When he came back, he sat on the stump and watched Delia turn the bird every few minutes. He tried to make his mind go empty, tried not to think of how he ended up with this odd woman in the middle of the woods, far from his parents' farm.

His thoughts landed smack-dab in the middle of the horrible thing again, when the woman jerked him to the present by asking a question.

"You a runaway slave?"

Jackson bent over, his hands covering his face, and sobbed.

The woman let him be. When he had cried out all his tears and caught his breath with a few hiccups, he looked at her across the fire. She tore off a piece of the bird and handed it to him on the end of a stick. "It's hot," she said. "Don't burn yourself."

Jackson chewed the stringy meat and swallowed. "It's good."

"You can call me Delia," the woman had said. She handed Jackson a tin cup of hot coffee and another piece of meat. "That biscuit will help fill you. Brush it off good first. There's ants crawling on it."

"I'm not a runaway slave," Jackson said.

195

"My pa was Cyrus Jackson, a freeman. My ma was free, too. They had a farm, almost as long as I remember. Those men . . . they were wrong to come after us."

"Your ma and pa send you to school?"

"No. There wasn't no school. But they could read and write, and I was learning real fast."

Delia looked at him with her eyebrows raised like she didn't believe a word he said.

"You got a book? I'll show you."

"No, I don't have a book. You'll have to show me another time. What's your name?"

"Andrew Jackson. I was named Andrew after the president."

"Imagine that," Delia said. "A president."

"Yes, ma'am. My pa said Andrew Jackson was a great general and served his country well. Later on, he said they should have named me after somebody else, but I don't know why."

Jackson got lost in another memory and sat quietly with the cup in one hand and a piece of meat in the other. He didn't want to start crying again, didn't want to remember the bad things. For a moment he thought about books, but that wandered into dangerous thoughts about sitting on his mother's lap as she read stories. With a shake of his head, he focused on the fire, then the food. He sipped the coffee, grimaced, but drank it anyway. The biscuit still sat on the tree stump. Jackson picked it up, dusted the ants away, and stuffed it into his pocket.

"You feel like moving on, young'un?"

"Yes, ma'am. Where are we going?"

"I'm not sure yet," she said. "We'll ride a bit and see where the road takes us. That sound good?"

It sounded good for a couple of hours, until the bad man found them. Delia told Jackson to fly like the wind, that the man was a bounty hunter and he'd be looking to drag Jackson to Kentucky or Tennessee or wherever a landowner would pay a fine price for someone like him.

"I don't want to leave you," Jackson said.

"Just git!" Delia yelled.

Jackson took off on Delia's packhorse, kicking her hard in the sides. She ran so fast he almost fell off. He didn't stop until a gunshot scared him. Then another. By the time he got his horse to slow down, Delia raced toward him, her left arm dangling at her side while she struggled to hold the reins and her revolver in her right. It wasn't going too well, because she kept leaning to the side. Jackson thought she would fall off any minute.

"Keep going!" she yelled. "We've got to get out of here."

After what seemed like hours to Jackson, she slowed her horse and finally found a place by a river where they stopped to rest. When they were ready to ride again, she had Jackson help her make a sling for her arm, using a long belt.

"Where'd you get this belt?" he asked. "It's way too big for you. Your pants would fall down."

"That's a long story for another time," she said as she struggled to get on her horse. "Let's get moving."

Jackson had to stand on a big rock to climb on his brown horse without help. "Where are we going?" he asked.

"To the town where my brother lives. It'll take a day or two."

With watching Delia to make sure she didn't fall off her horse, and with making sure they stopped to eat and find water, Jackson didn't have much time to think about the bad things.

Riding into Sangamon started out like it might be a good day. When the man at the store yelled about Miss Delia being trouble, Jackson realized it might not be so good after all. And later when he overheard Miss Delia and Miss Mary talking about Miss

Annie Gray and all the mean things she said, Jackson cringed, wishing he could shrink to nothing right then and there.

Finding Doc Hemmer and getting treated nice by the schoolteacher — with books and good food — made Jackson feel better. He tried not to listen to the grown-ups talk so he wouldn't hear any more about folks not wanting "his kind" in town. What did they mean by "his kind" anyway? In Jackson's mind, he was a good boy, a hard worker, and a God-loving Christian like his ma and pa taught him. What was wrong with that?

CHAPTER TWENTY-TWO: ANNIE'S CONVERSATIONS

Doc didn't stay at Annie's place any longer than necessary to move the Palouse to the back stall. He told her about seeing the intruders in the woods, though. She figured they were the same thieves she'd spotted around her barn. Annie didn't have time to walk into the village to gossip with those who might have more to tell. Much too much to do.

After Doc left, the goat wandered about the yard, pulling at weeds along the road, so she let him be. The mule drank at the water trough and seemed content. Annie paused at the barn door to confirm the Palouse could not be seen from the road or the door. Inside the barn, she secured the rear double doors.

Milking the cow was her next morning chore. She brought her clean bucket from the house, set the three-legged stool by the cow's flank, and began their morning conversation. "Cow, there are things going on in this town I do not understand."

As always, Annie's cow chewed her cud while Annie talked on and on. "I reckon I ought to clean out this barn now that we got us a boarder. Stinks like goat in here. Not you, Cow, you smell fine."

Talking when alone had not become a habit until Sarah married Jeremiah Frost. Before then, Annie had talked to Sarah.

In Annie's mind, all she ever did with Sarah was talk. The teacher's overindulgence in whiskey on the weekends was Annie's excuse for spending so much time with the young schoolmarm. Annie learned of Jeremiah's plan to marry Sarah and tried to warn him of her bad habits. Jeremiah told Annie never to speak ill of his wife-to-be again or she would suffer the consequences. Annie now kept her memories and opinions, including the whiskey drinking, to herself. She didn't want trouble. Choosing to rewrite their history, Annie now thought of Sarah as an acquaintance. What else could she do? Especially when Sarah avoided even the shortest conversation.

"A horse hiding in my barn, the doctor roaming town in the middle of the night chasing strangers away, that Pritchard gal come to town with all her baggage. What will Preacher think?"

Annie ducked the cow's tail as it swished past her face. She reached up and scratched the animal's rump. "Cow, I need to do something about that woman. And the boy. What was she thinking, bringing a boy like that to Sangamon?" It crossed her mind the Pritchard gal might have birthed the boy, and that made her think of how such a thing might have come to be. Her head felt like it might explode right there in her barn.

"Best not to imagine such things," she said. She continued to pull on the cow's teats until the udder felt empty. After returning the stool to its place outside the cow's stall, Annie carried the bucket into her kitchen where she set it aside to wait for the cream to rise. Outside again, she scattered cracked corn for her chickens. After the summer's dry spell, even most insects had disappeared, if you didn't count the grasshoppers. Without enough bugs to eat, the chickens needed grain, a hard cost to bear, but the only way to keep the hens laying and producing more chicks.

Annie continued talking, this time with her chickens while she worked in the yard. "I should ask Preacher to tea," she told them. "He said he liked my preserves. Honey cakes would be nice."

A few years ago, Annie had not looked forward to Preacher Claymore's return. He, too, had been a witness to Caswell Proud's murder. If he told everything that happened that day, he'd seal her fate. The thought of a hanging terrified her. But here was the preacher, staying in town for no good reason she could see, and he'd greeted her with a handshake and slight bow as though they'd never had more than the brief contact any preacher might have had with one of his flock. And a very devout member of his flock she had been. Even now, she often told townsfolk of her devotion to the Lord and her high regard for their former preacher, repeating quotations from the Holy Bible to remind folks of their Christian duty.

But what was her Christian duty when faced with the shocking return of Delia Pritchard, a girl who had run off and left her dead father and mother in a burning house and her own young brother an orphan? Some said the gal murdered her parents and should be hanged. Annie suspected Colin Pritchard believed that very thing. And the other rumors! Good gracious! Killing, thieving, probably whoring as well.

And yet, Delia remained in Sangamon, getting patched up by the doctor, and no one had made a move to punish her for her transgressions.

"I don't know what to make of that," Annie told the chickens. "And those men that wandered about in the dark? They were most likely looking for that Pritchard gal. Oh, she's on the road to hell, there's no doubt about that."

Inside the house again, Annie checked the milk bucket. She skimmed the cream and dumped it into the butter churn. Later she would decide whether to take her milk to the general store for sale before it soured and clabbered or use it in cooking. Curdled milk made the best biscuits and cornbread and even her honey cakes.

"I reckon I'll keep you right here," Annie said to the bucket of milk. It never gave her pause to hear her own words as she carried on her one-sided conversations with her animals and her possessions. Having no one else to talk to, except when she visited Doc Hemmer or walked into town, and not being inclined to make that walk often because the farm chores took too much time, Annie felt she'd go mad if she did not express her thoughts when she dared.

She did wonder, however, about the newer habit of talking to herself. Once she had even called herself by name. "Annie Gray, if you don't stop talking to yourself like this, folks will hear, and they'll think you've gone dotty. What will happen to you then?"

There was no good answer to that question as far as Annie could see. But she had learned to be discreet in other situations, so she could certainly be careful about keeping her thoughts to herself in public.

That evening she picked up her hoop and embroidery needle, prepared to finish the cross-stitch trim on the new pillow covers she'd made from the bolt of muslin purchased the last time the peddler came to Sangamon. During summer, with the sun still shining until late, she sometimes pulled her rocker in front of the open door and worked by daylight.

In winter, she put her quilting frame in front of the fireplace so she could work into the evening by the light of the fire.

"You're almost finished," Annie told her meticulous needlework. "Tonight, you'll be on my goose down pillow for the first time. Tomorrow I think I'll work on that dress I made. A bit of embroidery on the bodice will be smart. The ladies from the hat shop will be all aflutter because they'll have nothing that fine."

Annie looked up when she sensed movement. Mary stood in the open doorway, watching and listening. Annie flinched.

"I stopped by to see if you had extra eggs," Mary said. "Doc's hens can't seem to lay fast enough to keep the extra mouths fed."

Annie raised an eyebrow. "Perhaps if Doc didn't take his patients into his —"

"That's neither here nor there, Miss Gray. Do you have eggs or not?"

Annie huffed but got to her feet and set her embroidery in the chair. "I do. I'll get them." When she returned with six eggs in a basket, Mary transferred them to the pan she carried.

"Doc will deduct the cost from your account," Mary said.

As Annie stepped to the door and watched Mary walk away, she had a vague wish that the snippy, ungrateful woman would drop dead on the spot.

Chapter Twenty-Three: Delia Hears Jackson's Concerns

Delia didn't know why Mary marched out the door as though headed for battle. Her mission was only to buy eggs from Annie Gray's farm. No matter. Opportunities for Delia to prepare for her own departure didn't come often, so she welcomed Mary's absence.

Mary had provided an extra shirt and undergarments, a nightgown, and a new pair of socks. The socks were too big but better than the old pair with holes in the heels. Mary had thrown those away. Delia stuffed the extra shirt and undergarments in her saddlebags. Mary might not appreciate her keeping the borrowed clothes, but Delia had done much worse in her lifetime than help herself to things that weren't hers to take. Mary would no doubt "tut, tut" for a while, but Doc would only tell her to shrug off the loss and forget about it.

With all she'd been told about Sangamon

folks not taking kindly to Negroes, Delia might have no choice but to take Jackson with her when she left. He only had the clothes he wore on his back, but Mary had washed and dried them the first night. That would have to do for now. She thought of breaking into Jeremiah's store and taking what she needed for the boy but figured stealing from that man would have much worse consequences than helping herself to a shirt and underwear from the doctor's home.

What on earth would she do with the boy if she did take him along? She had to find where those abolitionists lived and take Jackson there. And she needed to get the sorrel mare out of the stable and use it for the young'un. Her plan to leave the horse as payment for the doctor would not work out after all. Instead of paying, she'd leave behind a debt. So be it. Plenty of folks owed her debts they'd never be able to pay, or want to pay, for that matter.

The more Delia thought about all she had to do — getting information from the doctor, removing the sorrel mare from the stable, and making sure the boy wasn't behind a barred door in Doc's cabin when she wanted to leave — the more she realized she must remain in Sangamon a little longer. About the time she worked her way around to that conclusion, Mary came in the front door of the doctor's office with her pail of eggs.

"Now we have enough for breakfast," Mary said. "Doc's hens can't keep up with Jackson's hearty appetite."

"We had nothing to eat for a couple of days before we reached Sangamon. Jackson is surely enjoying a full stomach."

Mary carried the eggs to the cookhouse, stopping along the way to tell Jackson to go inside the cabin and find a new book to read. "You've made a fine mess for me to clean up. Look at all those shavings from your whittling."

"Don't worry, Miss Mary. I'll take care of the mess. Do you have a broom?"

"You're a good boy, Jackson. The broom is in the cookhouse."

Running steps followed by the noise of sweeping told Delia that Jackson had hurried to do Mary's bidding. The clatter and rustle as Jackson dashed through Doc's office and into the bedroom, dragging the broom on the floor, suggested he did even more than asked. Delia sat in the rocking chair, still thinking about all she needed to do. Jackson ran to her side, sounding a little breathless. "How are you feeling, Miss

209

Delia? Can we leave this town soon?"

"I'm getting better, Jackson. Why do you ask? What's wrong?"

"Miss Mary won't let me leave and go to town. I want to see the horses. And talk to that girl who came by with her yellow parasol. I heard children playing, too."

"I reckon you're feeling lonely here with just us."

"More like having nothing to do. I reckon there'd be lots more books at that school. But she said I had to stay out of sight. I can be around the chickens, or in the cabins, or in the cookhouse, or right there on that bench, whittling sticks and then cleaning. I'm sure tired of all that."

Delia understood, but she wasn't sure what to say. Reaching for Jackson's hand, she pulled him a little closer and looked him in the eye. "Things aren't quite right in Sangamon Village," she told him. "It's not safe here for me, and it's not safe for you. As soon as I'm able to travel and take care of both of us, we'll be moving on."

Jackson whimpered his next questions, whiny sounds Delia had never heard from him before. "Why's it not safe here? Is something bad going to happen? Like with my pa and ma?"

"I don't think anything that bad will hap-

210

pen, young'un, but Sangamon is a hard place in a hard world. Some folks here are kind, but others are right hateful. They don't want us here. They might even run us out of town before we're ready to go if we don't stay out of sight. Someday I'll explain it all better. For now, mind what Miss Mary says. Will you do that for me?"

"I guess I will. But I sure am awful tired of whittling. And I read all the books two times."

"I'll talk to Doc Hemmer," Delia said. "Perhaps he has chores you can do."

"I can do lots of chores. I could even clean out that chicken house if he wants."

"Wow. That would be a big job. We'll see. Now I think Miss Mary called you to go inside Doc's cabin and get a book. You'd best git before she comes over and grabs you by the ear. Schoolteachers do that kind of thing when they want you to pay attention."

Jackson covered his ears with his hands and ran out the back door. Delia shook her head at the boy's quick ways and the sense of humor that had quickly replaced his worries. It was going to be a hard thing to let him go his way with strangers instead of riding on at her side.

Doc came in the front door of the office a

few minutes later, unwrapped the bandage on Delia's shoulder, applied the salve that smelled like horse liniment, then rewrapped the treated area in clean strips of white cloth. "It looks good, Delia. I expect the wound will be healed over in another day or two. You might want to start moving that arm around to get rid of the stiffness. If it hurts too much, I'll give you something, but it would be better if you stayed off the medicine. When you're walking, it can make you dizzy. Laudanum grabs hold of your mind like whiskey. Makes you think you need more and more."

"That's okay, Doc. I can bear the hurting now. I'll do what you say, move more and start getting my strength back. We need to talk about me and the young'un leaving soon as you say I can." There, she'd said it again. Her and the young'un going together. What a mess her mind was in when she couldn't decide from one minute to the next what she was going to do.

"We'll talk tomorrow morning, Delia. This evening, I'd rather not lock the back door from outside as I did while you were still using the pain medicine. You'll be here alone, so I want you to bar the door when I leave. If I get here before you wake, I'll knock on the window by your bed. Promise you won't grab that Colt and shoot me before you ask who's outside?"

"You won't be knocking in the dead of night, will you?"

"I hope not. But if someone from town has the sudden need of a doctor during the night, he'd come by my cabin first. Then I'd have to bring him here."

"I promise to ask who's there before I shoot."

Later that night, Delia woke from a dead sleep when a quiet tapping at the front door of the office set her nerves on fire. She had no idea how long she'd been asleep. No moonlight shone through the slats at her window, no sign of dawn turning the sky from dark to light. Nothing out there but pitch-black night and someone at the door.

CHAPTER TWENTY-FOUR:
BEAK AND MOOSE
ON THE PROWL

Beak had spent that previous morning berating Moose for causing them to get caught as they snuck through the woods after raiding the general store. The self-proclaimed expert at keeping quiet, tracking animals, and stalking humans, Moose was a blundering idiot in Beak's opinion.

That danged Moose charges through a thicket like, well, like a moose. No wonder the townsmen had discovered them. When it became clear they'd best beat it, they had scurried through the brush and run straight to their camp, gathered their horses and supplies, and moved from the woods to the river's bend near a big farm. There, they collapsed on the ground, trying to catch their breath while they waited to see if anyone followed.

The night grew still except for the occasional hoot of an owl or the rustle of small critters in the grass. The horses stood near a tree, heads drooping. An occasional swish of a tail or stamp of hoof against hard ground broke the silence.

Moose shoved his supplies to one side and stretched out on his bedroll. Beak stirred the fire and added a log. They didn't need the warmth on this mild September night, but it was easier to get the flame going in the morning to heat water and cook breakfast if they didn't let it die. *That's if we have anything left to cook.* Their food supply had dwindled drastically, and they had little to trade. The goods taken from the general store did not include meat or beans. They'd found a box of pellets and another of gunpowder. A pair of boots for Moose. A new gun belt for Beak.

He gazed across the land in the direction of the farm and barn he'd noticed earlier, but a cloud had drifted in front of the moon and none of the buildings were visible. At first light, he'd sneak behind the buildings and see if he could find food. He could gather eggs and milk a cow as good as any farmhand.

With still no sign the two had been followed by the men who surprised them in the woods, Beak followed Moose's example and cleared a spot on his blanket so he could stretch out by the fire. He didn't go

215

to sleep. With Moose snoring loud enough to wake the whole country, Beak figured he'd better stay alert. Not that he had much choice. He tried to count all the nights he'd lain awake, listening to Moose. It was a wonder he hadn't shot him in the head before now. Or beat his brains in with a big rock. The blessed silence would be worth the loss.

Sleepless nights are good for making a plan, Beak thought. As soon as he could see well enough to creep from the river to the farm buildings, he'd venture that way and see what he could find. He and Moose would be getting mighty hungry by morning, so even a hat full of cracked corn could be boiled for a spell and made fit to eat. Beak hoped for better than that, like maybe a cache of carrots or potatoes from a garden. Some farmers did their meat curing by salting a big chunk of beef or pork and letting it hang from the house or barn rafter. *Now wouldn't that be something?* A whole ham would feed him and Moose for days.

Through the next couple of hours, Beak's thoughts wandered this way and that, him figuring on what they should do next, where they should go, whether it was worth the trouble to keep on looking for that Pritchard woman and her fancy horse.

216

Dang, she's a purty gal. Feisty, too. I might of lit a spark in her if Moose hadn't got to her first. There was another good reason to get rid of Moose.

Nearly eight years ago he'd seen that girl for the first time, although from a far distance. She hoed weeds in a cornfield alongside a man and two boys. She and the man had glanced up, her eyes turning Beak's heart to jelly. He and Moose skedaddled when the man dropped his hoe and grabbed a long gun. Beak learned later that she came from this here Sangamon town and had run away after doing something so terrible she figured the law wanted her in jail. Beak didn't know what she'd done, but it was clear she was on the run.

The next time he'd spotted her, though, she'd ridden as close as she could get to the mouth of Cave-in-Rock and then sat there on her horse, looking all bedraggled as if she hadn't slept in a week. Her straggly hair hung loose from under a man's hat. Her face was dirty and her horse flecked with mud, like they'd galloped along the riverbank for a time. He recognized that light in those sparkling eyes when she focused on his face for only a few seconds, then looked through him like he wasn't even there.

Beak, who was standing on a flatboat

below the cave entrance, could have fallen into the water in a dead faint, but he held on to his wits and watched her dismount as easy as a man because she wore pants instead of a long dress. He near swooned like a girl. As soon as he could get off the flatboat, he had grabbed his horse's reins and led it through the shallows to the riverbank. Then he'd set out to find a way into the cave, hoping the gal was there, hoping the thieves and killers who often hid in the vast interior or the upper cave had not caught her before he got there.

He had turned away in a hurry when a gang of nearly twenty men appeared and milled about the area, some ripping apart luggage they must have stolen from riverboat travelers, a few gathered around a fire pit, tearing into a cooked animal like ravenous vultures.

A couple of years later, that big gang had been chased out of the cave and the whole Shawneetown area by a federal marshal and his posse. Beak returned, still thinking about the girl, wondering if she'd stayed around.

One of the women who still lived at Cave-in-Rock told Beak the cave now sheltered Hiram Biedler's five sons. She said that a gal stole a horse, a gun, and a bag of gold and disappeared into the woods. The Biedler gang intended to chase her down. Beak found her trail and followed, keeping his eyes and ears open for any sign of the brothers. He'd left Cave-in-Rock behind with a sigh of relief. He considered himself a thief of sorts, out of necessity. He didn't know how to do anything else. But the vicious outlaws and pirates who had preyed on Ohio River travelers for many years were far worse. And the Biedlers were the worst of all.

Beak lost the girl's trail that day and did not see her again until he and Moose teamed up. They caught up with her on the road north toward New Salem two months ago. More beautiful than ever in Beak's eyes, she now rode a big Palouse stallion, worth its weight in gold. She still had the mare she'd stolen from the Biedlers, too. And most likely she was a rich woman if what Beak heard was true. Beak's heart had beat fast and he couldn't think of anything to say.

"What do you boys want from me?" she had asked. "There's not much I'm willing to give except a bit of food."

"Just good company for a few miles," Moose had said. "We won't bother you none, will we, Beak?"

Beak had gulped and choked on his words.

Finally, he'd given up trying to talk and simply nodded.

"See," Moose had said. "We promise we won't be any trouble."

"A few days, then," she had said. "The first sign either one of you isn't keeping his word, I'm gone. I'm not afraid to shoot my way out of here if I have to."

Somewhere along the way, after the girl had enjoyed a little too much of Beak's moonshine, she told them her name was Delia, then a little about her younger days and running away from Sangamon. After that, Moose had ruined everything by grabbing her and trying to plant a sloppy kiss right on her mouth. She'd run off without even one word of good-bye. Beak had been trying to find her ever since. Lovesick and greedy, Beak's thoughts jumped back and forth between Delia's womanly assets, that big stallion, and the bag of gold he'd heard about.

Now he and Moose had come to Sangamon, still trying to find out if Delia had returned to her hometown, still trying to do a little food and supply scavenging before they had to move on. As the light broke in the east, streaks of pink clouds stretched across the horizon. Not being one to carry on about a fancy sunrise, Beak couldn't resist sneaking peeks at the sky while he pulled on his boots and added a log to their fire. By the time he was ready to go, he could tell the farmer's cabin from the barn and another outbuilding. They'd camped by the river behind the buildings, so getting into the barn without being seen should have been easy.

It took longer than he thought. His feet kept getting tangled in the tallgrass. Twice he tripped and fell to his knees. He finally got behind the barn and found it barred from the inside. He checked the windows but discovered all were shuttered and fastened.

He crept around to the front of the barn, staying in the shadows as much as possible. The heavy wood bar lifted easily, and Beak slid it to the side. The hinges did not creak, nor did the door scrape the ground as he pulled it open.

A mule had blocked his path and let out the most blood-chilling sound Beak had ever heard in his life. A goat answered with frantic bleats as it trotted toward Beak, its head lowered.

The front door of the cabin opened. A woman stomped outside with a musket in her hands. She spotted Beak, raised her gun and fired. Then she stepped to the corner of her front stoop and yanked on a rope.

Hellfire! The shot smacked into the ground by his foot, followed by the bell's loud clang that made his ears ring.

The crazy old woman had kept ringing the bell, again and again. Beak thought about shutting off that bell with a load of buckshot, but figured he'd better get the hell out of there before a whole posse of townsmen showed up. He dashed toward the river, zigzagging in case the old woman fired again. By the time he got to the campfire, Moose had thrown their supplies together and loaded the horses. The men mounted and rode away from the farm, away from Sangamon.

Away from the Delia gal.

Beak thought he might never see her again. He couldn't bear it.

"Wait," he called out to Moose.

"Cain't do it. Lookit what's coming."

Beak looked toward the farm. Three men on horseback approached from the direction of the town. When they reached the camp Beak and Moose had left behind, the men dismounted and put out the fire with river water.

"That's a posse, ain't it?" Moose said.

Beak kicked his horse into a canter and followed Moose across the open space. "I'm turning around as soon as those boys give up," he said. "I ain't going to places we already been."

"You want to find that woman, don't you?"

"Giving up on that one, Moose. What say we head west? We could hook up with one of those explorers."

"Phewf!"

"Don't like that idea?"

"Nope."

"C'mon, Moose. Tell me what you're thinking."

"I'm thinking we ought to head east where the pickings are easy. Nobody out here has money. There ain't any trains to rob. They ain't even got banks around here. I'll bet folks in this town trade for everything they get."

Beak knew Moose was right. He'd think on it while they rode east, at least until he was convinced those men from Sangamon had gone back to their useless little town that wasn't ever going to amount to a hill of beans.

Chapter Twenty-Five:
The Story of McAllister

When Delia heard the light knocking on the front door of the doctor's office during the night, Moose and Beak were the first two people who popped into her thoughts. If it truly was them who had caused mischief for Doc in the woods and then camped by the river near Miss Gray's farm, then maybe they'd learned she was inside Doc's office. Miss Gray had assured Doc she'd scared the man away from her barn before he saw the Palouse. Delia hoped that was true, but what if Miss Gray was mistaken?

Was it Beak tapping at the door? Or Moose? Annie Gray had fired her rifle. Maybe she'd hit one of them. Maybe one of them lay out there bleeding to death on Doc's front stoop.

Maybe Delia didn't give a hoot as long as it didn't come back on her.

She leaned her head against the door and listened to the other sounds. Scuffling, like shoes scraping across dirt. A rustling of the sparse, dry grass close to the house. The noises moved around to the shuttered window and stopped. A scratching as if someone checked to see if the shutters were secure. Then no more sounds for a time.

Delia gripped the rifle and padded across the office in her bare feet to the back door. She had her ear to the door when a cough gave her a scare. She jumped, then stepped away. Seconds later, a loud crash made her jump again — the sound of metal on metal, like all of Mary's pots and pans hit the floor at the same time. Delia unbarred the door and flung it open, aimed her rifle at the door of the cookhouse, and waited. An instant later, Doc opened the door of his cabin and stepped outside.

"Who's there?" he yelled.

A meek voice answered. "I'm sorry. It's me. I wanted to see Miss Delia and that Negra boy, but my pa said no, I should not come here ever again, and I mustn't consort with Negras, but I snuck out after Pa went to bed and came anyway." Jeremiah's daughter, Elizabeth, stepped out of the cookhouse and stood with her hands clasped primly at her waist. Her eyes widened at the sight of Delia and the rifle.

Delia pointed the weapon toward the

ground. No doubt she looked like a wild woman with her hair loose and unbrushed.

"I'm sorry," Elizabeth said. "I should go on home, I reckon."

"Yes, I reckon you should," said Doc. "I'll walk with you."

"You'd best mind your pa," Delia said, her tone sharp and meant to hurt. "I'm not up to talking to you. And that boy can't be your friend. He has chores to do. You go on home, and you stay there."

Delia turned and walked inside Doc's office, barred the door, and carried the rifle into the bedroom. She laid it on the floor next to the bed, then eased herself into the rocking chair. Her arm and shoulder throbbed. With small movements, she shifted her body until she felt more comfortable. Only after a few moments of rocking did she let her mind wander to the expression on Elizabeth's face, the disappointment and hurt obvious from her pouty mouth and the tears in her eyes.

I'm getting soft. Delia had never minded saying harsh words to children in the past. Of course, the children she'd known at Cave-in-Rock were ruffians. All had been exposed at an early age to the cruelties and violence practiced by their fathers, men who preyed on innocents and warred with those who tried to invade their territory or steal the bounty they'd gathered.

The boys went unwashed and unsupervised for days, only missed when the men needed a decoy or an expert pickpocket for a gathering. The girls? *Oh, those girls were a sight.* Their hair grew long, but no attentive ma ever helped brush a tangled mess. It was no surprise the mothers ignored their daughters. They were too busy participating in the raids, making fake money, or enticing folks on passing flatboats to come closer to Cave-in-Rock.

The girls also helped by luring travelers away from the crowds. They pilfered from saddlebags, and when needed, threw hunting knives hard enough to scare a grown man into a hiding place so the girls and the outlaws could make a quick getaway.

The outlaws kidnapped women, some poor and some rich, and took them as wives without benefit of a preacher, to put it a genteel way. Delia escaped that fate by shoving her hunting knife through the hand of the first man who threw her to the ground and tried to pull down her drawers. Made the butt of the other outlaws' ridicule, the would-be attacker never tried again. Neither did any of the others.

Delia had put up with the Cave-in-Rock

gang for eight years before they fled and left her to Hiram Biedler and his sons. Her education, her stubborn nature, and that sharp hunting knife protected her from the worst consequences of being a woman in a bad man's world. Her attitude toward the women and children still weighed on her mind. She had made no effort to befriend, help, or encourage them. They were part of the background. Delia could only handle her own survival, and for that she had to act the part. Faked cruelty was her weapon, faked indifference her suit of armor.

When the Biedlers moved into Cave-in-Rock, Delia knew it was time to set out on her own. Too smart to fall for her bluster, Hiram had his eye on her from the start.

The real end for the gangs along the Ohio River came when the law captured the infamous Horace C. Shouse and a judge sentenced him to hang. All the scum remaining around Shawneetown went to the spectacle. Delia watched as they brought the old outlaw in on an oxcart, him standing tall on the very coffin in which his body would soon rest. He seemed to flinch when the noose was placed around his neck, but a cloth bag covered his head, so no one knew for sure how Shouse looked. One of the men held the reins and led the oxen away, the support went out from under the outlaw, and he danced at the end of the rope until he died.

Delia had nightmares about that hanging for years to come, just as she did about the women and children she could have saved if she'd been willing to risk her own life. But even though she vowed never to do anything that might bring her to a similar end, she kept getting caught by trouble. After the hanging, she had grabbed what she could and hightailed it away from the river, thinking she might stop for a spell in Sangamon to see her brother. She could make amends for running away and leaving him behind. If he wanted her to stay, she could even make a new life, be safe and happy.

Dreams. Silly dreams.

Her father's horse was long gone, taken away by the first gang she'd lived with near Shawneetown. She took a risk when she stole the sorrel mare from Jack Biedler, but she didn't have much choice. She'd never have gotten away fast enough if she didn't have a horse. After taking a gun and the gold coins she found in a pouch under an outlaw's blanket, she'd ridden away from Cave-in-Rock, intending to ride alone for the rest of her days, or until she worked up the courage to go home to Sangamon.

That first evening, she camped in a small clearing, leaning against a rock wall that looked hand built, as if a farmer had partially cleared a piece of the land. She saw no signs of recent occupation — no cabin, no smoke from a campfire — so she settled in, sitting next to her small fire pit. She'd shot a rabbit from horseback earlier. Now skinned and gutted, the carcass roasted over the flames on her hand-hewn spit.

The horse whinnied and stamped its hooves. Delia reached for the rifle and got to her feet, crouching a little as she squinted to see across the prairie that surrounded her camp. A shadow moved closer through the dusk.

An answering whinny announced a visitor. A man on a Palouse stallion and leading a packhorse stopped well away from her fire. "Don't shoot me," he said. "I mean you no harm."

He clipped his words, his way of speaking different from any Delia had ever heard. She stood straight as a post and pointed her gun at the ground. "You alone?"

"I am."

"What do you want?"

"I have hardtack and a block of cheddar in my pack. I'd be willing to exchange for a bit of that hare."

Delia stared at him for a few seconds while she figured out what he said. Finally, she set her rifle against the rock wall and picked up a stick to poke at the fire. "That would be fine."

The man led his horses to the same clump of brush where Delia had tethered the mare. After removing the saddle and packs and setting them aside, he rubbed his horses with a big cloth and used a bucket to give the horses water and a small amount of grain from his supplies. All three horses were grazing by the time the stranger had retrieved the promised biscuits and cheese and brought them to the fire.

"My name is Owen McAllister. What might I call you?"

"Delia is good enough. You don't sound like you come from around here."

"No, I'm from Scotland. You know where that is?"

"Of course, I know where that is. Do you think I look stupid?"

"No, of course not, but you're . . . well . . ." He motioned toward her with an up-and-down wave of his hand.

Delia flushed as she realized what he meant. She hadn't brushed her hair in weeks. Most of her possessions had ended up in the Ohio River a week ago when she tried to escape a posse chasing after river pirates. She hadn't bathed or washed her clothes, either. More than likely, she'd need to scrub her head with kerosene to get rid of the lice that kept her scratching all night. "I lost my things in the river," she said. "I don't have nothing left for barter."

"You have folks?"

"Yes, that's where I'm headed."

"You want to clean up before you get there?"

"Why, you fixing to give me a bath?"

McAllister laughed. "I think you can arrange for your own bath. But I could give you a change of clothes and a brush. The pants would be large, but you have a belt. You can roll up the pant legs and shirt sleeves. It would be clean clothes to wear while you wash those things you have on."

"You fixing to clean me up for some special reason?"

"I might," he said. He walked to one of his packs and pulled out a pad and pencil. Staying on his own side of the fire, McAllister flipped the pages one at a time so Delia could see his drawings. Done in black pencil, the sketches showed all sorts of people, many just their faces and others on horses or doing work.

"You want to draw a picture of me?"

"Why not? You're interesting. You look different from other women. You're out here alone on the prairie. I draw the pictures and listen to the stories. When I go home, I'll write a book."

"Pfff." Delia looked away, then put her hand to her hair. The matted knots would take forever to untangle. Cutting it all off with her hunting knife made more sense. "I don't think so. I'm not telling my story to a picture-drawing drifter, and I don't have time for a bath."

After returning his pad and pencil to his pack, McAllister pulled his hunting knife and passed it through the flames a couple of times, then sliced off two chunks of cheese. He handed a biscuit and a piece of cheese to Delia.

A few crumbs of cheese dripped into the fire and sizzled on the red-hot wood coals. Delia turned the rabbit to cook the other side, then munched on her biscuit and cheese. She wanted to gobble the food but didn't want this stranger to see how hungry she was. Eventually the meat cooked through, and Delia ate her fill after signaling McAllister to help himself. She jumped up and gathered more wood to keep the fire burning, then pulled her blanket across her lap as she leaned against the rocks. Now content and drowsy, she would have liked to wrap herself in her blanket and go to sleep, her rifle at her side. But Owen McAllister still sat across from her, his pad propped on his knees and his hand moving the pencil around. The soft scratching of pencil on paper blended with the crackling of twigs and branches as they caught fire.

In a while, he put the pad and pencil aside and stretched out on the ground. His folded blanket served as a pillow under his head. He hadn't said another word to Delia. Soon he snored the soft, rhythmic sounds of deep sleep.

Delia threw her blanket aside and jumped up, stretching, trying to force herself awake. With the excuse of checking the horses to make sure their reins were securely tethered, Delia wandered around the fire. She gave her sorrel mare half of her remaining water. The Palouse nuzzled her shoulder. She patted his neck and ran her hand across his back.

When she turned toward the fire, she stood only a few feet from McAllister's drawing pad. He had not moved, had not stopped snoring. She edged closer, then picked up the pad and flipped past the pictures he'd shown her earlier. The drawing he'd started as he sat by the fire was a bare bones sketch of a woman, but certainly not Delia the way she looked today. She recognized herself in the eyes, the mouth. McAllister had imagined her the way she could look, the way she had looked when she was young and civilized.

Civilized. Now there was a thought.

She'd gone to wild ways from which there might be no return. The civilized Delia no longer existed. She tore the sketch from the pad and fed it to the flames.

When Delia returned to her rock wall, she put the blanket around her shoulders and leaned against the smooth stone, watching the fire, watching McAllister, occasionally letting her eyes close to give them a rest.

When she woke, Owen McAllister and his horses were gone. He'd left a feed sack on the other side of the fire pit. Inside she found the clean clothes he'd promised, a full water bag, a flat cooking pan, a tin cup, a small bag of ground coffee, two of the biscuits, a piece of the orange-colored cheese, and another sketch to replace the one she had burned.

Only a few embers glowed red, but Delia stirred the fire and added new twigs from the bushes. She heated enough water in the pan to make coffee. As she studied the new drawing, she found it more to her liking. It felt right to see her hair all scraggly, poking out from under a man's wide-brimmed hat. McAllister had even shaded one dirty smudge across her right cheek. Delia had folded the drawing and put it in the feed sack with her newly acquired supplies.

Delia snapped to the present when Doc returned from escorting Elizabeth Frost to her father's cabin.

"You okay now?" he asked.

"Shoulder's hurting a little, that's all. Too much strain on it, grabbing and pointing the gun. It'll be fine."

"Come bar the door again. I'm going to look in on Jackson."

When the doctor left, Delia secured the door, went into the bedroom, and got dressed. She wanted to check on the Palouse but figured she'd best not wander about in the dark, especially near Annie Gray's farm.

While she waited for morning light, she snooped through the doctor's office, checking the contents of all the cabinets, the labels on bottles and jars, his tools and surgical instruments. There were stacks of paper, too, but most seemed to be notes on his patients. She looked for anything with Colin Pritchard's name on it but found nothing.

In the bedroom, Delia looked through the books stacked on a small table by the bed. Most were books for children. When she found a copy of *The Water-Witch,* she set it aside with her own things. She had not read a book in years. A story of pirates and romance would take her mind off her troubles.

CHAPTER TWENTY-SIX: CONFRONTATIONS

Once the posse from Sangamon no longer followed, Moose and Beak had camped for the night. Perhaps they had relaxed a bit too much, Beak thought as he opened his eyes. Five men on horses stood no more than ten feet from their fire. Rough-dressed, unshaven — a motley crew of highwaymen in Beak's opinion. He rubbed his eyes and sighed in resignation. He and Moose didn't have much to steal, except for the horses.

Moose sat nearby, his back against a tree and his mouth hanging open. Sound asleep and making enough racket to wake the dead.

Beak reached over to shake Moose's shoulder, giving him a hard shove to boot. "Wake up, you idjit. You were supposed to be the lookout."

"What? What's wrong?" Moose scrambled on his knees toward Beak.

"Look there, you old fool. We got com-

238

pany." He pointed toward the five intruders, then did a double take. "Aww, hellfire and damnation. Ain't that the Biedler brothers?"

The Biedlers didn't seem amused, especially the one Beak recognized as Jack, the oldest. Jack dismounted and handed his reins to one of the twins.

Beak grabbed for his rifle.

One of the mounted outlaws drew a long-barreled pistol and pointed it at Beak.

Beak let his rifle stay where it was and raised his hands. "We ain't aiming to hurt anybody. And we ain't done nothing wrong. Come on, Jack. Take what you want and let us be."

Jack Biedler walked toward the tree and picked up Beak's rifle. "We'll take this," he said. Then he strolled over to Moose's rifle and picked it up. "This one, too. And your horses. Git over there and saddle up."

Beak leaped to his feet and walked to the horses, dragging the blankets in one hand to place under the saddles. He finished both horses in record time. "There. It's done," he said.

"Load those saddlebags while you're up," Jack ordered.

Beak did as he was told.

"Thank you, kindly," one of the others

said. "We'll be on our way now."

Jack held the reins and walked his bounty away from Beak and Moose, west toward the Village of Sangamon. The remaining four hadn't left yet, so Beak dared not breathe. The Biedlers had a reputation for not leaving witnesses.

Sure enough, Jack himself stopped and looked back, aimed his long-barreled pistol at Moose, and fired. Moose dropped at Beak's feet. Beak gawked at the hole in Moose's forehead, then closed his eyes and waited. The gun fired at the same instant a powerful blow struck his skull.

The sun already beat hard on the road in front of the doctor's office when Delia unbarred the front door and walked outside. The clouds scudded across the sky, the winds up high more forceful than those closer to the earth. At tree level, the barest of breezes gently moved leaves on the tree between Doc's office and the road. Delia returned inside to see if Mary had arrived to prepare breakfast.

The door to the cookhouse was open. Mary hung the pot to boil over a roaring fire.

"Is there anything I can do to help?" asked Delia.

"Only see if the hens have laid more eggs," Mary said.

Delia ran to the chicken house. She returned with four eggs to add to the six Mary had brought from Annie Gray's farm the evening before.

Mary handed Delia a cup of coffee and set the eggs on the table by the fireplace. "How are you feeling this morning?"

Delia raised her left arm and slowly rotated her shoulder. "It's good," she said. She showed Mary the back of her hand. Tiny red blotches marred the skin around the knuckles. "The hens didn't want to give up their eggs."

Reaching for Delia's hand, Mary looked closer. "They didn't break the skin. These will fade soon."

Mary tended to her chores, turning her back to Delia as she spoke. "With that shoulder on the mend, I imagine you'll be wanting to leave soon." She glanced over her shoulder and met Delia's gaze, then returned her focus to the potatoes she sliced into a pan of melted bacon grease.

"I reckon I will," Delia said. "I'm going over to Miss Gray's farm shortly to see how my stallion is doing. I need to check with Doc about the mare. If it's still at the stable, I'll need to get it for the young'un to ride."

"Where will you go? What will happen to Jackson?"

Delia took a deep breath and let it out. "Now those are mighty good questions. I don't know where I'm going after I leave Sangamon. And I don't know what I'm going to do about Jackson. I can't stay here, and I can't leave Jackson here when I go."

"Jeremiah asks every day if you're ready to ride yet. He says you're going to bring hell and damnation on this town if you stay."

"He should know, seeing how he's so high and mighty. Perhaps God is whispering the future in his ear."

Mary paused with her slicing but didn't turn around. "Jeremiah does good things for this town."

"I'm sure he does," Delia said. "But he hasn't always been as good a man as you say he is today. When I was a girl, and that mean old wife of his ran the store, Jeremiah Frost had an eye for all the ladies and girls who weren't attached to a man who might shoot him for sleeping around. I fought that man off until I finally threatened to tell his wife."

Mary seemed to concentrate even harder on her potato slicing.

"You've lived here for a long time," said

Delia. "Didn't Jeremiah bother you?"

"I was in a bad way," Mary said. "I didn't leave my house much, didn't talk to anyone. After my boy died and my girl ran away, I thought I might go to bed and stay there until I died. I don't think Jeremiah would have found me to his liking."

Delia thought of asking more questions about Mary's life, then let it pass. What did it matter? Why should she care? She'd be leaving soon with no hope of ever returning. She set her empty coffee cup on the table. "I'm going to walk on to Miss Gray's farm to see my horse. Where's Jackson? I could take him with me."

Mary pointed her paring knife toward Doc's cabin door. "I think he's inside with Doc. They were looking at pictures from one of the books." Mary hesitated a moment then added, "I don't recommend you take the boy with you. Miss Gray has been acting a mite strange lately, and she's talked against you and the boy. And you shouldn't go alone. The folks in town —"

"I'll push my hair under my hat and carry my rifle like I'm going hunting. If I walk to the woods and follow the river, who's going to see me?"

"One of the men could be out hunting or fishing. Or you could run into those two strangers Doc scared off."

"I'll be watchful," Delia said, unsure why Mary warned her against trouble. From the way Mary had acted before, she'd be fine with a mob running Delia out of town on a rail.

Delia turned her back on Mary's cautions, fetched the long gun, and headed toward the woods, checking in every direction for signs of men on the prowl. With her hair hidden, she was sure she looked like a man from behind. Walking like a man, however, proved more difficult. She tried to mimic the loping swagger of the men she knew, but finally gave up.

Taking the long way to Annie Gray's farm gave Delia time to think. She had made it across the road and almost even with Miss Gray's barn when she paused to watch the swirling reflections in the slow-moving water. A twig snapped.

That's what I get. Thinking leads to mind-wandering, and mind-wandering leads to carelessness.

Delia turned slowly, putting her back to the river. Not ten feet away stood a hard-faced woman with a musket raised to her shoulder, the barrel aimed at Delia's chest.

"Drop it and put your hands in the air," the woman ordered.

Delia set her rifle on the ground and raised her hands. "Are you Annie Gray? I'm Delia Pritchard. Doc put my Palouse in your barn. I wanted to see him."

"I know who you are. Git on back to Doc Hemmer's place. I don't want you here."

"My horse —"

"I don't give two hoots about you seeing that horse. Belongs to Doc now, doesn't it? Leave it be. Git."

"I'm taking my rifle," Delia said.

"Turn away before you pick it up. If you even look like you're coming here, I'll fire before I speak."

Delia turned away, picked up her rifle, and took off along the river, setting a brisk pace until she reached the protection of trees and brush. There she stopped and bent over to catch her breath and calm her pounding heart. Her brother might have good reason for thinking Delia should leave town, but she didn't understand Annie Gray's feelings. There must have been a powerful lot of gossip about Delia thirteen years ago, especially with the fire and her running away. No telling what folks thought. Delia started walking through the woods, trying to make as little noise as possible. She ignored the path that led to Doc Hemmer's office and cabin and continued along the path that led toward the main street of town.

Chapter Twenty-Seven: The Preacher at the Cemetery

John was still hanging around Sangamon, unable to leave, but knowing he shouldn't stay, when a farmer rode into town on a buckboard pulled by two dray horses. He stopped in front of the general store and went inside to get Jeremiah. By the time the farmer brought Jeremiah outside, several townsfolk had gathered by the buckboard, pointing to the bodies.

"Found 'em on the road outside of town," the farmer said. "Both of 'em shot in the head."

"Anybody know these men?" Jeremiah asked.

"Seen them at the saloon," Colin said. "I'll bet they're the ones who broke into your store, Jeremiah."

"Then who killed them?"

"Wasn't the posse," Colin said. "We went along the river past Miss Gray's farm, then came back to town."

"Did you see anyone else on the road?" Jeremiah asked the farmer.

"Nope. If I had, I would've been spooked and kept on going. I need to gather my goods and head home. Help me get these men out of my wagon. You want 'em by the cemetery?"

Jeremiah threw up his hands and led the way, then helped Colin Pritchard lift the bodies off the buckboard and lay them outside the cemetery fence. He put three of the townsmen to work digging graves while he returned to the store to take care of the farmer. By the time that customer had hightailed it out of town, the dead men resided in the ground.

John had followed the wagon from the stable to the general store, watched the bodies get moved and buried, and now stood at the shallow graves with his head bowed in prayer. The other townsfolk had already drifted away. Jeremiah returned to stand beside John, his brow furrowed and his jaw working as though clenching and unclenching on its own.

"You're worried," said John.

"Worried, and scared. Two men murdered in cold blood and left on the road to rot. Who would do that?"

"Have you had this kind of trouble before?"

"No. We don't get many strangers here. The men scared off by Doc Hemmer were probably the same ones who robbed my store. Could be these two."

"There are plenty of outlaws on the road these days. The law's trying to catch them all, but not having a good time of it. I received warnings from federal marshals when they saw me out riding my circuit."

Jeremiah studied the two graves, then spat on the ground. "It's that Pritchard gal," he said. "These men were looking for her. I feel it in my bones."

"Oh, I don't think —"

"I'd bet my life on it. I said from the beginning she'd bring trouble to this town."

CHAPTER TWENTY-EIGHT:
UNWELCOME VISITORS

By the time Delia had walked through her fear of Annie Gray and turned it into anger, she reached the main road that led from the river to the town. Hidden by the trees, she moved alongside the road until the woods came to an abrupt end. Beyond a field of dried tallgrass, a dozen log cabins clustered around a grassy patch with a large fire pit at the center. Delia figured the smaller homes were one room. The larger ones may have started as one room but now had add-ons and lean-tos built of stone or mud brick.

Across the road sat the buildings Delia remembered from her younger days. Jeremiah's general store was the first business built in Sangamon, followed soon after by the blacksmith shop and stable, the feed store, and a saloon built of split logs and mud to fill the cracks. From a distance, it appeared the saloon had been rebuilt. New space had been added to the stable, but as far as Delia could tell, the sign had not been repainted since she'd left town thirteen years ago.

Time to make a decision. She could return to Doc Hemmer's office through the woods. She could wade through the tallgrass, staying behind the cabins, until she reached the road that turned toward Doc's place. Or she could walk out onto the road and stroll past each business until she reached the stable. Colin might be in front, doing his smithy work, or he might be in the stable, mucking out stalls. Either way, Delia could check on the sorrel mare and let Colin know she'd be taking the horse soon and leaving town.

A flurry of activity at the east end of the village caught Delia's eye. Men and women scurried away from the road, some dragging small children by the hand.

The noise of jangling spurs and clopping hooves grew louder.

A man by the stable shouted, "Get Jeremiah."

A woman yelled, "Ring the bell."

Delia moved closer to the road, still using the trees for cover, and leaned out far enough to see all the way to the junction. Five men on horseback had stopped in front of the saloon. Two dismounted and strolled

251

through the open front door. The other three stayed in their saddles, watching the curious townsfolk gather and disperse as they tried to decide whether the newcomers were friend or foe.

Delia gasped and backed farther into the woods. Her decision had been made for her. One of the men who had stayed on his horse was Hiram Biedler's oldest son, Jack. The other men were his brothers. They had all looked alike to Delia when she first saw them. She had once asked if three of them were triplets. She never got a straight answer. Idiots likely didn't know what the word meant.

Gradually, she'd learned that the two second-oldest brothers were twins. George and Thomas. They were nearly as blood-thirsty as Jack. The next to youngest was named Daniel, often referred to as The Drunk. The only one of the five even slightly capable of kind deeds from time to time was the youngest, Billy. He'd once given Delia a necklace he'd stolen from a riverboat passenger, but it had disappeared from her stash of possessions soon after.

The Biedler gang was part of the whole banditti network, doing the same kind of badness the highwaymen and pirates at Cave-in-Rock and Ford's Ferry had done before the Biedlers were chased out of Indiana and landed at Shawneetown. They sure wouldn't be in a little, no-account town like Sangamon unless they were searching for her. They wouldn't be good for the town, not good for the townsfolk, and definitely not good for Delia.

The years Delia spent with the gangs on their riverboat raids and stagecoach robberies seemed a lifetime ago. She thought she'd grown strong and tough and could handle anything. But these men disgusted her. They did not hesitate to abuse or murder the people they robbed, so why did she think they'd spare her life if she said or did the wrong thing one day? Slinking away in the middle of the night with nothing but the clothes on her back and the things she'd had the nerve to steal most likely had saved her life.

She'd escaped, but barely. She later heard they had come looking for her. They'd covered every inch of the land for several miles around their camp. It didn't matter she'd done them no real harm and had taken only a horse, a gun, and a sack of gold. The fact that she'd run away without asking permission earned her a death sentence. That, and stealing, of course. Horse thieves got hanged for their crimes, even when they stole from outlaws. Especially if they stole from outlaws. If they found her today, she'd be dead and buried before tomorrow.

Delia returned through the woods to reach Doc Hemmer's land, placing her steps with care as she watched for sticks that might snap, rocks that might cause her to stumble. She still had to cross from the woods to the doctor's office, but the tallgrass hid a lot. If anyone appeared, she would drop to the ground and hide or crawl to Doc's cabin, if necessary.

Delia hoped Mary and Jackson were inside the cabin or the cookhouse. *Jackson must not be seen outside.* Notorious for hunting escaped slaves and dragging them barely alive to their owners for the bounty, the Biedlers rarely lost one of their victims. With no other black folks in the area, the gang would assume Jackson a runaway unless Mary and Doc told them different. Doc would protect Jackson at all costs. But would Mary come to the boy's aid if she thought her own life or Doc's were at risk? That was not a sure thing.

No one approached Delia during her escape through the woods. She made it to the field of tallgrass. No one showed on the road beyond the doctor's office, and no one in either direction to the side. Tempted to run at full speed, Delia calmed herself and reasoned that a casual stroll across the field would be less noticeable. She wished she had the carcass of a rabbit or wild bird to show for her outing. Her rifle held loosely at her right side, she pulled her hat a little lower over her eyes as though to shade from the sun and walked across the field at a slow but steady pace. When she reached Doc's chicken house, she checked to make sure Jackson was not inside.

With a few more steps, she slid through the cookhouse door, stumbled to the bench by the table, and sat. She bent her head almost to her knees and waited until her heartbeat slowed. As she took stock of her body's reaction to the Biedler gang's arrival, Delia felt how stiff and sore her left arm and shoulder felt. Her body was soaked in sweat, and she still had the rifle gripped in her right hand.

"What on earth is wrong?" Mary said from behind Delia. "Did something happen at Annie Gray's cabin?"

"Oh, hell and damnation, yes," Delia said. "There and beyond. Where's Jackson? And Doc?"

CHAPTER TWENTY-NINE:
A NEW DILEMMA
FOR THE PREACHER

John Claymore sat on the porch of the feed store, his chair tipped back and his boots propped on the railing. Reluctant to get his horse and leave town, yet convinced he could do nothing useful if he stayed, his lack of a clear plan for his future kept him from moving on. Annie Gray barely gave him a glance as she marched past on her way to the general store. Colin Pritchard stayed out of sight as much as possible, coming and going through the back door of his stable. Doc Hemmer stopped long enough to say hello, then went on his way.

Dangerously close to falling asleep in his precarious position, John put his feet on the floorboards and brought his chair to its four legs. He stood and stretched. A few excited voices from the east road out of town caught his attention. Five men rode their horses into Sangamon and stopped in front of the saloon. The horses were shiny with sweat, the men dusty from their hats to their boots.

While three of the men waited on horseback, two dismounted and entered the saloon. In minutes, one of the riders returned.

"They seen her?" asked one still on his horse.

"A woman did come through a few days ago but now she's gone on west."

"She riding a Palouse?"

"That's what he said."

"You sure he's telling the truth?"

"I'm sure. Tom had him backed to the bar with a gun in his face."

"We'll see about that." The rider doing the talking glanced toward the feed store.

John leaned on a post by the railing, wishing he'd vanished into the store instead of gawking at the strangers. He had no doubt they hunted for Delia. With all the talk about her bringing trouble to the town, he was surprised someone in the saloon had lied about her moving on. Now the man on horseback nudged his animal with his heels and ambled toward John.

John leaned against the porch post, trying to look relaxed and not show his knees slowly turning to melted lard. He shoved his hands in his pockets to still their trembling.

The man stopped his horse in front of the feed store and tipped his hat so he could wipe his brow. "We're looking for a gal name of Delia. Stole a gun and a horse. There's nothing worse than a horse thief."

"I'm the circuit-riding preacher, stopping here for a day or two. Haven't met anyone by that name."

The man studied John's face, then looked him up and down. "You ain't wearing preacher clothes."

"I save them for the days I have prayer meetings. I'm about to leave and head over to Decatur."

The man nudged his horse again and moved on past the stable to the general store. He dismounted, tossed the reins around the hitching rails, pulled his rifle from its scabbard, and walked inside the store.

John looked toward the saloon. One man must have stayed inside. The other three remained on their horses as they watched the people on the road, most of whom edged away from the riders and disappeared into the closest business or cabin. A yell from the direction of the general store drew John's attention. The stranger who had gone inside pushed Doc Hemmer out the door and down the steps to the road. The bag of

258

cornmeal Doc carried flew out of his hands and split open, the contents spilling over the ground. Doc tumbled down the steps and landed on his knees. He yelped as he rolled to a sitting position and grabbed his right leg.

Jeremiah appeared in the general store doorway, wiping his hands on his apron. "He's the only doctor in these parts. Don't hurt him."

The stranger slowly turned to face Jeremiah and raised his rifle. Jeremiah ducked out of sight as the stranger fired, nicking the wood frame at the top of the door. "That's a warning," the stranger called out. "If I wanted to kill you, I wouldn't miss."

Without acknowledging the doctor, the stranger mounted his horse, the rifle still in his hand, and rode to the saloon. With a tilt of his head, he gave the other three men permission to dismount and join him. As soon as they were out of sight, John ran toward the general store to help Jeremiah get Doc inside.

"I think it's broken," Doc said, grasping his leg below the knee. "If you can get me to my office, Mary can help you set the bone and put on a splint. You need to warn Delia. There's a horse in the stable that she had the boy riding when they came to town.

That's the one she stole from the outlaws. You need to get that animal out of town before they see it."

"If I bring the horse here, can you ride?" John asked.

"I can lift myself, but don't know if I can swing my bad leg over the saddle."

"We'll figure it out. I'll be back." John checked outside before bounding down the steps and running toward the stable. He found Colin Pritchard cowering in the feed room, shaking like he had palsy.

"What if they know Delia's name is Pritchard?" he cried. "If they figure out I'm kin, I might as well be a dead man. Oh, I feel sick." Colin doubled over, holding his abdomen. "I'm gonna die, and it's all her fault."

"Stop it! Help me get that sorrel horse out here so the outlaws don't find it. I'm taking it and Doc to his office right now."

"There's no place at Doc's to hide a horse."

"I'll take it on to Miss Gray's barn where they hid the Palouse."

"They're going to see you and kill you. They're going to kill us all."

"Colin, get the damned horse!"

Colin's jaw dropped in shock at the preacher's language. "I'm getting it. Right now."

John turned to the front door of the stable and checked the road in both directions. The outlaws' five horses remained at the hitching rail in front of the saloon. The only other person visible was Jeremiah's young daughter, Elizabeth. She ran past from the direction of the store toward the saloon.

Jeremiah jumped down the steps. "Elizabeth, come here!"

She paused and shouted at her father. "I'm going to tell Miss Mary about the doctor and tell that boy to hide." John tried to get her attention as she ran past the stable, but she ignored his call. Not sure whether to chase her or get the horse out of sight, he chose to stay put.

Surely even the roughest scoundrel will not harm a child.

John hoped he had not made the wrong choice as he watched Elizabeth run past the feed store, getting closer to the saloon with every step.

CHAPTER THIRTY: WORRIES FOR JACKSON

Jackson recognized the alarm in Delia's voice and set his book down. He stayed in Doc's office and listened, both Delia and Mary talking loud enough for him to hear every word. Jackson couldn't make sense of Delia's tone and what they talked about. Something had gone wrong, but Delia didn't explain.

That's the way grown-ups behave sometimes, he thought. His own ma and pa would talk over his head, sound worried or scared, but when he'd listen to the words they said, everything seemed fine. No troubles, no bad weather, no taxes, no Indians. "Don't worry," they said.

But late at night, voices would wake him from sleep. Low, murmuring voices tinged with feelings that made Jackson's skin get prickly with fear. He couldn't get up to listen because his ma and pa's bed was on the other side of the same room. No matter how hard he tried, he never understood what troubled them.

He had a feeling Delia thought the same way his ma and pa did. She wouldn't want to make him upset, wouldn't want to frighten him, so she wouldn't tell him anything. He guessed she wasn't going to tell Mary, either.

What could it be? The bad man who had come to steal Jackson and sell him? The men who killed his ma and pa were set on killing him and Delia, too? Miss Annie Gray and Mr. Frost, who wanted Delia and Jackson to leave Sangamon right this minute?

What if Delia was going to die from that gunshot! The thought of her dying and leaving him all alone in Sangamon made his heart beat faster and his throat choke up something terrible. He didn't trust anyone but her to protect him from the bad men. Her and Doc. He wasn't sure that even Miss Mary would help him. And from what he'd learned so far, he sure knew Miss Gray would not.

Jackson pushed his toe against the floor to set his chair rocking as he focused on the drawings in the book he'd started to read. It had turned out to be a story that made his hair stand on end. He knew he would

have very bad dreams when he went to bed
that night.

CHAPTER THIRTY-ONE: WAITING FOR DOC

"Jackson is reading in Doc's cabin," Mary said. "Doc went to the general store for cornmeal and to see if the salve he ordered has arrived. Why, what's wrong?"

Delia decided not to divulge what she knew about the Biedler gang until Doc returned. Instead, she told Mary what happened when Annie Gray caught Delia near the barn.

"She's a fierce one, isn't she? And strange," Mary said. "Too lonely, I think. She talks to her animals, the river, and her butter churn. It's amusing to some, but I find it sad."

"She has no friends?"

"Sarah and Annie became quite close when Sarah taught school. Now that Sarah is married to Jeremiah, it seems the two women hardly speak to each other. Perhaps Annie felt abandoned. I don't know. It wasn't that long ago that Annie marched about town several times a week, doing her Christian duty to those in need. She provided care and food . . ."

Mary paused and turned away from Delia to busy herself at the fireplace. Delia gathered there was much more to the story of Annie Gray and the townsfolk, but Delia wouldn't pry. She had other things to worry about.

"I'm going to see what Jackson is doing," she said. She left the cookhouse and walked in the open door to Doc's cabin. The first time she'd been inside his living space, she had taken extra care to look the place over, noting the furnishings and the general tidiness. Jackson sat with a book in a rocking chair in front of a low bookcase made of split logs and flat rocks. He grinned at Delia, then held the book up for her to see. He brought the book to his lap and used his finger to follow the words across the cover as he read the title to her. "The Legend of Sleepy Hollow."

Delia remembered that tale from her own school days. "It's hard to read," she said. "And scary."

"I'm not scared."

"That's good. You need to stay inside this cabin today or in Doc's office with me or in the cookhouse if Mary is there."

"I can't go feed the chickens?"

"Not today, Jackson. There are bad men in Sangamon. I don't know what they want, but we need to stay out of sight and hope they go away soon."

"What kind of bad men? Are they the ones that killed my ma and pa?"

"Not the same men, but the kind that might stir up trouble."

"Like the headless horseman?"

"I believe they all have their heads sitting on their shoulders where heads belong."

Jackson closed the pages of the book and slid from the rocker to return the book to a shelf. He pulled out another one, showed the cover of an alphabet primer to Delia, then returned to the chair.

Delia examined the rest of the books, noting that most were texts on anatomy, medicine, and surgery. She casually examined the samplers on the wall, the rack holding three rifles, an open-faced cupboard that held clothes, and a box on the floor for boots and shoes. A door from the living area led to a small alcove holding a double bed and side table.

"Where do you sleep, young'un?"

Jackson scrambled off the rocker and walked past Delia, into the alcove. At the bedside, he stooped over, reached underneath, and pulled out a thick mattress with a folded quilt on top. He pushed the mattress back and returned to his chair and book.

"I'll be in Doc's office or the cookhouse if you need me. Mind what I said. Don't go anywhere else, not even the chicken house. You hear me?"

"Yes, ma'am."

Delia hurried through the open space between the cabins and slipped into Doc's office, more worried now than ever. Until Doc returned from his errand, she could not relax. She set her rifle against the wall, paced, then lay on the cot and closed her eyes. The old sights her brain played against her closed eyelids were far worse than what she imagined with her eyes open. Memories of the Biedlers killing people while she watched. Children thrown off a ferry and drowning in the Ohio River. The horrors never ended.

After fighting her worst fears for at least an hour, Delia got up and retrieved the rifle, then went to the kitchen to see if she could help Mary. The room was empty. The fire had gone cold. The dark cookhouse retained no heat. Delia shivered, but more from unease than from the chill of the room. Perhaps the unexpected emptiness had triggered an alarm.

Returning to the doorway of Doc's cabin, Delia looked inside. Jackson still sat in the rocker, a book in his lap, but now he had his eyes closed. Apparently, Mary had checked on him because a pillow had been stuffed between the boy's side and the rocker's armrest. Delia tiptoed to the alcove, but that room also stood empty.

Delia should have told Mary about the men in the town. It was foolish to think she would stay put in the cookhouse all afternoon. She might have gone to the school to check on Sarah and the students. Or Annie Gray's farm for more eggs. Even to the general store for something she'd neglected to ask Doc to purchase.

Delia had not checked the chicken house. She tucked her hair under her hat before she peeked around the side of the kitchen. No one crossed the tallgrass field between the woods and the building. No one stood at the edge of the trees. She slipped around the corner and hurried to the building. The hens inside clucked their disapproval at the intrusion.

Returning to Doc's office, Delia looked through the slats in the front shutters but saw no one. She went to the bedroom and picked up her rifle, then crept to the front door. Easing it open enough to stick her head out, she checked first to the right toward Annie Gray's farm, then to the left where the main road of Sangamon lay. Still no sign of Mary.

The quiet that hung over the road and field around Doc Hemmer's office and cabin should have felt peaceful, but Delia couldn't shake her sense of foreboding.

The sudden eruption of gunfire almost came as relief. Her senses had gone on high alert for good reason.

Jackson ran into the doctor's office. "What was that?" he shouted.

"I don't know, young'un. Get in the bedroom and shut the door."

CHAPTER THIRTY-TWO: TO THE RESCUE

The preacher ran to the stable to see if Colin needed help saddling the sorrel mare, then rushed to his room for his rifle. When he returned, he looked both ways again and found the road deserted, with one frightening exception. One of the five strangers now paced in front of the saloon, looking in the direction of the road that led to Doc Hemmer's office.

He saw Elizabeth! John's brief prayer that the outlaw would return inside went unanswered. The man staggered to his horse, tried to put his left foot in the stirrup but missed, stumbled, and cracked his head on the saddle horn. Under any other circumstances, John would have laughed at the outlaw's clumsiness, but now he held his breath, hoping the man would give up and go back to his whiskey.

Instead, the outlaw got his foot in the stirrup, swung his leg over the saddle, and kicked the horse's side to get it moving. The horse tried to rear, but the reins, still tied to the hitching post, jerked the animal back. John was grateful he couldn't hear what the outlaw said as he tumbled off the saddle and untied the reins.

John didn't know what to do. Jeremiah motioned him to hurry and bring the horse so they could lift Doc astride. Beckoning Colin to the front door of the stable, John decided to get Doc and the mare into the woods before he helped Jeremiah find his daughter. "Colin, we need your help. Come on."

"I can't!"

"Do it!" John gave the blacksmith the angriest glare he could conjure and took a threatening step in his direction.

Colin gave in. The two hurried the horse to the general store. Several precious minutes later, the doctor sat astride, his clenched jaw the only sign of pain.

"You'll have to do this on your own so I can make sure Elizabeth is okay," John said. "Head toward the trail through the woods that runs on the east side of the river road."

"The road would be faster," Doc replied. "If that man catches Elizabeth —"

"Not enough cover. We don't know where these men will go next. Take the trail until you reach the field behind your place. Wait there until I join you."

"You're going after Elizabeth?"

"I told Jeremiah I'd go around the cabins to stay hidden from the saloon, then come out on the road close to your office. It's faster than the woods or the road."

"Go! I'll be fine."

John hurried through the woods until he reached the cluster of cabins that had been built across the road from the row of businesses. Creeping from one cover to another, always remaining out of direct sight from the saloon, he gradually came close to Doc's cabin. There was no longer anything to hide behind.

A scream. Elizabeth.

The pounding of a horse's hooves as the outlaw raced by at full speed.

John ran across the tallgrass as fast as he could, but the brittle stalks caught him around the ankles. He fell hard, knocking the wind from his lungs and smacking his nose into the ground. His rifle hit the ground and fired. John rolled over on his back and lay still, waiting until he could breathe normally before trying to sit up. His nose felt on fire, but when he touched his face, there was no blood.

Before he had recovered enough to get to

his feet and grab his gun, Mary yelled that Doc was hurt. A mumbled conversation he couldn't understand followed — and then another gun fired.

A chill ran down John's spine. Fully expecting to find the outlaw standing over the bleeding child, John reloaded his rifle and made his way toward the road, prepared to retaliate whether God approved or not. As he rounded the corner from Doc's cabin, he stopped to take in the scene, confused at first, then slowly comprehending.

CHAPTER THIRTY-THREE: THE CHASE

A few minutes earlier, Jackson had been by Delia's side in front of Doc's office, staring in the direction of the saloon. "Lookit there!" he yelled.

Delia squinted to see what he pointed at. A child ran toward them, her face flushed and her arms flailing.

"Get inside, Jackson. Right now."

"But it's that girl." Jackson dashed off, racing toward Elizabeth and away from Delia.

"Oh, no, Jackson," she yelled. "Come back here."

Before Delia could stop him, another movement at the road's juncture by the saloon caught her eye. A man had mounted his horse and now cantered after the girl. As he drew near Elizabeth, he slid to the ground, dropped the reins, staggered and nearly fell, then charged after the girl. His gait was unsteady, his eyes bloodshot.

Drunk as a skunk. Just like Daniel Biedler. Nothing more dangerous, even to a child.

Jackson and Elizabeth met on the road before the outlaw could grab her. They were now close enough that Delia recognized the look of terror on the girl's face. Elizabeth screamed as the man tried to grab her shoulder, his fingers barely brushing the fabric of her dress.

A rifle shot cracked from behind Doc's cabin. The outlaw turned his head to look for the shooter and bent over like he thought he could dodge a load of buckshot. Jackson pushed Elizabeth toward the side of the road, then ran at the man's legs, hitting the unsuspecting outlaw from the side and knocking him off his feet. The man landed on his back with a thud and a string of cuss words not fit for the young'uns' ears. The outlaw's horse shied away, ran a few steps, and pulled the reins out of reach.

By the time the man struggled to his feet, Delia had yanked Jackson away by the arm. "Get that girl and run as fast as you can to Doc's office. Go inside and bar the doors."

This time, Jackson followed orders.

Delia stood her ground, her rifle pointed at Daniel Biedler's belly. "Why's a grown man chasing a little girl that's not his own?"

His hands dangled at his sides as he

studied Delia's face, looked her up and down, then stared at her weapon. "You're the one we're after, ain't you? Delia Pritchard. Didn't recognize you in that getup. Jack's going to string you from a big old tree when he catches you."

"He's not going to catch me."

Daniel glanced toward his horse, now a good six feet from his side. Delia took note of his scruffy, unwashed hair and beard, his falling-to-pieces, flat-brim hat and his dirty boots.

"Who did the shooting in the town?" she asked. "Anybody dead?"

The man shifted his gaze to look over Delia's shoulder.

She'd learned about that trick a long time ago, but to be on the safe side, she backed to the side of the road to see in both directions. Annie Gray and Mary marched toward Delia from the direction of the farm. Both carried long guns.

Mary studied the man Delia held at gunpoint. She sounded out of breath and her voice shook. "Has Doc come back yet?"

"No. But Elizabeth is here. I sent her and Jackson inside and told them to bar the doors."

"Who's this?" Annie asked, pointing her musket at Daniel.

Delia stepped closer to Mary and Annie, deciding on the spur of the moment to avoid naming the outlaw. "This piece of shit chased Elizabeth down the road. The child was terrified out of her mind. I think she knows what happened to Doc."

"I'll find out," Mary said. She ran to Doc's office where she pounded on the door and called for Jackson to open up.

Annie stayed by Delia's side, her relic of a musket pointed at Daniel's chest. "You know this man?" Annie asked.

"I might."

"Any reason to let him go?"

"Nope."

"What'll we do with him?"

"I don't know. Shoot him?"

Mary ran out the front door of the doctor's office, yelling loud enough to send the horse skittering farther away from the outlaw. "This one pushed Doc down the steps in front of the general store and broke his leg. Elizabeth watched him do it. She said the preacher and her daddy looked after him, but Doc is hurt bad."

"That solves our dilemma," said Annie. She raised her musket and fired.

Delia and Mary exchanged a shocked glance, then stared at the man who lay on the dirt road, bleeding from a hole in his gut. Annie might have just set up the whole town to die in a bloody massacre. Delia walked toward the outlaw's horse, coaxing it to stand still. When close enough to grab the reins, Delia hung onto the saddle horn with her left hand, ignored the protesting shoulder and arm muscles, and lifted herself into the saddle. She looked toward the saloon to see if any of the outlaws had come outside to investigate the gunshots, but no one was in sight.

"I'm going to get the doctor," Delia said. She pulled back on the reins as John Claymore ran around the corner of Doc's office to the road. He gaped at the bleeding man who clutched his stomach and moaned. John dropped to one knee and touched the man's arm.

"Get back," Annie said as she reloaded her musket and aimed at the outlaw's head.

John jumped to his feet between Annie and the injured man, placed his hand on the barrel of her gun, and gently pressed down. "He's going to die on his own, Miss Gray. Leave him be."

She pushed his hand away. "It's not merciful to let him die slow like that." She shot the outlaw again, this time aiming at the side of his head.

John averted his eyes from the bloody

mess and turned his shocked gaze on Annie.

"He tried to run down Jeremiah's little
girl," Annie said. "Only the Lord knows
what he intended to do to her."

Delia waved to get John's attention. "Let
her be, Preacher. These men aren't worth
our time and sure aren't worth feeling guilty
over. Finding Doc is more important."

John shook his head as though not believ-
ing the hardness of these women. "You
don't need to get the doctor," he said. "We
put him on that brown mare of yours and
set him on the trail through the woods. By
now, he should be close enough to see
across the field. He'll be worried about the
gunfire."

Delia loosened the outlaw's long gun from
its straps and made sure it was primed for
firing. She decided not to return to the
doctor's office for her revolver. For all she
knew, Doc had fallen off the horse and lay
unconscious in the woods. Or the outlaws
had heard shots and were chasing him on
foot. There was no time to waste. She
turned the horse toward the field behind
Doc's office and kicked its flanks hard
enough to make it rear before it galloped
away from the road. Once in the tallgrass,
she slowed the horse to a walk and headed

for the trees.

Half expecting to see Doc sitting astride the mare just inside the woods, and half thinking he'd be helpless on the ground somewhere between the field and the town, Delia urged the outlaw's horse along the trail as fast as she dared.

No Doc, no brown mare, no outlaws. The woods were quiet.

When Delia reached the main town road, she halted the horse. They waited quietly as she checked in all directions and listened for sounds of activity. No townsfolk remained in the open. At the far end of the road, the four horses still stood by the railing in front of the saloon, their only movement an occasional stamp of a hoof or swish of a tail. As she urged the animal out of the woods and onto the road, the quiet gave Delia a chill, a strange sensation with the sun beating so hard. Scared to death one of the outlaws would come out of the saloon and see her on Daniel's horse, she nudged it to a trot and headed for the stable.

Delia dismounted behind the building and threw the reins over the railing by the rear barn door. The door, apparently barred from the inside, did not budge against her shoves. She called out as loud as she dared. "Colin, let me in. Is Doc Hemmer inside?"

The bar slid against the door. When it opened a crack, Colin eyed her and the horse, then pushed the door open enough for her to enter. "That horse. You took it from one of the outlaws?"

"I did. He chased Jeremiah's girl and almost caught her."

"Bring it on in here so it's out of sight."

"Where's Elizabeth?" yelled Jeremiah as he came up behind Colin. Delia saw all the people and decided half the town had locked themselves inside the stable. Why Jeremiah hadn't gone after his own daughter was a question Delia decided not to ask. She had nothing to gain by showing him to be a coward.

"She's fine. She's with Mary and Annie Gray at Doc's office. They're armed and ready to protect the young'uns."

"You got that boy in there with my daughter?" Jeremiah's face turned red. He stepped forward as though to push Delia out the door.

Colin put his hand forcefully on Jeremiah's shoulder and gave him a shove away from Delia. "Forget it, Jeremiah. She saved your girl. That's more than you done."

Delia slipped outside and led the outlaw's horse inside the stable. After handing the animal's reins to Jeremiah, she followed

Colin to the stalls. Doc sat on a pile of straw with his back to the wall, a long gun at his side. The bad leg, which had been wrapped in torn strips of petticoat and a rough board for a splint, stuck straight forward.

"Damnation, Doc," Delia said. "What are you doing here? The preacher thought you'd rode into the woods and headed for your place."

"I tried. Danged horse bolted when it flushed a bevy of quail. Threw me off before we even got out of Jeremiah's sight. Colin saw the quail fly up and came out to check. He dragged me here on his own, then went back and got the horse."

Doc was safe, thank goodness. Now Delia had to face the prospect of getting him on horseback and through the woods without the remaining four outlaws seeing them.

"Colin, get that mare over here again, would you? With Doc on her, I can lead them along the river road and then cut through the woods. We need to hurry. The outlaws will be looking for the one that's missing."

Jeremiah pointed a finger at her and stepped closer. "One's missing? What happened to him?"

Delia tried to ignore his question, stepping closer to the mare and taking the reins from Colin.

Jeremiah shook his finger in Delia's face. "You'll get us all killed, woman!"

She swatted his hand away. "What might get you killed is keeping that outlaw's horse in here. I'd better take him with me and turn him loose by the river."

With this excuse to get the mare away from Colin's stable, another of Delia's problems was solved. When she wanted to hightail it out of town, she'd have both of her horses ready to go, assuming Annie Gray would let her have the Palouse without a fight. No guarantee of that, she thought, despite the woman's help saving Elizabeth and disposing of Daniel Biedler.

It took three men to get Doc on the mare. He held onto the saddle horn with both hands, his good leg secure with the foot in its stirrup. When Delia tried to guide Doc's injured leg toward the other stirrup, he gasped.

"You won't pass out on me, will you, Doc?" Delia asked.

"No. I will not pass out."

"Colin, get that outlaw's gun. Doc, you can hold the horn with one hand and the gun in the other, can't you?" Delia looked at Doc's face. He wasn't pale, wasn't even sweating.

Tough hombre.

"I can," Doc said. He held the rifle in his right hand, kept hold of the horn with his left, and like most experienced riders, relaxed into a slouch.

Delia went to the door, slid the bar aside, and opened it far enough to check the street in both directions. She found it curious the four remaining Biedlers hadn't gone hunting for their missing brother yet. With luck, she and Doc would be out of sight before one or more of them came out to the street. If the outlaws chugged one whiskey after another, they might not realize how much time had passed. Getting drunk, however, tended to make the gang meaner than ever. Delia wanted to get Doc home and that outlaw's horse out of sight before the Biedler bunch had a chance to stagger into the street, looking for people to kill.

With no one in sight to the east or west, Delia still felt her nerves tingling. "We're going out the back," she said. It would be easier to stay out of sight if she walked behind the buildings from the stable all the way to the general store and then cut across to the river. Delia checked outside once again, relieved to find the path deserted, as she'd hoped. She led the sorrel mare and the outlaw's horse outside. The door closed as soon as they were clear. The bar dropped into its grooved frame with a dull clunk.

Colin had not said good-bye or wished them well. Delia hoped those left inside would be safe, but she had no doubt the Biedler gang could get to the whole bunch. She briefly considered banging on the door and advising them to scatter to their own homes, but she did not follow through. She needed to move fast to get the doctor to a safe place where they could tend to his broken leg.

Frequently checking Doc to make sure he sat securely in the saddle and did not slump to one side or the other, Delia led the horses along the Sangamon River until they reached the bend where the river turned to flow along Annie Gray's farm. She turned the outlaw's horse loose and smacked him on the rump. He trotted toward the water, then stopped to drink.

The path through the woods had clearly been made by people on foot, most likely hunters, so was not as wide as it would be if frequented by folks on horseback. The mare balked from time to time when bushes and shrubs scraped her haunches. Snapped twigs caused her to dance sideways and yank on the reins.

Delia had tried to keep the reins in her

left hand, but the jerking and pulling set her shoulder on fire. She transferred the rifle to her left hand and continued through the woods with the mare's reins held securely in her right. Each time she turned to look at Doc's face, he seemed a little more tired, a little more pained. Still, he gave her a grim smile of encouragement. "We're almost there," he said. "Best stop where the woods end and rest for a few minutes. We should cross the field as fast as we can."

Delia crept to the edge of the tallgrass and looked toward Doc's cabin. Smoke spiraled from the cookhouse chimney. A few chickens ran around outside, and the back door of Doc's office stood wide open. One of the Biedler twins, probably George, judging by his long hair and scraggly beard, leaned against the doorjamb, looking toward the woods.

Delia retreated, pushing and pulling the horse to force it deeper under cover. "We have a problem," she said.

The bushes rustled and snapped. Delia looked over her shoulder.

Oh, no!

The outlaw's horse had followed them. Delia grabbed its reins and pulled both horses into the shadows.

Chapter Thirty-Four:
Mary and the Two Outlaws

After Delia had left, Mary helped Annie and the preacher drag the outlaw's body past the doctor's office and into the chicken house. The chickens raised a ruckus before running outside, then recovered quickly as they settled into a hunt-and-peck war against the few remaining grasshoppers in the garden. Dusting the ground with her apron, Mary reversed their path from the road, sweeping the cloth across the trail they'd left in dirt and grass.

"I'll stand watch," Annie said. "If anyone we don't know comes down that road, I'll run inside, bar the door, and hide the children."

The preacher glanced toward the trees. "I don't see Delia and Doc yet. She might need help. I'm going after them." He set out across the tallgrass field on foot, glancing back once to see Mary and Annie watching. He waved, then entered the woods and disappeared.

Knowing there weren't that many places anyone could hide in either cabin gave Mary the shakes all over again. Still, there was nothing else to be done. The two women had to hold down their makeshift fort and protect the children until Delia and Doc returned. Mary swallowed hard, willing herself not to cry. She needed Doc's teaching and moral support. What if he died? Would Jeremiah turn against her being the schoolteacher and fire her? Would she end up lost in her old life of poverty and despair?

When Annie walked outside to keep watch, she left the front door of the office partway open. Mary followed her to the door and said, "I'll be in the cookhouse and might not hear you unless you shout or come out back."

Annie nodded, then faced the road, her musket held in both hands and pointed at the ground.

Mary stirred the fire embers to life in the cookhouse and added a few twigs and dry grass, then laid a piece of firewood on top. The chicken she'd killed and cleaned earlier now rested in a pot of water that would slowly heat to boiling. Her flour-coated hands trembled as she mixed dough for dumplings. The front door of the office slammed shut, the bar slid into place, and steps rapidly approached. Mary started in alarm.

"Two men on horseback," Annie said as she stopped in the doorway. "I'll take the children into the office bedroom."

Thankful that Annie appeared to have her wits about her again, Mary wiped her hands on her apron and edged toward the shelves where she kept her supplies. Despite her earlier resolve to leave the cooking whiskey alone, a quick swallow from the bottle, a squaring of her shoulders, and a bite of jerky gave her courage.

That courage didn't last long.

The two men banged on the front door of the office, one shouting that the other was injured and needed the doctor. Mary hurried into the office but did not answer the door. *Perhaps they'll think the doctor is gone.* She tapped on the bedroom door and whispered, "It's Mary."

When she opened the door and looked inside, she could not see the children. Annie sat on the bed with the quilt hanging far enough over the side to drag the floor. Her rifle lay across her lap. There was no way to keep the men from going inside if they wanted. Mary had to hope for the best. She closed the door and left the children to Annie's protection.

Hopefully, the children would remain quiet. Even a small movement or a tiny sob might catch the outlaws' attention. Annie would only have time to kill one of the men, which meant Mary would have to shoot the other. She retrieved one of Doc's rifles from his cabin, already primed and loaded, and leaned it against the wall behind her. Delia's fancy new handgun lay under the thin mattress on Doc's high bed, within easy reach.

The men pounded on the door. Mary did not remove the bar and did not respond. A few seconds later the shutters at the front window crashed into the office, smashed in with the stocks of the men's sturdy long guns.

Mary jumped and backed against the bed, one hand over her mouth to suppress a scream. As the men climbed through the window, they separated and moved away from each other but in her direction.

"Which one of you is hurt?" Mary asked. She looked to the man with short hair as he stumbled toward the center of the room.

"Not me," the one with a scruffy beard said. "Are you hurt, Bud?"

"No, I ain't hurt. I'm drunk. I guess you heard us wrong, lady. We came here hunting for my brother. You seen a man on horseback come this way?"

Mary saw where the rifle was, wishing she'd hidden it, wondering what would happen next. Was she about to die? Or worse? Rubbery knees forced her to grab the side of the bed so she wouldn't fall. Fear of what might happen at the hands of these two ruffians if she fainted overwhelmed her. She was sure her face had lost all color.

"I saw no one," she said. "I was in the cookhouse and didn't hear you knocking at first. If you had waited a bit longer, I would have reached the door." She wrung her hands in mock alarm at the broken shutters. "The doctor will be very upset to see the damage."

"Where is he?"

"He went to the store. He'll be back soon."

"Something smells good. You fixing food? I could use a good meal," the bearded man said.

"And coffee," the other chimed in. "I need to get me thinking straight after all that whiskey."

Mary hoped both men would follow her into the cookhouse to get them away from the bedroom where Annie and the children hid, but only the short-haired man went with her. He walked completely around the tables and chairs, moving things, searching the shelves and sideboard. He picked up the knives and moved them to the table. Trying to quell the shaking in her hands and calm the tension in her shoulders, she turned her back on him. She walked toward the door to see what the other man was doing.

"Stay here," the man said.

Mary pointed to the wood box by the door. "I need more firewood." She glanced outside as she selected a couple of small logs. The man with long hair and beard took up space in the office doorway, staring across the tallgrass field toward the trees. Mary wanted to run outside and see for herself. What if the preacher had found Doc and already had him crossing the open space, in plain sight of this outlaw? Or Delia coming their way on the dead man's horse?

Mary called to the man in the office doorway. "Coffee is almost hot. You want to come in and sit a spell?"

He continued to search the distance another few seconds, then looked at Mary. He walked inside and sat across from his friend.

The one with long hair said, "Thought something moved over in those woods. I should take my coffee outside and keep watch."

"You think those scaredy-cats from town going to come after you?" the other asked.

"Could be Daniel out there. And that little girl he chased through town."

Mary cringed. Could they honestly think that outlaw would have dragged Elizabeth into the woods?

"We'll look for him after we partake of this fine lady's hospitality."

The outlaw with long hair leered at Mary. She shuddered. It wasn't the "hospitality" she dreaded as much as what followed. After years of being an outcast because of her lifestyle, she would prefer death over life after suffering an assault at the hands of these filthy animals.

Still, she could best protect Doc and the others if she kept the two men in the kitchen as long as possible. She went to her cupboard, pulled out the whiskey bottle, and set it on the table. Considering the two had already consumed what may have been a large amount at the saloon, perhaps they would pass out if they had even more. Both immediately poured whiskey into the coffee cups Mary had set on the table.

She left the coffeepot sitting on the fireplace rack and returned to her dumplings.

Once she'd kneaded the dough long enough, she set the bowl on a chair beside the fireplace. Using a long wooden spoon, she stirred the pot of chicken with shaking hands. Hot broth splashed onto her fingers. Willing herself not to gasp, she put down the spoon and formed the dough into round balls before tossing them into the pot. *So much work to feed these two slimy snakes.* It was a little early to toss in the dumpling dough, but if the outlaws were willing to eat half-cooked chicken, who was she to fret?

Mary said a silent prayer that Annie would go off her common sense again, march to the door of the cookhouse with her musket, and shoot one of these men. Mary could grab one of the knives off the table and stab the other.

It was a bloody fantasy, but she felt it might be the only thing to save her life. Without warning, as though in answer to a prayer, Annie trotted through the door, cackling and muttering incoherently. Unlike the Annie in Mary's fantasy, however, this dotty old woman was not carrying her gun.

CHAPTER THIRTY-FIVE: THE TALLGRASS

Delia pushed the horses deeper into the woods, her motions swift and frantic.

Doc paled. "What's wrong?" he asked.

"There's a man standing at the back door of your office. He's looking this way."

"One of that gang? We need to get home fast."

"Not a chance you're going, Doc. You can't walk, and you'd be no good trying to shoot from a running horse. You let me handle this."

"What are you going to do?"

"Get you off that horse and hide you behind the bushes. I'm going to cut through the tallgrass behind the chicken house and help chase these men back to hell where they belong."

"How are you going to do that without shooting yourself?"

"A little bit at a time, Doc. If I have to, I'll crawl."

"You don't have enough time. Take the horse."

"Yes, and if that's one of those outlaws standing there, and if he already knows we shot one of his gang, I'd be dead before they even knew I'm the gal they've been chasing all over the state of Illinois."

"They're here because of you?"

Shitfire! Why did I say that? Because she trusted Doc enough to tell him the truth, but she had no time to talk about it now. "Never mind that. Let's git you off that horse and under cover. You'll be a sitting duck if someone shoots into these woods."

Getting Doc off the horse was a struggle. He tried to swing his injured, immobilized leg across the animal by himself but failed to clear the horse's head. Finally, Delia stepped onto a large rock, reached across Doc's lap, and lifted his leg across the saddle as he leaned back a little to make the move easier. With his left foot clear of the stirrup, Doc slid toward the ground, easing his weight into Delia's uninjured shoulder and arm.

Getting him hid was a whole lot easier. Again, using her good arm, Delia supported Doc as he hopped toward a stand of brush and new tree growth, then held him under his armpits to lower him to the ground.

297

By then, Delia's left shoulder burned like it had been lit on fire. She shrugged off the pain as she led the two horses farther into the trees and closer to the river, so they wouldn't draw anyone to Doc's location if they whinnied or pulled free from their tethers.

With a rifle in each hand, Delia surveyed the distance across the field of tallgrass and noted where the sparse cover offered no place to hide. She would cut to a spot where she wouldn't be in a direct line of sight from Doc's office door. The man who watched from there a little earlier had disappeared, but no telling where he went or when he'd take up his position again.

Walking bent over proved hard enough, but trying to keep an eye on Doc's place at the same time pained her neck and back worse with every step. The muscles in her left arm jerked and quivered as she stretched them to their limit. The deep ache in her shoulder grew like a living thing, spreading into her clenched teeth. Slow steps, tiny movements. It would be disastrous to trip and fall, especially if one of the guns fired.

This is stupid! I'm going to get caught for sure.

What else could she do? If the outlaws were there with Mary or Annie, then the children were in danger. It would take too long to return to town for help. The cowards in Sangamon most likely wouldn't ride to the rescue anyway.

And the preacher. Where did the preacher go? The thought of the outlaws finding the dead man in the chicken house made Delia feel sick. They wouldn't hesitate to kill the preacher and both women. Then they'd find Elizabeth and Jackson. No time to whimper about a pained shoulder.

Delia thanked Providence that no enterprising farmer had yet scythed the grass and hauled it away for his barn animals.

After what seemed hours, Delia stood and stretched again. She let out a breath of disappointment. Only halfway across the field and already exhausted, she wished she'd never come up with this goldarned stupid idea.

She was lined up directly behind the cookhouse, which had no window at the back. Inching slowly to the right, more minutes wasted, brought the open door of Doc's office into view. Beyond, the front window was open. No one lurked in the doorway. No one sat on the bench outside the door. The window into the cabin's bedroom was shuttered.

What should I do?

A whole list of questions raced through Delia's mind, none to be answered until she got to the cabin. She moved through the grass toward the cookhouse, going as fast as she dared. No one shouted an alarm. No one shot at her.

The absence of sound from the kitchen and the cabin worried Delia most. She didn't know what Mary and Annie had done after she'd left Doc's office, nor where the children were, not even a clue if the preacher stayed or went to town. A wrong move and she could get herself or any of the others killed. Worst of all, she had no idea if only one man remained at Doc's place or if all four outlaws lurked nearby.

The chicken house was only a few feet away. Delia crept along the cookhouse wall, then crossed the dirt yard by the garden and looked inside. The hens sat on their nests, the dead outlaw on the straw at the back of the coop. Annie and Mary had done what was asked of them, but no more. Delia considered going inside to hide the body with scooped-up straw and chicken manure, but decided she had no time to spare.

From the chicken house, Delia crept to the cabin where Doc lived and slept. The windows in the sleeping alcove remained shuttered. No one was on the road between the junction and the cabin. Two horses had been hitched to the rail in front of the saloon. Delia peeked around the corner toward the front of Doc's office. Two more horses at that rail. The front door of the office was still closed. The smashed shutters hung from their hinges.

She leaned against the alcove wall to think. Routing out a couple of innocent men waiting for Doc would be more than embarrassing, especially if someone got shot. The horses looked like any other horses, the trappings like most others she'd seen over the years. She couldn't swear they belonged to the Biedlers, but who else would bust the window shutters loose like that? It had to be them.

Dang. Why doesn't somebody make a noise? Talk? Cough?

That open front window invited her to come closer and look inside. Hardly daring to breathe, terrified one of the horses would raise a ruckus, she inched along the front of the office, still hauling a rifle in each hand. She leaned one of the weapons against the wall next to the front door so she could ready the other to fire. A quick glance into the office showed the door into the bedroom closed, but the door that led to the cookhouse and main cabin open. Another quick look through to the cookhouse revealed the fire lit in the fireplace and two men seated on benches at the table, only visible as silhouettes against the flames. One man's head rested on his hands as though taking a nap. The other slumped forward, moving his hand from table to mouth. She did not see Mary, Annie, the preacher, or the children.

Delia slipped over the window frame and quickly passed from the cookhouse line of sight. Someone had to be in the bedroom with the door closed and the windows shuttered, but it might be a very nervous Mary or Annie with a rifle. Delia pressed her ear against the door. No sound.

If she knocked or called out before opening the door, the men might hear. If she opened the door even a crack without warning, anything could happen. One of the young'uns might scream. Mary might fire the long gun. Annie might start talking to herself.

Delia had to send a silent message into the room. She lifted one of Mary's Bible-quoting, cross-stitch samplers from the wall, removed it from its hand-carved frame, and slid the fabric under the door. It was no accident she'd chosen the one that said: "So do not fear, for I am with you."

In seconds, the door opened a crack. Annie Gray peeked through, saw Delia, and let her in. Delia put her finger across her lips and shushed the older woman, who appeared ready to speak. She then used her hands to ask Annie about the children by measuring their approximate height against her own hip. Annie pointed to the bed.

Now what? Delia thought. She couldn't send the three of them out the bedroom window. If one of the men came out of the cookhouse at the wrong time, they'd be only a few feet away from each other. Trying to get Annie and the children out the front of Doc's office would be equally risky. They would pass in front of the open window. Anyone who glanced that direction could spot the runners from the cookhouse. With two adults and two children trying to sneak away, one of the men could easily catch movement out of the corner of his eye.

Where is Mary? Maybe the cookhouse. Perhaps Mary fed the men to keep them away from their dead brother as well as Annie and the children. No doubt she was also holding her breath as she waited for the men to leave.

Delia couldn't count on help from the townsfolk, especially those who'd chosen to barricade themselves in her brother's stable.

She couldn't count on Doc. He wouldn't be able to get on his horse by himself. The preacher? Who knew where he might be?

She had to figure this thing out on her own.

"I have an idea," Annie said aloud. Before Delia could stop her, Annie propped her musket against the wall, strode out of the bedroom, and disappeared around the corner. The next thing Delia knew, Annie was babbling loudly about no-account doctors who never gave her the medicine she needed, Mary who spent more time hobnobbing with stray men than she did school teaching, and the little girl whose parents let her play all alone in the woods by the river where she could fall in and drown. Speaking even faster, Annie rambled about shooting noises from the town and her mule that got scared and run off.

Annie's voice faded toward the cookhouse.

"What are you doing here?" Mary yelled. Then softer, "She's gone dotty. Don't hurt her. She doesn't mean any harm."

Delia assumed those words were directed at the men.

Mary's voice again: "These aren't stray men, Miss Gray. They're waiting to see Doc."

"They won't see him today," Annie cackled. "He's gone over to Decatur."

"Oh, my!" Mary said. Then in a quieter voice, she added, "I'll have to take her home and stay with her for a while. When she gets this far from her house, she always gets lost and confused. I don't know what we're going to do with her."

A rustling came from under the bed. Jackson lifted a corner of the quilt. He looked scared, his eyes wide and his lips trembling. Delia shushed him and motioned him to get back.

More voices came from the cookhouse, so she quickly closed the door between the bedroom and Doc's office.

Mary talked to Annie as if speaking to a child. Delia heard a fierce whispering from Mary, then Annie raised her voice and cried, "So do not fear, for she is with them." The next few sounds were easy to identify. Light footsteps crossed the room toward the front door. The bar slid across the door frame. The door creaked open. Heavier footsteps with the jangle of spurs. The creaking of leather as men mounted their rides. The clopping of horses' hooves on the dried dirt road. Sounds faded.

Delia checked the office, then ran to the front door which stood ajar. Both horses were gone. Delia leaned out the door and looked left. The two men on horseback rode toward the saloon and junction onto the main street. To the right, Mary and Annie Gray ambled toward Annie's farm.

With a sigh of relief, Delia returned to the bedroom and raised the quilt, calling the young'uns out.

As soon as the men disappeared from her sight, Delia intended to take the children into the woods, get Doc on his horse, and get to Annie's farm without the Biedlers spotting them. She'd have Jackson, the mare, and the Palouse all in one place. They could hightail it out of Sangamon before any of the Biedlers knew what happened.

First, she had to find the new Colt that had been placed on Doc's worktable. No way she'd leave that gun behind, even though she now had enough rifles to fight off the gang by herself.

The children watched as Delia searched every nook and cranny in the doctor's office, so engrossed she did not notice Elizabeth and Jackson go outside. A few minutes later, when she triumphantly recovered her Colt from under the mattress on the tall bed, she turned to the children. Shocked to see an empty room, Delia quickly checked outside the front, the bedroom, and finally ran to the cookhouse. There she found the

Jackson stirring a pot of chicken and dumplings while Elizabeth stood next to him, holding a tin plate.

"Hurry," Delia said as she poured water on the fire in the fireplace. "We're going into the woods to get Doc."

"I should go home now," Elizabeth said. "I'm very hungry."

"I'm hungry, too," Jackson said.

"We have no time to eat right now. And Elizabeth, I can't let you go home until those men are gone. After we get Doc, we're going to Miss Gray's farm."

"Is Miss Gray crazy?" Jackson asked.

"Yes," Delia said, "crazy like a fox."

Chapter Thirty-Six: Delia's Plan

Gathering everything they needed took a few more minutes. One of the muslin sheets from the bedroom worked as a pack to drag the rifles across the field. The children carried lighter loads, mostly food they'd gathered from Doc's cookhouse. The jerky, hard biscuits, and a jar of honey would have to do for now.

Jackson pointed toward the chicken house. "I could look for eggs."

"No! You stay out of that chicken house," Delia said. She ran to the front window, stuck her head out to check in both directions. She could no longer see Mary and Annie, and the two men on horseback had disappeared. Leaning a little farther out the window, Delia counted the horses in front of the saloon. Only two. Were the others tied where she couldn't see them, or had the men circled around to the river road or gone to search for the missing outlaw in the woods?

It didn't matter. She couldn't wait any longer. They needed to get Doc and head for the farm. She wanted to send the children along the road to Annie's alone, but felt she couldn't trust Elizabeth to follow instructions. The girl wouldn't mind her own father. She'd likely disobey Delia, too. Delia had to keep the children at her side. And they needed to leave immediately. She grabbed her saddlebags and tossed them onto the sheet with the guns, then tied the opposite corners of the sheet together to make a secure bundle.

"We're going now. Move as fast as you can, straight across that field. Watch your feet and don't trip. No talking. If you must tell me something, whisper. Don't yell." Delia led the way, frequently checking on the children, scanning in all directions for signs of life. They made it to the edge of the woods without mishap, although Delia had to slow for the children as they struggled with their makeshift baggage.

Another few minutes and they reached Doc's side. As Delia and the children broke through the brush, they found him wide awake, sitting up with the rifle pointed in their direction. Doc exhaled loudly as though he'd been holding his breath. He lowered the gun to the ground. "Is Mary okay?" he asked.

"She's fine." Delia gave Doc a quick report, then went to retrieve the horses. The mare raised her head and blew an exasperated sound as though tired of waiting. Delia flipped the reins of the outlaw's horse around a low branch and led the sorrel mare to Doc's side.

"Can you climb into the saddle, Doc?"

"I don't have much choice, do I?" Doc clenched his jaw as he struggled to his feet.

"I can help," Jackson whispered.

"You keep your eye on Elizabeth," Delia said. "Make sure she stays safe. I'll help Doc."

Sweat broke out on Doc's forehead and he grunted as he stepped onto a flat rock, stuck his left leg in the stirrup, and tried to lift his right leg over the horse. His pain was obvious to Delia, but also his determination. She put her hand under Doc's right calf and eased the leg across the saddle. When he finally sat upright, he took the rifle and grabbed the reins. "I'm ready. Let's get to the farm before anything else happens."

Staying in the cover of trees, Delia led the way along the narrow trail, again checking in every direction for signs of the outlaws. There would be hell to pay when the remaining Biedlers found the dead man in Doc's chicken house. Delia wanted Doc, Mary, and the children at Annie's farm, barricaded inside her barn with the horses before that happened. They dared not stay too long in Annie's cabin tending to Doc's leg because of the Palouse and the sorrel. Any one of the outlaws would recognize the horses and guess Delia hid nearby. They would feel no guilt about killing every single person in their way.

But Doc and the rest of the group didn't deserve to die. Perhaps they would be safe if Delia, the horses — and the young'un, too — up and disappeared.

Delia shook off her concerns. Doc and the children weren't out of danger yet. No sense getting ahead of herself. She retied the knot on the sheet and hoisted the pack onto the horse behind Doc, hoping the way she had it balanced would keep the pack in place. For a moment, she considered the outlaw's horse, debating whether to leave it in the woods untethered or still fastened to the branch. Untethered, it might follow the mare, an unnecessary risk. She turned away.

At the river, she motioned Doc to keep the horse and children under cover while she scouted ahead. In minutes, she returned to lead them along the water's edge, past where the road turned north toward the junction. From this distance, Delia could not see the front of the saloon. She studied the front of Doc's office. No one seemed to be around. For midday, it was eerily quiet. She guessed most of the townsfolk still hid inside the stable. *Not a sturdy backbone in the lot.*

Urging the children to run straight to Miss Gray's cabin, Delia walked alongside the mare to make sure Doc didn't fall off. Once again, she lifted his injured leg across the saddle so he could slide to the ground at the cabin door.

After hurrying the children inside, Mary rushed out to help Doc hobble through the door. "Thank goodness, you made it."

Doc groaned when he stepped on a pebble.

"Easy," Delia said. "We'll take it slow." She tried to sound calm, but fear of taking too long turned her body into a mass of jangling nerves. Once they'd moved Doc inside and settled him on Annie's bed, Delia rushed to retrieve the guns and her saddlebags and lug them into the cabin.

Finally, Delia led the mare to the barn where she placed her in the stall next to the Palouse. The mule and goat grazed in the yard. Neither animal seemed alarmed by the strangers and their bustling about the cabin and barn. Delia left the barn door ajar for Annie's critters, then joined the others in the house.

Doc had stretched out on a narrow bed in the front room. Mary pulled his pants leg open at the tear.

"The break looks clean," Mary said. "No sign of protruding bone."

Delia looked over Mary's shoulder and frowned at the bruises already forming from knee to ankle. No doubt the leg had suffered even more when Colin dragged Doc from the woods to the stable, not to mention getting on and off horseback. At least the skin wasn't broken.

Annie heated water and rummaged through her supplies.

"Annie says she has morphine," Mary whispered with a warning nod toward Jackson and Elizabeth. "And whiskey."

"I could use a little of that whiskey myself," Delia said.

Mary's mouth turned down and she sighed. "I gave my whole bottle of whiskey to those two outlaws. I thought if they got drunker than they already were, they'd pass out in the cookhouse, and I could get Annie and the children away."

"They might be sleeping it off at the

saloon."

Doc raised his head off the bed. "*Your* bottle of whiskey?"

"The cooking whiskey," Mary said.

He laid his head on the pillow. "I didn't know you had a taste for strong drink. Do you sample my laudanum as well?"

Mary jerked the torn pant leg aside and poked at the knee.

"Ow, Mary, that hurt!"

"Sorry."

She wasn't. Delia was sure of that. The last thing they needed was the kind and gentle Doc turning cranky and bossy when they most needed his help.

Annie handed Mary a jar. "Brandy from my own apples," Annie said.

Mary took a sip, then offered it to Delia. After a healthy swallow, Delia gave the jar to Mary. She tasted the drink again while Doc struggled to give her access to his leg to replace the splint. Mary set the brandy down without offering it to Doc.

Doc eyed the jar. "Might I remind you who the patient is here?" he said.

"Might I remind you of your manners?" Mary replied. She picked up the jar and helped him push his head and shoulders up enough to swallow the drink, then let him lie down on his own as she returned the

314

brandy jar to the table.

Annie brought a hot, poultice-soaked bandage to wrap around Doc's leg, followed by dry lengths of cloth to keep it all in place with the splints.

"That stinks," Doc said.

"It sure does stink," Jackson said as he wandered close to Doc's side.

"Lessens the bruising and eases the pain," Annie replied. She waved Jackson away. "Now go on back there with Elizabeth. There might be a piece of cake on the sideboard."

"Cold would be better to take down the swelling," Doc said.

Annie put her hands on her hips and glared at the doctor, clearly tired of his bad humor. "Where do you think I'd find a cold poultice on a warm day, Doctor Hemmer?"

Delia was seeing a different side of Doc and his ability to handle their precarious situation. When he was healthy and doing his doctoring, he gave off an air of self-confidence and reassurance. This sudden change was unexpected, especially after his stalwart courage escaping from the main road in Sangamon.

Doesn't matter, Delia thought. She didn't plan to stick around and figure out any of them.

"Delia," Doc said. "You have a lot of explaining to do."

"Me?"

"You said that gang came here looking for you. If you've brought trouble to this town and to my house, we deserve to know why."

Delia shook her head at her mistake. Now she had one more problem. How much should she tell Doc, Mary, and Annie about her life and the troubles she brought with her to Sangamon?

She looked around for the children and found them sitting on the floor at the back of the cabin, heads bent over a picture in Annie Gray's Bible. When she returned to Doc's bedside, Delia had made up her mind.

Chapter Thirty-Seven: A Confession

"It's a mighty long story, Doc. I ought to take Jackson and the horses and head south before those men get here. Once they're sure I'm not in Sangamon, they might go away."

"With that dead man in Doc's chicken house?" said Mary. "We're not any safer than you are."

"What dead man?" Doc yelled as he swung his legs to the side of the bed and tried to sit up. He yelped and turned pale but succeeded in getting upright. Sweat beaded on his forehead and his skin turned another shade of pale.

"Miss Gray, didn't you say you had morphine?" Mary asked.

"I don't want morphine," Doc said. Then he leaned to see around Mary. "Miss Gray, where did you get morphine?"

Annie ignored him as she bustled about her fireplace, poking up the fire.

Clearly exasperated, Doc returned his attention to Delia, who had started edging toward the front door.

"First tell me about the dead man in my chicken house," Doc said. "Mary, what do you know about this?"

"Ernest Hemmer, you do not talk to me in that tone of voice," Mary said. "I don't know what's gotten into you today."

"I'm sorry. Would you *please* tell me what happened, so I know why there's a body on my property?"

"I will tell you," Annie said. Wiping her hands on her skirt, Annie planted herself in front of the doctor. She let the story unfold slowly and dramatically, describing Elizabeth's terror and the outlaw on horseback who had almost caught up to the girl when the three women intervened. "I shot him," Annie said. "When Delia left to see if you were dead or alive and bring you back, the preacher helped Mary and me hide the outlaw's body. We intended to save the children and ourselves."

"But two of them came to the house," Doc said. "What if they're searching the woods? That other horse you left tied to the tree. Did it belong to the dead man?"

"Yes," Delia said. "I was surprised you didn't ask why I left it there."

318

Doc waved the comment away. "I had my mind on other things."

Mary picked up the story at that point and described what had happened in the cookhouse. "Then Delia returned and told us you were safe."

Annie continued from there, explaining why she and Mary had ended up on the farm, while Delia returned to the woods with the children.

During the time Annie told the story, Delia had checked outside a dozen times, peering through the windows or the door long enough to survey the countryside.

"Still too quiet out there," she said. "It's worrisome."

"Your turn, Delia," Doc said. "It's time to tell us why those men are looking for you."

Delia wasn't eager to leave her lookout post. She was even less interested in talking about her past while their lives were in danger. She *could* take Jackson now and leave. Then she'd never have to tell her story to these people. But she owed them for saving her life and for taking care of the young'un despite their fears. And Annie Gray. That woman had come through like a guardian angel, even though she'd clearly expressed her wish to see Delia and the child leave Sangamon as soon as possible.

Mary was right about the body in the chicken house, too. Once the Biedlers found their brother's body, they'd kill everyone in town.

Perhaps she did owe Doc, Mary, and Annie an explanation.

"Annie, you need to keep watch," Delia said. Annie walked to the window and leaned against the wall so she could see outside while listening to the others talk.

Delia dragged a rocking chair closer and sat. She clasped her hands in her lap and looked Doc in the eye. "You aren't going to like this," she said.

To Mary and Annie, Delia added, "You lived in Sangamon at the time of the Pritchard fire, when I ran away. Do you know what happened?"

"I remember the fire," Mary said, "but that's all. I didn't leave my cabin often and rarely talked to the townsfolk except for Miss Gray."

"I heard many stories about the fire and how your parents died," Annie said. "I didn't know what to believe. You were such a lovely child. I couldn't believe you'd done anything wrong. But Jeremiah told me you murdered your mother and father, then set the fire to destroy their bodies."

"Jeremiah knew only what my brother told

him. He made up the rest of that story on his own," Delia said. "I didn't tell Colin everything. I'm not going to tell you everything, either. But I want you to know I did not kill my mother. My father did that. He'd beaten her for years, and this final time he strangled her before she even got out of bed."

"Then you killed your father and set the cabin on fire," Doc said. He stared at Delia with a look that seemed to combine horror and compassion.

As she continued, Delia wondered which of Doc's emotions would win out. "After I left Sangamon, I rode south along the river road, then crossed at the bridge and kept going. Farm folks gave me food and water, and some let me sleep in a barn or shed. I did my best to hide, thinking Jeremiah would set the law on me. I didn't light in one place for long until I crossed the Ohio River. I worked on farms, helped clean houses, and finally got a good job as a washerwoman in a house where women . . . which is neither here nor there. A couple of years later, the town closed that bawdy house and I was on my own again. I still had my pa's horse, so I went exploring. After a time, I found the gang on the Cave-in-Rock side of the river and the pirates across the water at Ford's Ferry."

Shaking her head as though she could hardly believe her own story, Delia looked at Annie and Mary. Both gazed back with an interest that seemed more shocked than sympathetic.

"Preying on the riverboats proved an easy way for those men to get rich, but they needed women to do the hunting and cooking and help with the stealing. The men left me alone after I showed my hunting knife and acted a little crazy, but they let me stay on because I made a good thief and didn't mind robbing rich folks.

"Until the Biedler gang caught me, I didn't understand how dangerous a life I chose. They were even more violent than the other gangs. They shot folks for no reason, even tortured some. The Biedlers had such a bad reputation they caught the attention of federal lawmen after the marshals thought they'd already chased all the rats out of the cave. With me riding alongside the Biedler brothers, my name and description got bandied about and at least one bounty placed on my head. Once, I even saw a wanted poster with my face front and center."

Mary gasped and placed her hand over her mouth. "A bounty? Dead or alive?"

"I'm sure dead would be fine with the law and the Biedlers."

"Oh, my," Mary whispered.

Delia cleared her throat. "Hiram Biedler, the old man, was caught and hanged from a tree by a posse of men sick of the gang's raids and killings. After that, I kept seeing myself hanging from a tree. Nightmares kept me awake. I didn't want to die that way. The rest of the Biedler gang escaped from the posse and turned to robbing stagecoaches and wagon trains. They stirred up trouble all over the state of Illinois, and I rode with them because they said they'd kill me if I ran. I kept them in line by sharpening my hunting knife where they could see. They let me be, like a dog they'd trained to fetch but would go for its owner's throat if threatened. They used me as a shill to cheat gamblers. I lured innocent folks into traps. I was a tool, another weapon. I'd almost forgotten what it was like to be a person separate from the gang.

"But the fear of getting hanged from a big old tree grew bigger than the fear of being alone. Jack Biedler had taken away my father's horse long ago, so I returned the favor and stole that young sorrel mare and a few other things, and I ran for my life.

"I'd almost started to feel safe when I met

a man who saw through the ratty, disheveled mess I'd become to the woman I hid inside."

Delia got up and reached into one side of her saddlebags. She pulled out McCallister's drawing and returned to the rocking chair. Placing the paper in her lap, she unfolded it, smoothing the creases. The picture of the wild and uncivilized Delia forced her to remember the beautiful woman McCallister had drawn earlier. She recalled the thoughtless thing she'd done, tossing that picture into the flames as though she could never make that Delia real again. And now, she lived among normal people, her body and mind cleansed of the past. *Almost* cleansed of the past. She still had the rest of the Biedler gang to worry about.

Annie walked across the room to look over Delia's shoulder, studied the drawing for a moment, then returned to the window to keep watch.

Mary placed a hand on Delia's shoulder. "Who drew that picture?"

"And what does it have to do with anything?" Doc said.

Delia looked up at Doc for a moment, wondering how this annoying fellow had replaced the patient doctor she'd met when she first arrived in Sangamon.

"Go on," Mary urged.

"I had finally run away from the Biedlers and started to feel safe. After a month or so, when I tried to figure out where to go and what to do next, I camped out for a couple of days to catch up on my eating and sleeping. By then, I was a mess. My clothes were torn, I was dirty, my hair tangled worse than a rat's nest. I'd shot a rabbit and had it roasting over a fire when this man rode up on the Palouse. He stayed long enough to eat and rest, draw his pictures, and then he left in the night. When I woke up, I found this picture. It was like him telling me I could be a better person, that this scruffy outcast could change. I could be a good woman. That's when I decided to come to Sangamon, talk to Colin, see if I could set things straight with him and be a family again."

Delia carefully refolded the drawing and slid it into the pocket of her pants. "I guess you can see I have a ways to go. And as far as Colin being family to me, I don't think that's going to happen."

Doc looked at Delia expectantly, as though waiting to hear more. "This story isn't over yet, is it? That man rode off on the Palouse, the very horse now hidden in Miss Gray's barn. And you still haven't told us how you came to be riding with Jackson."

"You're right, Doc," Delia said. "There's a lot more story to be told."

"Men on horses are coming this way," Annie said. She opened the door and walked outside, closing the door behind her.

Delia jumped up in alarm. "She shouldn't be out there alone."

"Nothing to be done about it now," Doc said. "Mary, give me one of those rifles. Elizabeth, take Jackson to the pantry and be quiet."

Delia picked up another long gun and took up a position by the window, hoping to hear any exchange between the men and Annie Gray. Mary came to her side with another rifle. An occasional pop from the fireplace interrupted the silence inside the cabin. Outside, leather squeaked, hooves thudded against the packed dirt road, spurs jangled when at least one of the men dismounted. Annie's mule brayed from close by. Mary jumped at the sound and slapped her hand over her mouth.

Annie's voice sounded strong and clear to those inside. "Don't be getting off your horse here, young man. I got no time for palavering. My cow needs milking and eggs need gathering and the weeds in my garden need pulling. I've work to do."

"Hold on," a man's voice said. "I want to know if you've seen a woman on a Palouse horse come into this town or anywhere hereabouts."

"What's a Palouse?" Annie said. Her next words were unintelligible to those inside the cabin. It sounded like nonsense words mumbled and jumbled. The sounds grew fainter as though she walked away while talking.

"That other woman, the one that did the cooking, said this one was going dotty," another man's voice said. "Should I shoot her?"

"Nah. Leave her be. Let's go to the doctor's office and see if the other one is there. She had food and whiskey."

More jangling of spurs, creaking leather, and horse-walking sounds moved away from the cabin. Delia leaned far enough toward the window to see the four men and their horses ride toward Doc's office.

They're going to find the body. We don't have much time.

CHAPTER THIRTY-EIGHT: IN ANNIE'S BARN

"We'll be safer in the barn," Delia said. "When these men return, they'll find no sign Annie had visitors. I don't think they'll follow her. They'll think she's possessed."

"I'll take one of the long guns and the children first," Mary said. "Then I'll help you with Doc."

She opened the door and made sure no one lurked on the road. "Elizabeth! Jackson! Run to the barn as fast as you can. Let's go!" Mary returned in minutes. "Annie brought the mule and cow inside, checked on the goat, and barricaded the back door. She told the children to sit on a pile of straw by the stalls and make little straw dolls. And to be quiet."

Delia glanced around the front room of Annie's cabin to make sure they'd left nothing behind. She tucked the jar of brandy and a handful of cloth remnants for clean bandages into her saddlebags, then replaced the lid on the poultice jar and set it on the sideboard. Mary and Delia got on each side of Doc. With his arms across their shoulders, he hopped with his weight on his good leg and dragged the bad. They stopped only long enough for Delia to grab the saddle-bags with her free hand and pull the front door closed.

Their progress was slow and painful. By the time the three reached the barn, Doc's face had gone white again and sweat ran down his back and chest, staining his shirt with wet stripes. They settled him next to the children on the pile of straw and gave him one of the long guns.

Annie placed a box of shot and gunpowder in his lap. "I hope you won't need this," she said.

Doc gripped the rifle in both hands.

The front of the barn where the three women waited kept them separated from Doc's position. Delia ran back to the cabin for the rest of the rifles, then tried to look too busy to answer more questions. She checked the load on each long gun and the revolver, examined the two front barn windows to make sure the shutters were secure, then cracked the barn door open enough to see the road in both directions.

Long minutes passed. Birds chirped. A

hawk screamed. No one came. One of the horses whinnied, then quieted. Every sound, even the occasional rustling from the straw pile, grated on Delia's nerves.

Still no one came.

"They could be cleaning out the chicken and dumplings and finishing off the whiskey," Mary said. "After they take everything they want, maybe they'll go to the saloon. With luck, they might get sick. That chicken wasn't cooked all the way."

"Maybe," Delia said as she thought how close the children had come to eating from that very pot.

"Or maybe not," Annie added. "How bad do they want to find you, Delia?"

"They want to kill me, and they want the horses."

"How'd you get that Palouse?" Annie asked. "You said it belonged to the feller that drew that picture. Did you steal it from him?"

"Not from him," Delia said. She leaned against the door after looking outside again. "I came across that artist fellow again a day or so later. He was sprawled on the road. Dead. He'd been shot in the back and left there to rot in the sun. I looked around for his pack and his drawing goods but could find nothing. Even his boots were gone.

"I heard noises from the woods and snuck in there to see what I'd find. The Palouse nickered and shied away, his sides scratched and bleeding from brambles. He had burrs in his tail and mane. I guess he'd run off before the killers could catch him because the saddlebags were still in place. He was skittish, but he let me catch hold of the reins and mount. No one else came around, so I figured the horse was better off with me than left on the road. I got the mare to follow and kept on going."

"You didn't bury the body?" Annie asked.

"I had nothing to dig a hole with. I pulled him off to the side of the road and let him be."

Annie didn't say anything for a moment, then added, "You prayed over him, I reckon."

Delia didn't answer. Her attention had abruptly been hijacked by the sounds of gunfire. "Did you hear that? Came from the main road!"

Annie pushed Delia aside and slipped out the door. A few steps toward the road. A few more. Then Annie stood still, her hands on her hips, staring toward the junction. When she came inside, she went straight for her musket. "Can't see nothing or nobody. No horses in front of Doc's office or the saloon." She propped the gun against the wall by the door.

More gunshots echoed. Then silence.

The eerie quiet floated across the field and down the road, settling over Annie Gray's barn like a fog.

Delia watched through the slim crack at the door she'd propped open with her foot. Were the townsfolk in the stable shooting at the outlaws or had the Biedler gang launched an attack? She wished Colin and the others well.

A rustle of straw, followed by quick footsteps, warned Delia one of the children was on the move. Elizabeth scurried toward the door. "I want to go home," Elizabeth said. "I don't like it here. I'm scared."

Mary hurried toward Elizabeth and grabbed her hand. "It's not safe yet. Those men are dangerous. You saw what happened to Doc. And that man who chased after you."

"I know what happened on the road. Miss Gray killed that man dead." Elizabeth struggled to pull her hand free. Mary held on until Elizabeth let out a scream loud enough to scare the skittish horses. They stomped and whinnied. Elizabeth jerked hard and freed herself from Mary's grip. Mary and Annie, anticipating Elizabeth would run for the front barn door where Delia already waited, ran in that direction to head off the child.

Instead, Elizabeth turned and dashed to the back door of the barn. She slid the bar free of its frame, pushed the door open, and ran outside.

"Damnation," Delia said. "Get that girl in here."

The next thing she knew, Jackson jumped to his feet. "I'll get her," he said. He ran out the door before anyone could stop him.

"I'll go," said Annie.

Mary hustled toward the back of the barn, waving Annie away. "The girl is afraid of you. I'll take care of this."

"Here they come!" Delia yelled. "All four of them. Run, Mary, catch the children and hide by the river."

Mary picked up a rifle and ran, stuffing one of the bags of shot in her pocket. Annie closed the door and started to slide the bar across.

"Don't," shouted Doc. He began to scoot across the floor, dragging his bad leg and still holding his rifle. "I'll watch this door. Mary will need to get inside fast if she returns with the children."

Annie exchanged a look with Delia and strode to the front of the barn. "I should be out there acting like everything is fine," Annie said. "I'll go pull weeds in the garden. Let the mule out so he doesn't raise a ruckus. He likes to follow me around."

Delia stepped aside and let Annie and the mule leave.

Annie pushed the barn door all the way closed, whispering, "Bar the door."

Delia did as Annie said, then went to the front window and undid the latch on the shutters so they could be opened a crack. From that vantage point, she watched Annie drag a hoe from the wooden box by the garden. With her back turned toward the road, the mule grazing a few feet away, Annie chopped at weeds, broke dirt clods into pieces, even leaned over and pulled up a few carrots and beets and piled them on the dry grass that served as Annie's yard. When she could no longer ignore the sounds of horses approaching, she straightened, stretched, and leaned on her hoe to watch the men.

They stopped on the road in front of Annie, lined up like a mounted firing squad. One of the men slumped in his saddle, one hand holding onto the pommel, the other against his stomach. If he'd been shot, they'd be looking for Doc.

"What can I do for you gentlemen?" Annie asked. "I have fresh vegetables from the garden, water in the rain barrel —"

"I thought you was crazy!" one of the men said. Two of the others laughed.

The man who appeared to be injured bent over a little more. "What happened to the lady who brought you home? The one from the doctor's office."

"She went back to Doc's office," Annie said. "I reckon Doc is there by now."

The men watched Annie for a moment as though to read her thoughts. "Nah, there weren't nobody there. Say, didn't someone tell us that doctor went to Decatur?" one asked.

"I thought the doctor fell down the steps at the store," said another.

"Oh, bother. I'm an old woman. Can't keep up with everybody. If you don't want anything else, I'll get back to my garden." Annie started up a conversation with the mule and the weeds, mumbling mostly but then tossing in a cuss word when the old hoe couldn't cut through the woody stalk of a nettle. She tried to pull it out by hand, yelped as the tiny thorns bit through her callused fingers, and let out a few more cuss words.

Delia shook her head at Annie's ability to change her behavior from minute to minute.

From what she'd been told about the woman by Doc and Mary, Annie was once a Bible-quoting paragon of virtue, judge and jury to the town. If true, Delia wondered where Annie had learned all these cuss words. And how to act like a crazy person, for that matter.

Could be she really is crazy. If so, Annie could unintentionally reveal who she hid in her barn. A cold chill washed over Delia's shoulders as she imagined such a conversation.

Jack and his brothers talked among themselves for a moment, then turned their horses toward the doctor's office. Annie shifted her position and watched the men as they rode away.

She dropped the hoe and hurried to the barn, the mule following close behind. Delia quickly slid the bar aside and cracked open the door. The mule followed Annie inside. "They've stopped at Doc's office," Annie said. "They had to help one get off his horse. If they don't find Doc or Mary right away, they're going to search all over."

"That doesn't mean they'll come here," Doc said. "They might figure we're holed up with the rest of the town in the stable."

"We need to know what happened in the town with all that gunfire," Annie said. "I'll put on my bonnet, take the mule and wagon, say I'm going to the general store."

"That's a bad idea, Annie," Doc said. "That leaves us two here alone, and Mary out in the open with Elizabeth and Jackson. Once the outlaws figure out one of us had something to do with that dead man in the chicken house, they're going to hunt us down like animals. If we're not together, they can pick us off, one at a time."

Annie leaned against the wall. She looked at Doc for a minute, then at Delia, apparently trying to think through her plan. Her next words came out in a jumble of sounds, none of which made any sense.

CHAPTER THIRTY-NINE: WAITING IN FEAR

Delia exchanged a glance with Doc, then took a long look out the front barn door. The four horses stood at the rail in front of the doctor's office, their tails swishing at flies. Nothing else moved on the road or in the tallgrass behind Doc's place. Although she had no view of the open space between Doc's two cabins and the cookhouse, she could see the garden and the chicken house. Two of the hens flapped their wings and squawked as one of the Biedler brothers headed toward the chicken house door. He leaned inside, jerked back, then ran in the direction of the cookhouse.

"They found the body," Delia said. She glanced at Doc to make sure he heard.

"We knew that was coming sooner or later. They weren't going to leave town until they found him."

A noise at the rear of the barn caught their attention.

"It's me. Open up." Mary's voice. Doc used one hand to open the door wide enough for her to get inside. She had both children in tow and pushed them in ahead of her. The preacher, John Claymore, rushed in last.

Delia wished the children had hidden somewhere far from the barn. On the other hand, she was overjoyed to see Mary and the preacher. Delia met his gaze, relieved to see him alive, then looked away. Two more to fire guns when the Biedlers attacked. The battle was inevitable now. Could they survive? Delia thought they could. But she had to keep Annie on the premises, ready to put that musket to good use.

"You can't go to the general store now, Annie. You won't put them off with your strange ways anymore. They'll be searching every inch of Sangamon and all its surroundings for that dead man's horse."

John stepped closer to Delia. "I found it in the woods, its reins tied to a branch. I led it away from town and set it loose on the other side of the river. Dropped the saddle and trappings in the bushes. They won't find it anytime soon."

"That's why you stayed away so long? I didn't know what happened."

"I knew you'd gone after Doc, so I ran

across the field to the woods, hoping I could help. I must have passed close by without seeing or hearing you. When I reached the edge of town, I returned to Doc's place by a different path. That's when I found the horse. I may have made the situation worse if they're going to rip the town apart looking for it."

Delia looked at Annie. "That's why you can't leave us. Once they get inside Colin's stable and don't find what they're looking for, they'll come here. We need you."

"I won't quibble with that," Annie said. "If not for me, you'd all be dead by now."

Delia watched through the crack in the front barn door and beckoned Annie closer when Jack and two of his brothers came out of Doc's office, mounted their horses, and rode toward the junction. *What in tarnation?*

"One of the outlaws is still inside Doc's office," she whispered. "The other three are riding the other direction. What are they doing?"

"I told you so. I fooled 'em," Annie said. "Hell's afire, I fooled 'em." Her words sounded like the cackling of an ancient crone, not the educated and pious woman Mary had described a few days ago.

Delia leaned her head against the wall and fought the temptation to groan out loud.

What was the world coming to when the only protection two small children had against an outlaw gang included a doctor who couldn't walk, a preacher who'd be against killing, and three women? And one of those women was crazy enough to suddenly turn her musket on the whole lot of them.

"Annie, why don't you make sure that door is barred. Tell Doc he needs to watch Elizabeth."

Delia mostly feared Elizabeth would start screaming again. The outlaw still inside Doc's office would hear. "Mary, can you talk to the children, make them understand why they need to be quiet?"

"I already scared them witless with notions about those men and their guns. I'll tell them again." Delia watched as Mary shook her finger at Elizabeth. The girl's eyes grew wide, and her cheeks showed a patch of red against her pale skin. Tears welled up in her eyes. Jackson scrunched himself into a corner of the straw pile outside the Palouse's stall. The horse lowered his head over the railing and snuffled at the child's hair. Jackson reached up both hands to touch the Palouse's nose.

Delia turned away. She had her regrets now about keeping the young'un with her and bringing him to Sangamon. She might have saved his life for a time, but she'd brought him into a bad situation and put his life at greater risk. If anything happened to him, it would be her fault.

She'd be taking the blame no matter what happened. She knew when she came to town that the Biedler gang would stay on her trail until they found her and the horse she stole, not to mention the Palouse that had run off after they'd shot McAllister. What a ridiculous idea to come here for help. She'd also put her own brother in danger. The whole town, to be truthful.

At least Doc had given up asking questions about Delia's past. She'd left out a lot of things she didn't want them to know, things she never wanted anyone to know. Aware that she'd masked part of the truth and lied about even more, she still felt no remorse. Her story belonged to her and no one else. If by a miracle, they escaped this mess, she'd have to hightail it out of town fast. For a while, she'd thought Doc would give her a pass. Now she was afraid Doc's judgment, and Mary's, would be harsh. They might even send someone to fetch a marshal. Would the people of Sangamon want to see Delia Pritchard hang for her crimes?

They might.

What if she saddled the Palouse right now and took off? Raced along the river road to the bridge, crossed over, and kept going until the horse couldn't go another step? She'd have to leave Jackson behind. And the mare. Would the Biedlers chase her and leave the Sangamon folks alone?

Oh, damnation. The Biedlers probably wanted to get inside the stable to look for the missing horse, but the townsfolk had barricaded themselves inside. Now the gang would try again. She checked out the front door to see if the fourth outlaw remained at Doc's office. His horse was still there. Was the man left behind to keep watch, or was he injured and waiting for Mary's return?

Or maybe he didn't make it. If that was the case, if two of the brothers had died at the hands of Sangamon townsfolk, Jack Biedler would be furious. His rage would be directed at anyone who crossed his path, even those innocents hiding in the stable.

CHAPTER FORTY: MARY'S FEARS, DELIA'S DOUBTS

Mary warned the children again as Delia had insisted, then slumped to the floor, trying to hide her tears. After all her work to find peace, her life had spun out of control. She felt a touch on her hand. The preacher knelt between her and the others. He held Mary's hand as she wept, the tears staining the bodice of her blue smocked gown. She pulled her hand away, then frantically brushed at the hem of her dress, crusted with dirt and dung from the cow's stall. She had never been so frightened, even when her beloved David had died fighting Indians and left her alone with a baby.

"I did terrible things to survive," she murmured. "You remember me from before. But I never killed anyone."

"You didn't kill that man on the road."

"I would have, though. If Annie had not fired first, I would have done it."

"To protect the children."

"Yes. He was chasing Elizabeth."

"I know. I saw him come out of the saloon and go after her. That's why I left Doc and rushed through the woods alone. If it's any comfort, Mary, I would have shot the outlaw. I have never killed anyone. I'm trained to revere life, not take it. But I have come to know evil, and evil cannot be allowed to thrive."

Mary wiped her tears with the handkerchief she pulled from her sleeve. "You saved Doc."

She looked at Doc, who had settled on a pile of clean straw with his broken leg stretched out and newly splinted. She thanked their good luck the bone did not require setting. A crack, most likely. Still, it would be painful when he needed to move from Annie's barn to his office. She doubted he could use a chamber pot without an army to help him, so an even greater struggle would be the trips from his cabin to the outhouse.

Fancy that. I'm assuming we'll escape this mess and return to our normal lives.

From the other side of the barn, Delia watched the preacher comfort Mary. Earlier, he had sat beside Annie, touching the woman's shoulder. Annie had pushed his kindness aside. She seemed to have no use for a gentle word from any of them. She started to act as though Doc, Mary, the preacher, Delia, and the children were invaders, the enemy. The preacher had pulled Annie's gun from her hands and turned it over to the doctor to hold. Now the old woman sat on her three-legged stool and chatted with the cow. Elizabeth and Jackson watched with eyes wide and mouths hanging open. Delia hoped they wouldn't start giggling.

As she watched at the barn door, footsteps shuffled through the scattered straw. The preacher stopped at her side. "Do you want me to stand watch for a while? You need to rest."

"I'm fine. My shoulder hurts like the devil, but I feel strong."

"Has the doctor taken a look at the wound to make sure it hasn't opened?"

"Mary did that. It looks good."

"There's nothing I can do for you then?"

"Maybe later."

The preacher strolled to the rear of the barn to see to the children.

Delia returned to her vigil, checking the road in both directions. She wanted to talk to the preacher again when the danger had passed. She'd done so many wrong things in her life, committed so many crimes. She'd killed men. And she'd do it again. She hoped the preacher could tell her how to survive such a past without suffering from bad memories for the rest of her life. He could tell her how to make amends. She wasn't expecting salvation or anything silly like that. And if the preacher started talking about God, she might even tell him a thing or two about God not doing his job like he should. Or there not being a God at all.

But how could a man go through all that schooling to learn about preaching and praying if God didn't exist to preach about or pray to? Life was such a mystery. Delia didn't know what to make of it. She figured the preacher didn't know what to make of it, either, but at least she could ask.

CHAPTER FORTY-ONE: WHAT HAPPENED IN SANGAMON THAT DAY?

Delia knew what to do next. "I'm going to Doc's to check on the man they left behind. If he's dead, the gang is down to three able-bodied men. They're most likely going after the folks holed up in the stable. I can surprise them from the rear, take out at least two before they know what happened."

"You're not going alone," said Annie. She picked up her musket from where Doc had laid it aside and joined Delia by the front door.

Mary took a long gun from those propped by the door, looked at Doc, then joined the other two women. "If those men want the Palouse, wouldn't it be best if we took him along? He'd be a good bargaining tool."

I'd also be a good bargaining tool, Delia thought. "Yes, you're right." Delia returned to the Palouse's stall to put on his bridle and reins, then looked for the artist's fancy saddle.

"Doc, where's the saddle?"

"Still at the stable."

When she faced the others, she saw John had also taken a gun and moved toward the door. There was no time to worry about the saddle now.

"Preacher, you've got to stay here. Doc can't protect the children by himself. Not against three men if they get past us. Bar the door after we leave. Jackson, you help keep Elizabeth quiet. Sit there by Doc and don't make any noise."

Jackson didn't answer but moved closer to Elizabeth.

The preacher frowned, apparently disturbed at being left behind while the women took on the job of wiping out the rest of the Biedler gang. He started to speak as though to protest, then shut his mouth without saying a word.

When Delia, Annie, Mary, and the Palouse were outside, Delia heard the bar move into its slot, securing the door against easy entry.

Delia touched Mary on the arm as they began to walk toward the junction. "When we get in front of Doc's, you go check on that man inside and see if he's dead or alive."

Mary trotted over to the window and peered inside. "He's laid out on Doc's table with his hands crossed over his chest. The whole front and side of his shirt looks bloody."

"How are we going to do this?" Annie asked. "We can't walk up the road in plain sight."

"I thought about crossing the field and going through the woods," Delia said. "But if they finish their business before we get there, they'll come this way to gather their dead and might come after you out of pure meanness. We need to stay between the gang and your barn. When we get to the junction, I'll let the Palouse go with a slap on the rear. Jack Biedler will stop whatever he's doing to chase that horse."

Mary's jaw dropped as she glared at Delia. "Jack Biedler? You know these men? I thought —"

"I know them. Leave it be."

"Dear God," Mary said. "Are we going to die this day?" A fresh rain of tears dampened her cheeks. Her hands shook so hard she nearly lost her grip on the gun. Delia reached to steady the muzzle but grabbed it instead when Mary let the weapon drop.

Delia placed a hand firmly on Mary's shoulder and shook the woman gently. "We need you."

"We're not going to die," Annie said. "I'd

feel it in my bones."

"I can't do this," Mary whispered. "Defending myself or the children is one thing, but hunting those men like animals? No, I can't."

"They are animals," Delia said.

Mary shook her head vehemently and shoved Delia's hand off her shoulder. "I'll stay with Doc and Preacher and watch out for the little ones." She took the weapon out of Delia's hand and ran toward the barn. She did not look back as she slipped inside.

"Well," said Annie. "I guess it's up to you and me and the cowardly bastards hiding behind their barred doors and shuttered windows."

Delia glanced at the barn, wondering if she'd made one more mistake, a mistake that might end her life and others this time.

"Don't weaken now, young lady. Let's get on with it." Annie tucked her musket under her arm and marched on toward the junction. They saw no one between the farm and the junction. Delia led the Palouse forward and caught up with Annie. At the sound of another gunshot from the direction of the main street, the Palouse balked and pulled backward on the reins, almost jerking out of Delia's grasp. She stopped and calmed the horse. Annie, whose determined stride hadn't paused at the interruption, seemed not to notice Delia lagging behind. She said nothing when Delia reappeared at her side.

As they drew close to the saloon, no one rounded the corner to come their way. No laughter or loud talk sounded from inside. No clinking glasses or chairs scraped across wood floors. No gunfire. No sounds of creaking leather. No voices.

An eerie silence had fallen again.

The smell of burning wood tickled Delia's nose. A small plume of black smoke rose above the main street. Delia reckoned the location to be at or near the stable. "They're trying to drive the townsfolk out to the street," Delia said. "That stable will go up like kindling wood soaked in lamp fuel."

Delia and Annie broke into a run, Delia quickly outpacing Annie, who wore a long skirt. Dropping the reins of the Palouse, Delia kept going, faster and faster. As she rounded the corner at the junction, she spotted the three outlaws standing in front of the stable, their rifles raised and pointed toward the door. Delia stopped, planted her feet in a wide stance to maintain her balance, aimed the rifle at Jack Biedler, and fired. He dropped to his knees, then fell forward onto the road.

The other two outlaws, the twins George and Thomas, turned and crouched, ready to fire. Delia dropped the long gun to the ground and pulled the Colt from her belt. Before she could shoot, a gun fired from behind her.

George Biedler fired as he toppled to the side. His shot hit the ground, raising a cloud of dirt and dust. Taking aim at Delia again, he hesitated a second too long. Delia raised the Colt with two hands and shot him in the chest. He sprawled on his back, his hand stretched out with the gun still in his grip.

Thomas Biedler had raised his long gun and aimed it at Delia, but his rifle wavered as he shot into the air. He fell and grabbed his leg with one hand, then raised his gun and aimed at Delia with the other. Before he could pull the trigger again, Delia shot him in the shoulder. His weapon dropped to the ground. He grabbed his arm at the elbow, holding it close to his side. He bent his head in surrender as Delia took a step closer.

Delia turned to acknowledge Annie's help, but discovered a flustered Annie struggling with the musket. "Wouldn't fire," she yelled. "Somebody else shot that man." She waved a hand in the vague direction of the saloon.

Delia focused on the saloon first, but then her gaze was drawn to the hat shop. The barrel of a long gun poked through the shop's window.

Delia's Colt hung at her side as she turned to study the downed outlaws. *Do we kill them all? Lock them up and send for the marshal?*

As she remembered the bad things Jack Biedler and his gang had done to so many people, including women and children, she couldn't think of one single reason to let any of them live. They'd killed innocents traveling along the Ohio River on flatboats. Later, as they moved around the state, they'd robbed and killed farmers and stage-coach travelers. Delia moved past the twin who clutched the elbow of his injured arm and shoulder, past the twin sprawled on his back, unconscious if not dead, and approached Jack Biedler. He moaned and tried to turn over but failed.

Still unsure whether to kill them all or lock them up, she looked at Annie for guidance. Annie struggled to reload her musket and paid no attention to Delia.

From the direction of the hat shop, two ladies walked out their front door and approached, rifles ready to fire. Before Delia said a word, Annie aimed her musket and shot the unconscious outlaw in the face. She then approached the outlaw who sat in the road with one arm raised and the other hanging at his side, blood staining the sleeve in a widening patch of red.

"Don't kill me," he cried.

Annie put the barrel of her musket to his head. He tried to jerk away, tried to use his good arm to grab the gun. He missed. She pulled the trigger, but the musket misfired again.

One of the ladies moved closer, nudged Annie out of the way, and placed the barrel of her rifle against the man's ear.

He screamed, "No, no," as he attempted to scoot away. She pulled the trigger. He fell sideways, his head hitting the road with a *thunk*.

Delia looked at Jack Biedler. Was he breathing? Did she care? "It's over, Jack. You're not going to hurt anyone again." She kicked at his side. He groaned. She raised her Colt and shot him in the back of the head.

At that moment, the front doors of the stable flew open and banged against the walls as townsfolk rushed outside, coughing and hacking from the smoke in their lungs. The plume had turned into a cloud that hung over the town. By the time everyone abandoned the stable, some herding horses into the street, flames roared through the hay and straw, burning through stalls and troughs as though they'd been built of paper.

They had no time to form a water brigade from the river to the stable. The building, including the blacksmith shop, was engulfed in flames. The stunned townsfolk backed away and watched the destruction of Colin Pritchard's livelihood.

If there had been a wind that day, the whole of Sangamon's businesses might have burned. But in the absence of even a breeze, the rest of the buildings and nearby cabins would likely be spared.

Jeremiah confronted Delia and planted his hands on his hips. "Where's Elizabeth?"

"She's with Doc, Mary, and the preacher in Miss Gray's barn."

Jeremiah grabbed one of the fully tacked up horses and mounted, taking off for Annie's farm at a gallop. His wife, Sarah, walked away from the dead men, saying nothing to the women who'd saved their lives. Annie started to follow Sarah, then stopped at Delia's side.

"Your horse ran away."

Delia scanned the road that led to the saloon and the junction, but no Palouse. She acknowledged Annie's words, then turned toward her brother, hoping for a chance to offer a comforting word.

Colin Pritchard stared at his lost business, the rubble and debris that littered the ground around the burning building. His shoulders slumped, and sooty tears ran down his cheeks. Delia wanted to put her hand on his shoulder, but she feared he'd push her away.

"I need to get to my place," Annie said. "I'll look for your horse. The preacher can help." She didn't wait for a response, but walked away, her old musket cradled in her arms.

Delia tucked the Colt into her belt, picked up the long gun, and followed Annie. The hat-shop ladies had disappeared without a word, taking their mysteriously newfangled rifles out of sight. Most of the townsfolk continued to watch the fire in silence. Delia suspected no one had even noticed the two ladies and their guns.

The dead lay sprawled where they died, left behind for the townsfolk to bury.

As Delia caught up to Annie, she wondered if the woman was even the slightest bit demented. Annie sure hadn't acted that way when they confronted the outlaws. She'd killed the first outlaw, the one who'd chased Elizabeth, without pause in front of

357

Doc's office. And moments ago, she'd murdered another. Annie Gray was a dangerous woman.

Rounding the corner at the junction, they ran into Jeremiah, now leading the horse with Elizabeth in the saddle, her hands gripping the horn. The girl raised one hand to wave at Delia and Annie.

Jeremiah stopped in front of Delia. "Elizabeth says the Negra boy saved her from harm two different times. She said she'd be dead if not for him."

"He's a good boy," Delia said. "He's suffered big troubles for such a small child, but he has a warm heart and a joyful soul. He tries to do good."

"If you can find someone to take him, he can stay in Sangamon and go to school here. Sarah will make sure he learns enough to get along in the world."

"That's kind of you, Jeremiah," Annie said. "I spoke cruel words when they first came into town. I have reconsidered. I'll make no trouble for the boy if he stays."

"But you have to go, Delia," Jeremiah said. He stared at the road as he talked, apparently unwilling to look Delia in the eye as he gave his pronouncements.

"I agree," Annie said. "There's no place for you here."

Hurt but not surprised, Delia looked at Jeremiah's stony expression and Annie's pursed lips. Thoughts charged through her mind like a flock of barn swallows. She walked around Jeremiah, patted Elizabeth on the knee as she whisked by, and moved on toward Doc's office. She went inside through the front door, which the outlaws had left standing open.

As Mary had reported earlier, one dead outlaw lay on the doctor's table. Billy, the youngest of the brothers, the one who'd been kind at least once in his sorry lifetime, would do no more good deeds. Delia propped her rifle against the wall and dumped the body onto the floor by tipping the thin mattress and rolling him off the table. She gripped him by his boots, dragged him out the door, and left his body by the side of the road.

The body in the chicken house came next. The smell made the air in the small building nearly unbreathable. Still, the hens sat on their nests, seemingly oblivious to the odor. They clucked their disapproval of Delia's presence as she wrestled the dead man's corpse out the door, past the cookhouse and cabins, and around to the road. She dumped him next to the other outlaw and left them for someone else to haul away.

Jeremiah had stopped to watch, never once offering to help. "We'll have a common grave outside the cemetery," he called. "Tell Doc we'll have these bodies gone within the hour."

Annie had kept walking, so she reached the barn ahead of Delia. The door flew open and Mary rushed out.

"We were so afraid. With all the gunfire and your horse running here like he'd been shot at, I thought you'd been killed. What happened? Are they gone?"

"The gang?" Delia said. "All dead. You're safe now." She looked toward the barn, avoiding Mary's gaze, fearful of saying something unkind.

Mary stepped into the barn and came out leading the Palouse with Doc on the stallion's bare back. Jackson and the preacher followed.

"We prepared to escape out the rear door if even one of the outlaws remained alive. What should we do now?"

"Return to Doc's office, I reckon. Let's cross the road here and get to the cookhouse from the field. There are things on the road Jackson doesn't need to see up close."

CHAPTER FORTY-TWO: DELIA ACCEPTS HER FATE

"Jeremiah won't soften his mind about you," Mary said, as she and Delia changed the bedding on Doc's patient bed and helped him lie down. "He and Annie, like most of the townsfolk, are set in their ways. It's a miracle they're willing to let Jackson stay here and go to school. If it's okay with everyone, Jackson can live here with Doc. I'll help out when I can."

"That's very kind of you," Delia said. "What about you, Doc? Is it okay with you that Jackson live in your home?"

"I have no objection," he said. "But could we focus on taking care of my leg? I need both of you helping. We need to adjust these splints, so I can get up with the crutches. Mary, if those outlaws didn't drink all your cooking whiskey, please bring it in here."

"It's all gone, Doc."

"Wouldn't a dose of your laudanum be better?" Delia asked.

"Don't use the stuff," Doc said. "Whiskey's bad enough."

Delia shook her head. She figured whiskey was worse because it was easier to get.

"I'm not sure that bone is aligned right. You and Mary need to set it."

Mary put her hands on her hips and laughed. "Oh, Doc, it's set fine. When we rewrapped your leg, we cut the pant leg open and checked it very carefully."

"I want to see for myself. Unwrap it. If I decide it's not right, you'll have to pull one way and Delia the other."

"Me?" Delia's alarm must have shown clearly on her face, because Doc reached out a hand and patted her on the shoulder.

"You'll be fine. Mary and you together will do the work while I tell you how. You can start now by taking off this contraption you all put together. It served its purpose but it's not good enough."

"You said you thought it would be fine."

"I did. We didn't have a choice. We couldn't take the time to set the bone right then with killers running around shooting people."

Doc raised up on his elbows to watch as Delia removed the splint. They stared at the bump below Doc's knee.

"That looks bad," Delia said.

"Yep." Doc eased back until his head again rested on the pillow. "We got our work cut out for us this time. Only the Lord God knows how messed up this leg might be. At least the bone isn't sticking through the skin, so we don't have to worry about gangrene."

Mary shook her head as she peered closer at the bump. "That's not bone, Doc. If you could get your eyes on the right place, you'd see it's a big bruise with swelling. Look. When I poke it, it's squishy." Mary pressed her finger into the lump, demonstrating the softness of the tissue.

Doc yelped, then put his own fingers on the bump and poked at the injury to confirm Mary's diagnosis. "Perhaps you're right. Are you sure the whiskey is all gone, Mary? I'd still like that drink," he said. "The bump hurts something fierce where you poked at it."

Mary whisked out of the room and returned with the empty bottle.

"They had set their cups aside and passed around the bottle for drinking," Mary said. "It's disgusting. Even if they'd left a drop, it might be contaminated with a foul disease."

"Doc, you'll have to show a little grit," Delia said. "We got to get you patched up before I leave this place for good."

Mary looked up sharply and met Delia's gaze head-on. "You can stay here as long as we need you," Mary said, her expression sad but firm. "A few days at the most."

"I want Doc to look at my shoulder one more time to make sure it's healing okay."

"I can do that," Mary said.

"Look, I can ride the Palouse up to the general store and get that whiskey. No sense in letting Doc suffer. It won't take long."

Mary agreed, asking Delia to check on the townsfolk and see how they were recovering from their horrifying day. "If anyone else needs doctoring, tell them we'll do our best here at the office."

As Delia walked the horse along the main road, she didn't receive any signs of recognition, much less gratitude. No one looked her in the eye or acknowledged her presence. She tied the Palouse's reins to the railing in front of the general store and walked inside, her head held high and her back as straight as a soldier's.

Jeremiah and Sarah stood at the counter, Jeremiah looking huffy and superior with his palms planted flat on the counter, while Sarah stepped behind him and seemed merely curious. "What do you want?" Jeremiah asked.

"Doc's leg is giving him a lot of pain. He

wants to use whiskey to ease his suffering. Mary asked for a bottle. She said to put it on Doc's account."

"Plenty of whiskey here, now that the saloon has its own working still." Jeremiah picked a bottle off the shelf and slid it across to Delia. "This is the kind Mary likes," he said. "She says it's powerful enough to tenderize a cut of buffalo, should we ever have such a thing. It will work fine for killing Doc's pain."

Grateful that Jeremiah talked to her at all, Delia reminded Jeremiah to add the bottle to Doc's account. He pulled out a ledger and jotted the note on a page labeled ERNEST HEMMER at the top.

Delia threw a thank-you in Jeremiah's direction and started toward the door. Jeremiah was busy with his bookkeeping, but Sarah watched Delia leave, her gaze hard to figure out. *Strange lady.* Delia carried the bottle of whiskey outside and stuffed it safely in the saddlebags she'd emptied before leaving Doc's office.

Riding the Palouse, headed toward the doctor's place, Delia decided everyone she saw acted a bit strange. She expected the townsfolk would be buzzing with gossip about the day's events, the fire and the shootings, Elizabeth's safe return, and more.

Instead, they went about their business quietly, as though pretending nothing out of the ordinary had happened.

Unless they shut up because she'd come to town, and they'd return to their bustle and chatter as soon as she left. A disturbing thought. Delia prodded the Palouse to move a little faster, on past the destroyed smithy shop and stable and the saddle she'd need to replace somehow, past the saloon, and the turn to Doc's office at the junction. She stopped at Doc's to take the whiskey into the cookhouse, intending to return the horse to Annie's barn before helping Mary with Doc's leg. Mary insisted they get all the doctoring taken care of first.

Mary poured a generous portion of whiskey into a tin cup. She took a big swallow, then offered the cup to Delia. The drink went down easy, even with the burn. Delia whispered her thanks. Mary bit off a piece of jerky and then handed the chunk to Delia to clear the whiskey taste and smell from her mouth.

They walked into the office, both women hesitating at the door. Two male voices carried on a conversation inside. Delia rushed forward, then stopped and let out a sigh of relief. The preacher stood beside Doc's bed with one hand resting on the injured man's shoulder.

The muscles in Delia's shoulders and neck relaxed. She had been worried about the preacher earlier, before he'd shown up at Annie's barn. She'd feared for his safety from the outlaws, while worrying he might have run away from Sangamon like a dastardly coward. When he returned, safe and uninjured, she focused on the danger and what to do about it. She had no time to feel relieved. Now, she acknowledged her interest in the preacher's welfare, but only to herself.

"Did someone tell you what happened by the stable?" she asked.

"Yes. I'm sorry I wasn't there to help."

"You can be of use now," Doc said. "Mary and Delia are about to put new splints on my leg and wrap it so I can walk with crutches. If you help Mary, Delia can sit over there and rest her shoulder." He looked at Delia and motioned her away. "Your shoulder survived far more exercise today than I would have prescribed."

Delia looked longingly at the full whiskey bottle, wishing she could get a cupful to sip, but the presence of the preacher made that impossible.

Impossible. Because I don't want him to think poorly of me. And yet, strong drink is the least of my sins.

"I have done this before," the preacher said. "I'm a better doctor's assistant than I am a saver of souls."

"I'll see to the young'un," Delia muttered. She edged out the back door of the office and went to search for Jackson.

CHAPTER FORTY-THREE:
TIME TO GO

The days turned into a week while Doc hobbled from office to cookhouse to cabin and back as needed. He struggled with the crutches. The bottom edges of the leg splints extended an inch or so below his boot to make sure he did not put his full weight on the bone while it healed. The day he slid the splints up and tentatively let his foot touch the floor relieved a lot of anxiety for all of them.

Delia intercepted the glances between Doc and Mary and got the message. *Time for me to go.* Before anyone said a word, Delia packed her bags and tied up her supplies in her bedroll. She had taken a saddle from one of the outlaws' horses without asking permission, but no one had raised an objection.

Mary seemed relieved that Delia was preparing to leave. Delia felt the same need to break the bond the two women had formed over the past several days — days when they sipped a little whiskey and talked. Talked too much about too many things.

It had started that first night Doc went to sleep early, exhausted by events and sedated by strong drink. Both women had tired of Doc's "get this, get that" affliction, as Mary called it.

That evening, Mary had perhaps taken a few too many sips from her overfilled cup. She began by telling Delia about the years she lived in poverty, supported only by her mentally damaged son and her daughter whose wild ways got her pregnant. "That girl had to care for a baby when she could barely care for herself."

Delia reciprocated with stories about her stay with the outlaws and river pirates, glossing over her worst crimes.

Then Mary, after imbibing a little more, told Delia about the day Caswell Proud died. "Annie's the one who did it," she said. "I've never told Doc about this, and I never will. He might someday tell the wrong person. No one else in town knows except the preacher. Annie and I never speak of that day. It's like it never happened.

"That's the way it will go with the five men killed here," she continued. "You saw how quickly the bodies disappeared from in front of Doc's office? And the three on the street by the stable? They're buried outside the cemetery fence. No one will speak of this again, at least not to me or Annie. The outlaws all died before the townsfolk ran out of the stable to escape the fire. They don't know for sure who did the killing. They won't ask. They don't want to know. They can trust Annie and me to mind our words. They don't trust you in that same way. They won't rest until they see the last of you."

Delia didn't much care what the townsfolk thought or who they trusted. She wasn't welcome. Her brother had not come by to see her. She wouldn't approach him again. She did pay one last visit to the preacher, who still hadn't left town. With the room behind the stable no longer available, he had slept in the schoolhouse on a couple of the mats used for the youngest children's naps. His horse, which had been freed from the stable during the fire, had not gone far, but his saddle was lost in the flames. The preacher planned to ride bareback south from the town and retrieve the outlaw's saddle and trappings where he'd hidden them in a dense thicket. Delia gave the preacher a small packet of the gold she'd stolen and asked him to give it to Colin as a gift from an anonymous donor to help rebuild his business. The preacher agreed without asking any questions. One more thing for Delia to appreciate about John Claymore.

Delia walked to Annie Gray's farm to pick up the Palouse and let the woman know she was leaving. Annie, already prepared, handed Delia a package of baked goods and salt-cured ham. In an unexpected gesture, Annie placed her hand on Delia's arm and gave it a squeeze. "Find a new path, Delia, travel a safer road. Do you know what you'll do next?"

"The preacher told me about groups of people in covered wagons wanting to travel west. I might go to St. Louis and see what that's all about."

"Good," Annie said. "If I were a younger woman and not already getting strange in my thinking, I believe I'd consider that as well. Go with God, Delia."

Delia could hardly believe this was the same woman who had once threatened to shoot her and had killed at least one of the outlaws. She patted Annie's hand and thanked her, then mounted the Palouse and walked him to Doc's office.

She had one final good-bye left, the one

that would be most difficult. Mary told her Jackson was in the cookhouse, using his whittling knife to cut up carrots for the stew. Delia stepped inside, let her eyes get used to the dim light, then sat on one of the benches at the table. "I'm getting ready to head out," she said.

Jackson didn't look up. He kept his eyes on his fingers and the knife as he continued his work. "I know," he said.

"You'll be safe here. When I see you again, you'll be smart as can be after all the schooling you're going to get."

"If you leave here, you ain't going to come back. Not ever."

He was right. She shouldn't lie to him. "I could write you letters," Delia said. "Jeremiah already has a corner of his store set up to handle mail. Somebody's going to carry letters and packages back and forth from Springfield."

"Miss Delia, I don't know how to write yet."

Tears welled up in Jackson's eyes, even though he wouldn't look directly at her. The feeling was contagious. She fought her own tears but knew the shine in her eyes would give her away. She got up, went to Jackson's side, and pulled him close in a big hug, the biggest and longest hug she'd given him since rescuing him months ago. "I'll be seeing you, young'un."

Jackson did not answer, but Delia had already headed for the door. She didn't turn to wave or give him any indication she might change her mind. With no need to speak any more words to Doc or Mary, Delia walked around the outside of the cabin and hurried to her horse. She mounted, then hesitated for a moment as she thought about riding along the main road so everyone would see her leave and know that trouble was on its way out of town. No, she thought, better to leave it be.

She walked the Palouse past Annie Gray's farm. Annie chopped at weeds in her garden. She glanced up once, then returned to her task.

Delia guided the Palouse along the river road to the bridge, then crossed it to travel south. She would never go east again. That was where all the memories of Cave-in-Rock, Ford's Ferry, and the outlaw gangs could stay and die their own slow death. She would travel west when the road turned.

Keeping her pace slow while she thought through the last few weeks and all that happened, she wondered if she could change her life and her way of doing things.

The fast clip-clop of a horse's hooves

brought her to a quick halt. She turned the Palouse and pulled her long gun out of its strap.

She recognized the horse immediately as its head came into view. The sorrel mare. A small black boy on the mare's back.

"What the hell are you doing here, young'un?"

"I decided to go with you, Miss Delia."

"Hellfire, Jackson. What do you want to do that for?"

"Miss Mary said Mr. Jeremiah told Elizabeth I could not play with her or any of the other children, that I had to go to school and then go straight to Doc's place. I could have learning, and I could have a place to sleep and food to eat, but that's all. I walked to Miss Gray's farm, saddled up this horse all by myself, and I'm here. I'm not leaving, so you better let it be."

And that's what Delia decided to do. Let it be. She dismounted to tighten the cinch on Jackson's horse and adjust the stirrups, then offered him a drink from her water bag before she mounted the Palouse once more. They rode together, heading south and west as soon as the road turned, and had long talks about covered wagons and herds of buffalo and wild Indians that still might take a white man's scalp. They were passing through Springfield when they found the way blocked by hundreds and hundreds of Indians on foot, guarded and pushed along by soldiers.

"Where are they going?" Jackson asked.

"West, Jackson. Just like us. The government says they have to cross the Mississippi River and go live on special lands so the farmers will be safe. Some of these Indians had a bad habit of killing white people. Others wouldn't give up their lands."

"Why?"

Delia hesitated. "People hurt each other for lots of reasons. White men and Indians alike. You'll understand better when you get older. Let's wait for these people to move on past and we'll tag along for a while."

"Seems like there's always trouble no matter where we go, Miss Delia."

"That's true," she said. "That is for sure a true thing."

CHAPTER FORTY-FOUR: ABOUT DESPAIR

Jackson received one more lesson in the sadness of life as they rode for days behind the Indian tribe. Children got sick and died. Old people fell in their tracks, unable to walk another mile. The soldiers loaded them onto travois pulled along by those younger and stronger, who willingly cared for their elders in their last days.

"What's happening to those people?" Jackson asked, pointing to several bodies placed by the side of the road.

"They gave in to disappointment and despair," Delia said.

"What's despair?"

"Despair, Jackson, is the result of losing everything you've ever owned or loved and realizing there's no hope those things can ever be replaced."

"I think I might have some despair," he said. His shoulders slumped, and tears leaked from his eyes. It gave him a real bad feeling to think that he might die like those Indians had.

"Jackson," Delia said, patting him on the back and then squeezing his shoulder, "you might have a little of that despair for now. But you have hope, too. These folks are going to a new place because the soldiers are making them go. They can never return. And they don't have one bit of choice in the matter. For you, it's different. You'll be with me. We can go to one place to check it out, and if we don't like it there, we can get on our horses and go somewhere else. We have choices, and we have freedom."

"Freedom to go back to Sangamon if we want?"

Delia laughed. "Sure. If we decide we want to take a little trouble back to Sangamon one day, we can do that very thing."

CHAPTER FORTY-FIVE:
A SURPRISE MEETING

After Delia and Jackson had watched the Indians continue straight west toward the Mississippi River, they turned their horses south toward St. Louis. Plodding along the dirt road, swaying back and forth in their saddles, they didn't talk much. Two days' ride south from Springfield, Jackson called out. "There's a man up ahead. He's sitting there, watching us."

Delia looked up and squinted against the sun, trying to decide whether she needed to pull her rifle from its scabbard.

"It's the preacher! Hey, Preacher," Jackson yelled. "What are you doing here? I thought you went to St. Louis."

Delia reined in the Palouse and patted his neck as she watched the preacher ride closer. A slight hitch in her breathing and a little jump in her heartbeat meant she was tired, she told herself. The preacher greeted Jackson with a big grin. "I got partway to the city and changed my mind," he said. "I decided I'd return to Sangamon."

"What for?"

Delia shifted in her saddle, afraid of what the preacher might say. "Jackson, you shouldn't ask so many questions. If the preacher wants you to know, he'll tell you."

"I do want you both to know. I left a piece of me behind in that town, and I finally figured out I left it with you two."

"Was it your heart?" Jackson asked with a sly smile.

"I think it was."

Delia quickly looked away when he tried to catch her eye. *This man is crazier than Annie Gray if he thinks I'm worthy of even the tiniest piece of his heart.*

She decided she'd set him straight before the day ended. "We're going to stop for the night when we get to those trees," she said. "I was fixing to hunt, shoot a bird or two, get a little sleep."

"I can shoot," he said. "And I have saddlebags full of jerky and hardtack. I'm willing to share my food for a place at your fire."

"One night," Delia said. "Then we'll be heading south."

Later, as the preacher and Delia sat across from each other at the campfire, they had little to say. Finally, the preacher stood and approached her. "May I sit next to you?"

Delia nodded, a lump in her throat as she contemplated what she must tell him and what she hoped to hear in advice and comfort.

"Preacher, I *am* glad to see you. I don't know about this 'piece of your heart' business, because I'm not worth a piece of anything. I am the worst sort of woman you'll ever meet. I reckon you want to fix everything you see that's broke, but I don't think you can fix me."

Delia glanced around the camp to check on Jackson. He seemed to be in his own world as he rubbed down his horse. She avoided meeting the preacher's gaze, wanting only to get this talking over with. *Lordy, I've done more talking in the last two weeks than I did in my whole lifetime before. I'm so tired of talking.*

"I don't want to fix you, Delia. You're a better person than you think you are. And you should call me John."

"I keep thinking of you as Preacher. That might be better for now. I want to tell you about things I did that weigh on my mind. There are nights I can't sleep for the bad thoughts. When I do sleep, I have awful nightmares."

"Okay, I'm the preacher for now. But one

day, Delia, I'd like you to think of me as a friend."

"You may not feel that way after I tell you what I've done."

"Go on."

"You already know the story of why I ran away from Sangamon. I was sixteen and scared I would be hanged if the law caught me. Women rarely traveled alone, but the roads were full of men of all kinds. Good men of means traveling by stagecoach, farmers and ranchers meeting in small towns, Indians looking for trouble, thieves and killers stealing money and lives."

The preacher cleared his throat and looked into the campfire.

Delia clenched her hands in her lap, determined to finish her story. "I killed men to protect myself, Preacher. I shot two of the Indians who killed a farmer I worked for. I killed the man chasing after Jackson. After I joined the outlaws at Cave-in-Rock, I was party to robbing folks . . . and worse."

"I've traveled on roads near Shawneetown many times, Delia, knowing the stories about these men, but I never ran into them. I'd begun to think it was all legend. I'm grateful for that, or I might be telling you of my own sins."

Sins. The word made Delia stop and

think. *Was it a sin to kill a man in order to protect myself or Jackson? Would I do it again?*

"It was a bad time," she said. "It didn't matter if folks traveled on the roads or rode ferries and riverboats. Thieves and killers didn't care. I suspect the Biedlers murdered the man who owned the Palouse. His name was Owen McAllister. He drew fine pictures. Even drew a beautiful one of me I couldn't bear to look at. I didn't feel beautiful, so I threw it in the fire. The picture I still have looks like the old me with wild hair and a man's clothes." She paused as though lost in thought, then continued. "The Biedlers tracked me for weeks and would never have given up. When I met Owen McAllister, I didn't realize the gang had come so close. I never thought to warn McAllister. That weighs on my mind."

"You couldn't have known what would happen."

"When old Hiram got himself killed, his oldest son, Jack, led the gang. He made me lure riverboats to shore with pitiful cries for help and set me to work collecting the valuables from the stagecoaches they robbed. So many bad things. They shot people, kidnapped and took women by force, threw little children in the river to drown. I couldn't stop it from happening, but now I can't get those things out of my mind."

Until these last words, John had appeared to listen with interest. Now he sat still, his forehead creased and sadness in his eyes. "How could a caring God let this happen?" he asked.

"God didn't give a hoot about Cave-in-Rock, Preacher. If He even exists, I reckon there are places He leaves alone, just to see what will happen. When I stayed with the Biedlers, I chose to live in hell, and I'm sure your God didn't like that much. I didn't like it much, either. I made terrible choices in my life, and now I can't forget."

"By leaving Sangamon when you were young, you thought you spared your brother from great suffering," John said. "And not so long ago, you saved Jackson's life."

Delia wrung her hands and forced herself to go on, her voice growing louder and more frantic. "I left women and children behind when I escaped from the Biedlers. I don't know what happened to them. I might have helped them escape —"

"Shhh. You might have gotten them all killed and you along with them. Who would have saved Jackson then?"

"Taking care of that young'un may be the

one good thing I've done in my life. He's mighty important to me now."

The preacher reached for Delia's hands, pried them apart, and held them in his own. "Delia, your past no longer matters, if you want a better future. I'd like to be the other most important person in your life and help you be safe. Would you allow me to ride with you and Jackson?"

She pulled her hands away. "I don't know what to say, Preacher. What are you asking of me?"

"Please call me John. I'm no longer a preacher. Only a man who needs a friend."

Delia looked around the camp until she spotted Jackson, snuggling into his bedroll. "Jackson, John here wants to ride with us for a time. Is that a good thing?"

"Yes, ma'am."

"Okay, then. You'll be our friend, John. Ride with us for a time. Then we'll see."

Those words brought a light to his eyes and a smile to his lips. Delia felt dangerously close to tears. She poked at the fire with a stick, then added more wood. The night air smelled better than it had before. The breeze blew softly through the trees, rustling the last dry leaves of fall. The new moon shone bright and full of promise. When Delia stretched out in her bedroll, she had one thought in her mind. *For a time. Then we'll see.*

ABOUT THE AUTHOR

Pat Stoltey is the author of two amateur sleuth mysteries (*The Prairie Grass Murders; The Desert Hedge Murders*), one thriller (*Dead Wrong*), and the first Sangamon novel in the Frontier Fiction line (*Wishing Caswell Dead*), all originally published by Five Star. *Dead Wrong* and *Wishing Caswell Dead* were finalists for a Colorado Book Award. Pat lives in Northern Colorado with her husband, her Scottish terrier named Sassy, and a brown tabby who answers to Kitty Cat. Memberships include Mystery Writers of America and its Rocky Mountain chapter, Sisters in Crime and its Colorado chapter, Northern Colorado Writers, and Pikes Peak Writers. Please visit Pat at her website/blog (https://patriciastolteybooks .com), on Facebook (https://www.facebook .com/PatStoltey) and on Twitter (https:// twitter.com/PStoltey).

Printed in the USA
CPSIA information can be obtained
at www.ICGtesting.com
JSHW020739030324
58230JS00004B/4